TERROR TRAP

Dianna lay on her back on the floor of a damp stone cellar. Her hands were tied behind her, and strips of duct tape covered her mouth. Straw was piled deep on the floor, and in her nostrils was the familiar, hideous, zoo-animal stench. The difference was that now the smell was omnipresent, overwhelming.

I'm in the icehouse, she realized, in the large square pit below the surface of the earth.

Through the window she saw that her car was gone from the space where she had parked it in the driveway. And there chained to the sugar maple tree in the backyard was a lump that reminded Dianna of a rhino sleeping on the grass. Esau.

Dianna slumped to the floor. What are they going to do with me . . . ?

HUNGER OF THE BEAST

JOHN DRIVER

JOVE BOOKS, NEW YORK

HUNGER OF THE BEAST

A Jove Book / published by arrangement with
the author

PRINTING HISTORY
Jove edition / May 1991

ISBN: 0-515-10567-8

Jove Books are published by The Berkley Publishing Group,
200 Madison Avenue, New York, New York 10016.
The name "JOVE" and the "J" logo
are trademarks belonging to Jove Publications, Inc.

PRINTED IN THE UNITED STATES OF AMERICA

10 9 8 7 6 5 4 3 2 1

To Sensei Yoshiteru Otani
His smile and his words will always be with me.

Together, we rowed into the fog
And through the fog.
How blue, how vibrant
Is the vast sea.

—Shiki

PROLOGUE

Esau want booteful.

Down in the stone-walled pit, just below the surface of the earth, it was wet and cold. Esau lumbered from fieldstone wall to fieldstone wall, his oversized feet scattering the straw on the earthen floor. From ankle to instep each of his feet was covered with a mat of tangled, mud-caked hair, and his soles and heels were callous shoe leather—toughened by a hundred thousand steps on the hard-packed earth.

Esau hate small place. Esau want darkness come. Sometimes, only sometimes, when darkness come, they put on chain and let Esau play in big place.

Esau want be outside. Esau like big place. Can run. Big place have living things. Good smells.

He made a low-pitched growl and struck at the sheet-metal door with his right fist.

"Garrrrghga!"

His big knuckles left an inch-deep impression, but the door did not come open for him—as it had one time before.

In three shuffling strides Esau covered the distance to the only window in the stone-walled space. Like everything else in the room, the window was encrusted with filth. Steel bars were set in the thick wall and kept Esau from breaking the two soundproofed layers of glass that separated him from the world of wonderful things.

The window was his salvation and his entertainment—his one hope. It was his only tangible link to the world outside. If there was any kind of breeze, a trace of the scent of horses or

1

geese or flowers would waft its way through the cracks around the windowpanes.

And if he was lucky, he would see people and the driveway and the cars that came and left.

Once, after he escaped that time when the door had been left unlocked, they had begun to board up his window, but Esau had gone wild—roaring and kicking, beating on the door until they had no choice but to uncover the glass once again.

He looked down the driveway and was disappointed. No people were coming, not today.

Esau want booteful.

He tested the air. No new smells either.

His nose was keen—able to discern between the most subtle of aromas, between scents that would confuse a bloodhound.

Soon they come and take Esau with horses to other place.

They did it every year when the seasons changed, when it started to get warm. They locked him in the darkness of the horse truck and took him on the long drive north, away from the many people who would arrive with the summer weather.

Esau want stay here, not go other place. When Esau not here, many people come. Esau smell this. When Esau return, people smell everywhere. On horses, inside where Goody Mama lives. All over big place. Esau want stay. Esau want play with different smells . . . with different bootefuls. . . .

Dog smell.

Esau knew the dog was coming toward the cellar long before the animal made the slightest move in his direction. The German shepherd had a particular scent of fear that told Esau the dog was thinking of him.

Esau hate dog.

The German shepherd slunk to the window, sniffed, and growled a low challenge. It was a male dog, and Esau could sense the blood lust in the animal's tone. Esau hissed back. The dog barked, taunting, daring, then bared his teeth in a parting snarl and trotted off.

Hate dog. Why they not let Esau be free like dog?

Esau had an old debt that he longed to settle with the German shepherd, but it went even deeper than that. Esau's hatred of the dog was in his protoplasm. He had despised it from the first day it had been brought to the inn. It was the kind of visceral reaction a cobra would have to a mongoose. The very smell of the breed burned Esau's nose; a mere glimpse of the German shepherd evoked an urge in him to do battle, to strike out and kill.

Esau want break dog.

Esau moved to his shelf and his eyes peered over the contents. There was a pile of worn magazines, a pair of child's scissors, a box of broken crayons, a comb with missing teeth, a stack of worn baseball cards, a hairbrush with twisted nylon bristles, a collection of chipped bottles of cheap cologne, and a razor with no blade.

He pulled the light cord, taking fumbling care not to break the string, as he had done so often in the past. The bare bulb cast hard-edged shadows on the fieldstone walls. Esau took up the plastic brush. His meaty palm dwarfed it. Painfully, he pulled the brush through his tangled, oily hair. Out came burrs, twigs, and occasional clumps of matted curl.

Esau went to his stack of magazines, brushed aside the tattered and yellowed *Sports Illustrated*s until he came to a Sunday fashion magazine supplement. Esau was searching for another picture for his collection. The walls around him were already covered with his favorites. On every peg or nail there were pictures of men—perfect men, ideal men, "booteful" men. They were ultramasculine, sporting the latest fashions— bare-torsoed athletes, Adonis-like weight lifters. The pictures were cut from movie magazines, newspapers, sports sections, and muscle-building manuals. Each had the letters ESA awkwardly printed next to the man.

Esau took the pair of child's paper shears and with a painstaking clumsiness began to cut out a picture of a male model wearing a Ralph Lauren tuxedo. Esau's hands were black with grime. The tips of his large fingers could barely fit through the loops of the scissors. His nails were the width of quarters, some long and pointed, others split and broken. A rug of hair covered all the exposed skin from Esau's arms to the backs of his hands.

Holding an aqua-colored crayon in his fist, he wrote "ESA" beside the male model's too-perfect face, breaking the crayon on the last leg of the A. With an angry cry Esau threw the crayon to the floor. Taking another, he drew an arrow from the word to the man and jammed the cutout on a nail already holding a half dozen or more similar pictures.

Esau stood admiring his work for a moment, then returned to the magazines, thumbing page to page with a panting eagerness. Finally he came to a photograph that pleased him: a bikini-clad lady advertising a Caribbean vacation.

Esau want booteful.

Esau remembered the straw-haired booteful he had found, and their one night out in the big place. It had been so good.

Booteful had 'ove Esau.

He was sure of it.

Esau moved quickly to his favorite standing place and posed, admiring the shadow on the wall cast by the naked bulb at his back.

If Esau had been standing squarely, facing the wall, the light would have cast an accurate shadow—one of a man of oversized proportions: long, hulking torso, one side distended; stocky, powerful legs; thick, gangling arms that hung almost to the knees, the right arm reaching lower than the left.

The true image of Esau would have shown his hunch: a monstrous, ill-conceived pregnancy perched on the left shoulder. But Esau knew that this was not the way he looked, not Esau.

Esau booteful.

That was why he stood so that his shadow hit the wall at just the right angle. The distortion of this shadow on the fieldstone compensated for his own lack of symmetry.

If he tilted his head to the side, positioning himself with the right bend of his body, his dark image was proportionate, pleasing, just like the men in his collection of pictures.

That was the way Esau looked. He knew it. He was handsome, as handsome as any man could be. His shadow proved it. His shadow told him he was perfect.

He reached down and stroked himself where it felt so good. He smiled.

Esau booteful.
Esau want booteful.

PART I

A kanji (Japanese character), pronounced "do" or "michi,"
that may be translated as "a road."

A journey of five thousand
miles begins with one step.

Chinese proverb

1

Dianna's apartment was small even for a studio, but she had sacrificed space to live in privacy in a charming brownstone with good light and a working fireplace, on a tree-lined West Village block. Framed four-sheet show posters of various hits and flops she had been associated with decorated the walls.

Her title, which appeared in very small print on some of the posters, was Assistant Producer, and she knew all too well that the words had little or no real meaning to anyone in the business. Assistant Producer could be anything from a schlepper, to a secretary, to, on occasion, a serious-minded, intelligent, and creative person.

Dianna put herself at the top of the latter category.

No sooner had she entered the apartment and tossed a suitcase on the kitchen counter than the phone rang. Dianna knew who was calling and automatically decided not to answer. Instead, she began rummaging through her bureau, gathering pieces of clothing.

When the phone stopped ringing, Dianna thought, Well, what do you know, Arthur's cooling off, he only let it ring thirty-two times.

But Dianna knew him well enough to expect his persistent knocking at her door within five to ten minutes. It was only last night that she had told Arthur it was over for good, and she knew he would be panicked. That was why she had no time to lose.

From a shelf that also held plays and theatrical textbooks, she grabbed a battered copy of *Fodor's Guide to New England*. Quickly she jammed everything into the suitcase.

Before leaving, Dianna went to the window for a quick check of the street. Right again—Arthur's balding head was just emerging from his double-parked Saab. "Son of a bitch," she cursed and stormed out the door.

With suitcase, tote bag, and laptop in hand, Dianna ran up one flight of stairs to the roof, across to the adjoining brownstone, and down its stairway. On the street she hurried to the corner and hailed a cab.

Dianna gave the cabbie the address of a rooftop parking lot over a shipping terminal on the Lower West Side. It was a popular and inexpensive place (at least by New York standards) for keeping a car. It wasn't easy to get to, but the location was fine for a vehicle that was only used on weekends.

Weekends? Who am I kidding? Dianna thought. This is only the second time I've driven the car this year, and what is it, March? No, April.

She asked the cabbie to load the suitcase into the trunk of her four-year-old Honda Acura. As he heaved the bag in, he muttered, "Lady, this had better be worth my time."

Unperturbed, she told him if he wanted to get paid, he'd better stick around until she got her car started. After the engine roared into life, she gave the man the fare, threw in a dollar tip, and said, "It would have been more, if you hadn't started complaining."

The cabbie turned red and climbed out of his car—looking as if he might take a swing at her. Dianna immediately regretted her comment.

She was suddenly aware of the isolation of her surroundings. The wind whistled off the Hudson, bringing a faint industrial smell from New Jersey. It was a gray afternoon, and the two of them seemed almost lost among the rows of empty cars covered with layers of settled dust and grime of the city.

Wanting to hide her fear and dissolve the possibly dangerous situation, Dianna took out another dollar. To save face she quipped, "Here, let it be a lesson to you."

"Fuck you, lady," said the cabbie, but his hand snaked out and grabbed the offered bill. With a squeal and a small cloud of burning rubber, he gunned the cab out of the parking lot.

By the time the clock on the instrument panel read five-thirty, Dianna was escaping Manhattan via the West Side Highway.

Not a smart thing to do, telling that cabbie off, she thought. He might have turned out to be a weirdo and could have decided to smash me in the face or hit my car or . . .

"Too impulsive," Dianna criticized herself aloud, thinking of her mother's favorite comment: "The LaBianca mouth is going to be the end of you."

2

It had been a long afternoon, starting with the Saturday matinee. The show was in its third year and a little tired and ragged due to lack of attention from the original creative team. Dianna half wanted to stay and take some notes to pass along to the stage manager, but this afternoon was her weekly Za-zen session.

On her way out she stopped at the box office door and knocked twice, paused, knocked twice again, and after being checked through the peephole, was admitted. It was part of her job to look in at the daily ticket count. Not that it really mattered, but Sy said it helped to keep everyone on their toes. Three pale men glanced up at her and, without any acknowledgment, resumed thumbing through stacks of money and credit card receipts.

One of the counters spoke at her in a monotone, "Arthur called."

Another man handed her a wrapped bouquet of a dozen roses that had been delivered to the box office. "Guess who sent 'em." All three men exchanged a look and grinned. Dianna tried to remain businesslike but was red-faced as she checked over the figures for the day's box office wrap.

As Dianna took a small elevator up to the offices above the theater, she could still hear the men counting in her head—ten for the theater, ten for me, ten for the theater. . . .

What a strange world is the "legit" theater, she thought. So much glamour when perceived from a seat in the twelfth row center, and so much backbiting, infighting, money-grubbing, one-upmanship, pride, gigantic egos, and bullshit, when experienced firsthand. But I guess that's why I'm here, she admitted to herself.

Sy was in his office, behind his heavy maple desk, drinking a Doctor Brown's cream soda. Sy was the FM or Der Yiddishe Field Marshal, as everyone in the office referred to him behind his back. Short, balding, heavyset, though he had to be over sixty-five, he always seemed to have the energy of a two-year-old after a nap.

He's amazing, she thought. In the last year he has laid two catastrophic bombs on Broadway at a combined loss of almost six million dollars, and here he is on the phone hustling up another easy million-plus for his next production.

Seven years ago Sy had branched out from being a successful seafood restaurateur into a second career as a producer. It had all happened when, as a stage-struck investor, he had had the good fortune to get involved with one blockbuster hit.

Dianna plunged in, "I need four weeks off."

"Forget it."

"I quit."

"Good. I don't have to pay unemployment."

Dianna turned and walked out to her desk in the larger office just outside Sy's door. After a moment the old producer appeared, his hands in his pockets.

He studied her while finishing off the soft drink. It was clear she was upset. "What's the matter? That married schmuck giving you trouble? You want me to make a phone call? I'll have somebody break his arms and legs."

"I've got to get away from him and the city."

"You're pregnant?"

"Sy, no jokes, please. I didn't take a vacation last year."

"So? You were busy."

"Or the year before that."

"I sent you to Philadelphia, when was it, just last month?"

"That was a year and a half ago and I was there only on business."

"Take off tomorrow; it's Sunday. You'll have a long weekend."

"Four weeks."

"Four days."

"Three weeks. . . . Look, Louis can cover for me."

"Two weeks, or I take out an ad in the help wanted."

"Deal."

"But you got to do some work on that kid's . . . What's his name?"

"Kronenberger."

"Yeah, you take his script with you and bring it back all done." Sy turned and walked back to his desk, immediately picking up the phone. "Hey, Dianna, what was that last title he gave us for his play?"

"*Remembered Jewels.*"

"What do you think?" he asked her.

"It sucks."

"Well, then get out of here. And I don't want to see your face till you come up with a really good title."

Dianna dug the Kronenberger play out of a stack of manuscripts and stuffed it in her bag. Now that she had the FM's okay, she knew she should make haste. She took a few seconds to check through her stack of messages, just to make sure that there wasn't something genuinely important. Most of her memos requested her to call Mr. Arthur Berkeley, and every single one of them was marked "urgent."

Though of modest proportions, her desk peeked out through a little streaked window onto Shubert Alley—the best location in the room and proof that even as assistant producer she was second only to the FM in the office pecking order.

Pressed under the desk's glass top were two photos. One was a family portrait taken when Dianna was seven. As the only girl and the youngest, she was posed in the center of the grouping. Her four brothers, two of them identical twins, stood around her, wearing an assortment of football uniforms. Mother and father, a well-dressed and warm-looking couple, were on the far right, and a Catholic priest stood at the other end, football tucked under his arm.

The other picture had been done by a portrait photographer and displayed a teenage Dianna decked out in full riding gear, holding a handful of prize ribbons. She stood eye to eye with a glistening thoroughbred.

Dianna took the time to retract her computer into the special hideaway compartment that was built into her desk. She liked to keep the presence of the machine a secret from as many people as possible. She gathered all the necessary working software and the data disks for the Kronenberger script, put them in a hard plastic box, and dropped it into her bag.

Dianna knew the FM. If she didn't get out of the office fast, he would start finding various pretexts to keep her from going or, at the least, he would come up with more work for her to do while away. Grabbing her purse in one hand and her laptop computer in the other, Dianna was out the door.

3

After leaving the office Dianna had to make one other stop before she could be on her way. It was an appointment that she kept at four o'clock every Saturday afternoon between shows, a time which allowed her to be back at the theater before the half-hour call of the evening performance.

A taxi dropped her off not far from the Hudson River in the Chelsea area, outside a partially converted loft building. The brass elevator cage smelled of freshly ground coffee and olive oil from the two still-functioning businesses left in the soon-to-be-converted-into-an-expensive-co-op building.

Dianna pressed the seventh floor button, which was labeled Zen. As the car rose, Dianna smiled and thought, How simple it would be, if enlightenment could be reached by putting out a finger and pressing a button—like pressing a reformatting command on a word processor or merely flipping a light switch. Yes, a light switch would be appropriate. If it only worked that way.

She knew the label beside the button must have been her teacher's idea. "Zen," a signpost, a perfect instruction—one of his little philosophical jokes set out like a booby trap for his students to trip over—or perhaps be enlightened by.

For the first time in the last six months Dianna was actually looking forward to going to the Zendo and seeing her Roshi, her teacher, Sanjiro Takahashi.

The elevator door slid open on a brightly lit space divided into rooms by paper doors and walls. Dianna slipped off her shoes, put on a pair of *tabi* socks, and padded across the lacquered wood floor. The sheen of soft light reflecting off the

14

orange-brown oak planking made her feel warm and at home.

Waiting for her turn to see the Roshi, Dianna sat on a small cushion in the Za-zen position of meditation—back straight, legs in an ankles-against-thighs figure eight. She quickly fell into her pattern of breathing—in, out, count ten breaths, then start again. Try to find yourself in the space between breaths. What should she think about? Her koan, her philosophical problem? But she wasn't supposed to try to think about the answer.

As the old teacher constantly reminded her, she was not to consider his questions and proverbs with a logical approach. "Do not be rational" was one of his most frequent remarks.

Whenever Dianna had asked him questions like, "But how do I answer a problem if I don't consider it rationally?" the old man would say "Meditate," or throw up his arms with impatience and shout, "Just consider it!" or "Just answer it."

Zen, Zen, Zen. It brewed in her mind like the virus of a plague, a hopeless maze of koans and wise-sounding phrases.

Lately, the growing agonies in her shoulders and legs from the difficult sitting position had made Dianna ask herself the same series of questions:

Why do I endure this pain?

Why do I ponder a koan, an unsolvable riddle, when I already know the answer?

Why do I waste hours here that I could spend on some other activity that was fun or creative or would help me to meet people?

With every passing day her motives for attending the Zendo seemed to grow more vague and conflicting. Dianna had at one time found a feeling of peace and security in the place, but now many of the rituals seemed a waste of time.

And then there was the quest for satori, the ultimate state of enlightenment. What the hell was enlightenment anyway? A thing of a dream? A thing intangible and unattainable? Perhaps a myth, perhaps even a lie?

As Dianna knelt into the Za-zen position, she was obsessed with thoughts of the many much-more interesting ways she could be spending her time.

She was a breath away from quitting the Zendo forever.

She thought, It's time to start with a fresh slate—a clean, just-formatted computer disk out of the box—time to get rid of all the unwanted baggage in my life. I have to get away. I need time alone, time to think everything out.

Outside the Roshi's door she struck the small gong that announced her desire for learning. It was said that the master could tell the state of a disciple's awareness merely by the nature of the sound.

Dianna surprised herself and rang the little gong rather well. Her thoughts about giving up, the impending renouncement that she knew she would soon make, left her with an easy, I-could-care-less feeling that translated into a defiant, smooth strike.

As she bowed and entered, the Roshi spoke, "Have a nice trip."

Dianna tried to cover her surprise. "How did you know I was leaving?" She had brought him one of the roses from Arthur's bouquet and laid it carefully, almost tenderly, before her teacher.

"Why else would you have so much happiness?"

The shaven head of the old priest glowed with reflected light. His eyes wrinkled into dozens of little crow's feet as he stared through her. "So, what is the sound of one hand clapping?"

Dianna lowered her head, dreading her answer. Then after a long beat she whispered, as if in an apology for her failure to grasp the ungraspable, "Mu."

"Mu" meant no or nothing or nothingness. Dianna was supposed to be answering in a particular state of mind. Like the challenge of the ringing of the gong, a perfect answer was in the way she spoke, which in turn was a product of her state of mind and her depth of understanding.

But whenever Dianna attempted to give the answer, all she could summon up was a halfhearted utterance, an untruth. The feeling of failure was becoming unbearable.

But today the Roshi only frowned a little and shook it off with a smile. "I think perhaps today is not the day for us to speak of this question. Ignore fear, ignore negativity, press on."

This is strange, thought Dianna. Usually they would end up discussing the koan for a good part of the session. "What is the sound of one hand clapping?" was her assigned koan, the philosophical conundrum that she had been contemplating, meditating on, grappling with . . . for the last four wasted years.

Takahashi studied her long and carefully in silence. "I think, perhaps, you have set yourself on a path of changing."

"Yes, I think so," she replied.

The Roshi appeared to be slightly disturbed and looked away from her to that distant point, to that far-off horizon he always seemed to focus upon when his mind searched for an explanation or some hidden meaning. "There are many paths. . . . Do you know of the samurai?"

"Only what I've seen in a few Japanese films."

For Dianna's taste, she found them too obsessed with death and swords and slashing people to pieces in frenzies of bloodletting. The Roshi ignored her look of slight distaste.

"In feudal times, the samurai warriors spent their lives in constant fear. You see, they were all professional soldiers. At any moment a samurai could be called upon to lay down his life in the service of his lord. So, a samurai warrior always had to keep himself in readiness, practicing his martial skills constantly.

"You see," the Roshi continued, "if a man is shaking with terror in a sword fight, no matter how great his ability, he is surely a dead man. Is this not true? So, for the samurai to, as you say, 'cope' with his fears, he borrowed certain things from the masters who taught Zen. What did the samurai borrow? Ah, so simple."

Yeah, I'm sure, thought Dianna, anticipating yet another concept as clear as a bucket of mud.

"In order to be able to fight without worrying about death, they learned to die before a battle, to die in their minds. You see, once a person is dead he has nothing to be afraid of, yes? Very smart of the samurai, yes? Ignore fear, ignore negativity, press on." Takahashi smiled a broad grin. This last phrase was his favorite personal bit of philosophy and it always peppered his teachings.

What does this have to do with getting my boss to raise my salary or finding a man I could love, or getting back into the shape I was in college?

The Roshi held up the rose and gently inhaled its aroma.

Dianna felt a pang of envy as she studied his blissful boyish face. How I wish I could enjoy that scent in the way that he is now enjoying it—so perfectly, so totally. How can he appreciate something with such a childlike joy? What is it that he knows? He understands something, believes some truth about life and existence that I can't seem to get a handle on.

He continued, "It is interesting that the samurai have the cherry blossom for their symbol, a flower of great beauty but also of special usefulness. These blossoms are the father and mother of cherries, are they not?"

Dianna nodded in patient agreement.

"You see, the samurai hoped that their time on earth would be glorious, but they were prepared for their lives to be short." The Roshi paused for emphasis. "Exactly like the cherry blossom. This is how they spent their lives, preparing to fall like a blossom falls from the tree."

Dianna shrugged her shoulders, her thoughts already wandering off, trying to decide whether she should head to Maine or Virginia Beach. She felt him probing, studying her in a way he had never before attempted to. But if he was looking for an answer, the Roshi did not seem to find it. His eyes drifted once more to that infinite point on the horizon. He made a quiet assertion of fact.

" 'To live life to its fullest, you must at any moment be ready to die.' "

And in the split second that Dianna was about ask a question, Takahashi rang the bell next to him, signaling the end of the session.

4

A fifteen-minute walk from the Zendo brought Dianna almost to her apartment on Bank Street. She was troubled because of the session. It was unlike Roshi Takahashi to vary from his normal routine. He had seemed unsettled, and being unsettled was not usual for her teacher. But Takahashi was right about one thing—a change was in the air. Cut all ties with Arthur Caller Berkeley. And perhaps cut all ties with Zen?

I wonder if the Roshi knew I was thinking about quitting the Zendo? she asked herself. Dianna had a suspicion that somehow he did.

And how easy would it be to cut all ties with Arthur? Her last year and a half with him had been both a heaven and a hell. He was generous with his money; he was usually thoughtful. But it just wasn't sensible to love someone who couldn't be there when she needed him. What was the point of a "relationship?" that could be reduced to a twice-a-week dinner and romp in the sack.

Too long. The time has come.

The irony was that the moment she had said good-bye he had started to want her more. With her final we-can't-see-each-other-ever-again ultimatum, his efforts throughout the day to call, to see her, to communicate had steadily intensified.

What a piece of work is man, she thought, to become obsessive and possessive only as he is losing that which he has for so long taken for granted.

Ah, but Arthur has had it all for so long. He deserves to suffer a bit. How sweet is the taste of justice, she thought as she turned the corner onto Bank Street. Anticipating the worst, she

19

stopped under a streetlight and checked in both directions for Arthur's Saab.

To hell with the guilt, she decided. When I'm ready to die, I'll stop having adventures.

In college, if Dianna felt like having a date with a certain guy, one she would rather not let life go by without getting to know, she would simply ask him out. Share a house in Montauk with three men she had never met? No sweat. So now her latest dare would be a hasty off-season trip to . . . Vermont.

Sure, Vermont, sounds good. Why not?

There were flowers waiting for her in the entrance foyer.

She felt guilty but didn't pick up the bouquet—if it were gone, it could tip off Arthur that she was home. This is going to be a bigger readjustment than I thought. It's going to be drastic.

5

It was one of Esau's favorite boyhood memories—riding in the front seat beside his father in the shiny red 1960 Ford Galaxy. It took them almost four hours to drive to Boston and to find a lot to park in near Fenway Park. But for Esau, every minute of the trip had been a joy.

They didn't go many places together and certainly not far from home—Esau's father spent a lot of time away from Fenwick, in Boston or Washington, representing the interests of the Massachusetts banking community. But last week had been Esau's birthday, and yesterday his father had come home. This morning he had dressed his son in a heavy overcoat to help hide his lumpy figure, put a baseball cap low on his head to try and cover the red birthmark on his face, and then took him on an outing.

It was difficult for both of them to be in public. The stares and nasty comments hurt Esau and drove his father into long silences. And there had been more than one occasion when Michael Wilkinson had lost his temper and fought off insulting words with fists.

For a nine-year-old, Esau was large, almost a hundred and fifty pounds, and his dad had trouble convincing the ticket taker that he qualified for the under-twelve admission price. But when the man saw Esau's enlarged features and heard the boy make a guttural gurgling sound of glee, he took the money from Esau's father and sold them a pair of box seats in an empty section of the stadium.

It was Bat Day—a free bat for every kid under twelve—and after another round of explanations from his father, Esau was the proud owner of a shiny boy-sized baseball bat. Esau was wild with his new toy, and because Mr. Wilkinson didn't want to risk his hurting anyone, he took the bat from the boy, telling him that he could have it to play with later.

Esau had never been able to comprehend the rules of baseball, but that didn't keep him from enjoying the game. The organ music and the fresh smells of the stadium had an stirring effect on Esau, and he got a great thrill out of watching a player hit the ball. And then there were these wonderful delicious things called hot dogs. He ate six of them before his father told him, "No more."

It was very special for the boy to be with his dad and out among other people. There had been a few of the usual mouth-dropping stares and several frightened looks, but mostly the two of them were left alone. The cheering excited Esau, and whenever the crowd reacted, Esau would stand up and snort his approval right along with them.

The Red Sox lost that day, but Michael Wilkinson seemed to enjoy himself anyway, and once when a runner scored, he put his arm lightly on Esau's shoulder. It was the most fun they had ever had together.

Later, in the parking lot, Esau's father opened the trunk and put away the extra jackets that Goody had packed for them. Mr. Wilkinson had given in to Esau's protests and let him carry the bat. Esau had gone wild every time a ball, even a foul ball, flew all the way out of the park, and he imagined doing it himself—taking that big swing and hitting the ball just like the players did.

The bat was like a stick in Esau's hands. The momentum of his swing turned him around in a circle, and he cried when the shiny bat broke against his father's head and his father didn't move again.

For many years, until Esau came to understand death, he imagined that his father had only gone away on one of his long trips. He wasn't really dead. He was at the big exciting place with all the people, eating hot dogs and watching the most wonderful thing on earth—a baseball game.

6

Three hours and one hundred twenty-five miles later, the April wind buffeted Dianna's Honda with stiff gusts that kept nudging the car toward the highway's center line. Dianna kept a tight grip on the steering wheel, but as she climbed higher in the Berkshires the winds became even more powerful. The car automatically downshifted into a lower gear to negotiate the steep grade of the two-lane road.

Along the highway the trees were lackluster and barren, the earth a dull gray, and above, a light cover of clouds began to gather, blotting out the last rays of the setting sun. To some, the scenery might have seemed dismal and depressing, but to Dianna, it was near idyllic. At that moment, she would gladly have eaten her supper off the earth beneath the leafless trees.

Dianna rolled the window down an inch, letting in the bracing pure air. Since she had come to work for Sy, she had driven the Honda only on those few weekends when she had managed to talk him into giving her time off.

It was a poor investment, Dianna knew, to have the car depreciating in the lot, but it was important to her to have a means of escape from the oppressive confines of the "Big (cement and asphalt) Apple." It seemed to her that every day New York was deteriorating, becoming more litter-strewn and more beggar-riddled, becoming more like some B-movie, third-world slum. No, thought Dianna, I will never give up my car.

The expensive Acura had been a gift from Mommy and Daddy. Dianna had thought long and hard before accepting the vehicle. "Gifts" from her parents always came with obligations, hidden "strings." Dianna conceptualized them as fish-linelike umbilical cords—transparent, very strong, with hooks in the end that set deeply under the skin. That was the price for being born into the privileges of her family—having to play a continual game of detaching and untangling one's self from these little umbilical cords.

Dianna's childhood had been spent between the environments of a Westchester equestrian set and Shubert Alley. Her parents weren't fabulously wealthy like her grandparents, the Dupres, but they lived very well. From the time she could sit still through a complete act, Dianna was taken to every show that came to Broadway, mostly using complimentary tickets provided by her father's clientele.

He was a cosmetic surgeon, one of the best in New York City. His patients included big names in theater, film, fashion, and even several national politicians—many of whom kept the use of his services a closely guarded secret. Dianna had often jokingly threatened to steal a few juicy medical files and send them off for release in the *National Enquirer* or the *Star*.

A blast of wind rattled the Honda. Night had fallen, and Dianna's arms were beginning to ache from the struggle to keep the car in the middle of the lane. Her destination was an inn in southern Vermont that, at least from its photograph in the guide, looked chock-full of atmosphere. Dianna had marked several places listed in the five-year-old book—all were purported to have an abundance of Vermont charm and had riding stables on or near the premises.

She glanced at the plastic statue magnetically clipped over her glove compartment. It had once been a figure of the Virgin Mary, but now it wore a tiny, makeshift robe and held a miniature begging bowl in its one supplicating palm. The statue's former long hair had been scraped off with a knife so that the figure appeared bald. The altered caption on the pedestal read, May Mary *and Buddha* Protect Your Volkswagen.

Louis, a friend who worked with her at the theater, had doctored the statue and given it to her as a kindly barb directed at her concocted beliefs. He had come across her job application form at the office and gotten a good laugh when he saw Dianna's entry for religious preference—Zen/Catholic.

Dianna knew that her two faiths were often hopelessly

incompatible. Yet there were moments when the two seemed to blend in a strange way, like Scotch and milk.

She glanced back at the laptop on the rear seat to make sure it hadn't fallen off on a sharp turn. How Dianna loved the machine for the things that it did so well and so quickly, but on the other hand, how she detested it for what it symbolized to her and what its very presence in the car revealed about her.

She was tempted to stop on a bridge and toss the portable into a gorge.

No typing. That was one thing she had insisted throughout four years of college dramatics. Dianna had sworn by all the saints that under no circumstances would she learn to type. To her, having duties at a typewriter or a word processor carried the connotation of sit-at-desk-all-day-and-pound-out-correct-copy-of-other-people's-ideas. Having the machine on her desk or in her car meant that she might be perceived by the world as a nonthinker, an office drudge, one of a faceless army of historically subordinate women. She loathed being on the wrong end of "Listen, would you mind typing this over for me?"

In fact, she kidded herself, when I come to power I will hire only male secretaries and treat them all with a superior attitude of complete condescension.

No, I really won't, she thought. If I ever do come to power, every one of my employees will be treated with equality and respect, and then they will all worship my name. It was a lesson that being a subordinate had taught her.

"But," she said aloud, thinking how she had broken her no-typing pledge, "you chickened out, didn't you, Dianna?

"You just didn't have what it takes to see it through.

"You just didn't have the patience to go a little hungry.

"You didn't have the courage to do without a credit card."

The renunciation of her vow was life's worst debacle—her most thorough and humiliating defeat. Dianna's face reddened as she relived her choice, remembering the shame she tried a little every day to justify and forget.

7

A road sign read, Ski Mount Snow Route 22.

Dianna hated the Interstate and had chosen the old, winding highway instead. Picturesque countryside interested her, not lanes of endless pavement.

High altitude winds were driving the clouds across the dark sky. The air was heavy and the rows of trees along the mountainsides bent in ripples under the strain. A light sprinkle raked the windshield and made Dianna flip on the wipers.

Driving was a panacea for Dianna, in a way an extension of her meditation. Once the rhythm of the road was established, it allowed her mind to wander and to consider. She continued to wrestle with her career choice. Ideals, she thought, ideals had forced her decision.

The realities of getting work as a performer in New York City had battered and ultimately defeated Dianna's goal to be an actress.

Dianna resented the fact that her academic theater training had not taught her many of the necessary "business" skills needed for success—practical things like getting an agent, having the right pictures, knowing how to audition, acting on camera, and so on. When she had started "making the rounds" in the city, she found that she was competing with a group of established actresses her age who were already masters of these vital down-to-earth techniques. Dianna was deeply angered that her school had misdirected her, left her to face the commercial world so unprepared, so ill-equipped to begin a professional career.

But as she relived her failure she asked herself if it would have been worth it even if she had stuck with it. Her dream as an actress was to play meaty and well-written roles. But they rarely seemed to exist for women under forty, and for women over forty the roles were limited to Lady Macbeth and parts that usually were played by name performers with a list of credits that filled a small book. Would she have those credits when she was forty? she wondered. And if she didn't, what then?

Dianna had managed to land a few things off-Broadway and in regional theater, but she had found the parts shallow and unfulfilling. Without making a name for herself, she couldn't get parts, and unless she could get the parts, she couldn't make a name for herself. Trapped in the catch-22 of "the business," she seemed at the mercy of every egomaniacal agent, director, and casting director. So Dianna had given up her ideal of being an actress for a long-range ideal of being her own boss.

Let's face it, she thought, I copped out.

Four years ago a help-wanted ad for a gal Friday had caught her attention. She put on her best two-piece Bergdorf suit, casually lied that she could type forty-five words a minute, and landed the job. For weeks she had conned Sy into thinking she was typing manuscripts at home, while she was in fact shelling out half her salary to pay someone else to do the work and spending long evenings at home mastering the keyboard of her word processor.

The rain came in waves that made Dianna dim her brights so the glare of the high beams would not be reflected back into her eyes. The wind rose to a howl as it battered the Honda. She suppressed a yawn and rubbed her fatigued eyes. Dianna had been four hours behind the wheel without a break.

She had to admit it was crafty of Sy to give her the Kronenberger script to finish. It was just like him. He'll get almost as much work out of me as he would have if I had stayed in town, she thought. She calculated it would take at least seven four-hour sessions to get it in shape. Four hours straight was all she could stand to stare at her computer monitor and juggle blocks of letters.

In most cases Dianna would never be allowed to have anything to do with the work on a script. But this was Kronenberger's first effort, and the FM had bought the play with no agent involved, telling the young man that it wouldn't work without rewrites and insisting that there be a provision in the contract for making revisions.

Dianna was pleased that the FM would give her such an important job. At the same time she had reason to be resentful. No one would ever know she was responsible for the changes. The FM was telling Kronenberger he was having the play rewritten by one of the greatest authors in the history of the American theater, who happened to be broke and needed to make some money under the table.

Dianna's suggestions on other scripts in the past had led the FM to trust and rely on her instincts. Dianna wasn't getting paid anything extra, but she took the assignment because it was interesting, a way to learn, and because it took her away from other dull jobs. But she still felt all the pressures of having to deliver.

Dianna knew that if her work didn't get the FM excited he would simply turn it over to some other ghostwriter until he had the script he wanted. The situation wasn't really fair, she admitted to herself. But the bottom line was it was teaching her a lot about scripts and about writing.

Little does poor Kronenberger know, she thought. Maybe I'll sign this next draft "by Arthur Miller/Dianna LaBianca."

She told herself, One day I will walk into the office and tell Sy what he can do with his uncredited rewrites and his phones and his typing. Then I will option a script or write one myself, if necessary, and produce my own production. My taste is just as good as the old macher's, I have the same connections, and one other thing that he is somewhat lacking—integrity.

Small twigs and branches were thrown down across the roadway. The car picked up speed through a series of downhill S-curves into a valley. Most of her driving had been done in and around the city, and Dianna was not used to these steep descents. The rain and the wind confused her sense of speed. The Acura hit ninety. Entering a sharp turn, the tires slid and Dianna realized she was moving too fast.

As she hit the brakes and went into a skid on the wet pavement, a tangled mass suddenly appeared ahead. The wind had blown down a heavy limb into her lane. She veered toward the double yellow line.

Then, from her left, headlights of a roaring semi truck bore down on her from around the oncoming curve.

To her right was only a narrow space between the fallen limb and a low guardrail.

The blackness of a sharp drop-off was all she could see beyond the edge of the guardrail.

8

In a split-second decision, Dianna braked and swerved the car to the right, narrowly squeezing past the end of the limb and the cables of the rail. The Honda skirted the gravel berm and started slipping toward the flimsy rail.

The driver of the huge rig slammed on his brakes, and the semi jackknifed toward her on the rain-soaked pavement.

Dianna jerked the wheel to the left. The car didn't respond and kept sliding for the edge.

"Mary, Mother of God!" shouted Dianna.

The truck engine growled as the driver accelerated to pull out of the jackknife.

The long trailer of the rig came at Dianna like the side of a steel barn.

Dianna's car hurtled toward the edge.

With a jolt the tires of the Honda finally dug in and swung the car back onto the pavement. As the semi gained speed, the driver managed to pull the wide-swinging trailer back into the proper lane.

The truck thundered to a halt fifty feet past the fallen limb. Dianna brought the Acura to a stop as soon as she had it under control.

Jumping down from his rig, the trucker ran toward Dianna's car and yelled, "You okay, lady?"

Dianna exhaled. "I'll be fine . . . as soon as my heart starts again."

The driver stood in the rain, looking over the edge of the rail. "You almost bought the farm, lady. Jesus, that's a long way down. I'll put out some flares and try to raise the 'man' on the CB."

After sitting motionless for a moment clutching the wheel, Dianna put the car in gear and drove on. Her sweating hands on the leather steering-wheel cover began to shake uncontrollably.

If I'd gone to the left toward the truck instead of to the side of the road, it would have been all over. That heavy semi would have demolished the car and me with it. Dianna had a vision of the driver scraping her car off the grill of his truck like a squashed bug.

Yes, I saw the end coming, no doubt about it—I "knew" that truck was going to hit. Wait a minute, what did I call out? . . . I shouted "Hail Mary, Mother of God," didn't I? I'm still as Catholic as I ever was. I spend the last four years living and breathing Zen, then when I'm put to the test, I turn into a rabid Catholic. I guess it's to be expected, she realized. *I've spent most of my life as a Catholic.*

Both the LaBiancas and her mother's side, the Dupres, were Catholic, and the two families took the religion seriously. Definitely too seriously, she decided. When she was a little girl, missing Mass was an act punishable by virtual disinheritance. Her four brothers had played football for their parochial high school, and nights before the games the entire family would gather at home to pray for the success of their team.

The very first weekend Dianna had escaped away to college, she stopped attending Mass. She remembered the freedom she felt that Sunday morning on campus when the chapel bells pealed out their call and she knew she had the luxury of staying in bed with a book. Still, there were compromises that had to be made to keep the tuition coffers open: Dianna still had to attend Mass whenever she was at home.

She pictured the phone ringing in the plush Westchester home and the folks getting a call announcing her death. Daddy, she knew, would react with his wild temperament: hysteria, tears. Mother would develop worry lines so quickly that within the year she'd be forced to have a third face-lift—free, of course, at the hands of her husband surgeon.

Why is it, Dianna wondered, *that to think of death is often to think of it in terms of the reactions of those around us?*

9

Cold. Wet. Want out. Want play big place. Cold time too long. Want flowers come. Want smells come. Want out.

The rain outside made Esau restless. The winter had been long, and he knew the rains would soon bring the flowers and that meant the coming of spring.

Esau took the photograph of Anne off the nail on the wall and studied her face.

Want play with booteful.

What a fantastic hot, dry night it had been, the September evening he had gotten out of the icehouse, and how good was the feeling of freedom. That previous summer, the reservoirs had fallen to their lowest point in years, and the heat had continued well into the fall evening when Esau first saw the straw-haired booteful walking in the cemetery, in the place of the dead stones.

Smell! What smell! Esau 'ove booteful's smell.

He could recall perfectly all the smells of that night, a night fraught with the aroma of falling leaves, a pungent scent that had an exhilarating effect on him, like a dose of caffeine. When the air was dry, Esau's sense of smell was especially acute.

He had been allowed outside for his evening feed and was chained to his tree when Jacques came to get him and put him back in the cellar for the night. The French Canadian had been drinking, and when the man shut the heavy icehouse inner door and tried to lock it, he only half turned the key and the dead bolt did not quite set.

Esau knew by the sound of the door's closing that something was different, and after Jacques had gone, he discovered the

32

open lock. An outer door was still held in place by a slide bar, but it was an easy matter for him to work the door back and forth, wiggling the hinges loose from the wood of the dry-rotted door frame.

As Esau crept outside, he felt a joy of freedom that he had not known in years.

"Gaaagh-ga! Heeeeoooo!"

Free! Smells! Free!

He loped across the grass with a sideways skipping stride and disappeared down the bridle path, into the moonlit night.

Esau played for an hour and a half among the trees and on the forest bed, scratching and rolling himself in the earth and leaves, wallowing like a happy hog. His frolic was a demented romp of celebration. How good it felt to be outside. How wonderful were all the different smells that he came across—spoor of raccoon, fox, insect droppings, and unusual aromas like the urine that the squirrels tried to spray at him from the trees.

As Esau played, Anne Spencer Caufield was only a mile away taking a walk to cool off. She was glad to get some time apart from the other Children of the Bread of Life. Since seven that morning, Anne had baked 144 loaves of whole grain raisin bread—enough to feed the Family for three days, with many dozens of loaves left over to sell in town. Her face still felt a tingle of the heat from the fires of the huge ovens. Sometimes the pressures of continual sharing were too much to handle, even for the good-natured young woman.

She had struck out to the south along the narrow trails that wound through the forest. The Vermont moon was half-full and colored Anne's blond hair with a river of silver-blue.

She came to a bridle path and took it west until she arrived at the old family cemetery that she sometimes visited, a place that overlooked a splendid moonlit view. Anne leaned against a mausoleum with a large W etched at the top and took deep breaths of the bracing air. She could feel the tension ease from her body.

She was ready to move on, back home or out West. Anywhere. Her stay with the Children of Bread had been a unique experience, but now Anne was ready for something else. She wasn't even sure exactly what, but she didn't see herself in a lifetime career as a semiprofessional baker.

Behind her, around the corner of the crypt, a twig snapped. Anne wondered if it was the tall, lanky young man who was her sometimes lover.

"Jimmy?" She spoke the name into the quiet night air.

Another loud footfall, then the sound of irregular, heavy breathing came from just around the side of the stone cubicle.

"Jimmy?"

The realization that she was in a graveyard came to the forefront of her mind and took her by surprise, catching her in a moment of frozen fear. Then a word came from behind her like the growl of a large animal, filling Anne with terror. It was spoken deep in the bass register, in jarring masculine tones, with a thick-tongued diction.

"Booteful."

Anne tried to run, but a giant hand, hot and callous, grabbed her arm and held it like a steel-toothed trap.

"Booteful."

When she looked around, Anne was too terrified to scream.

Trying to live up to his twisted vision of how he should behave—how he should act in order to be romantic—Esau lifted Anne in his arms.

Esau be booteful. Do booteful thing.

He intended to casually put her on a low granite headstone, but Esau didn't know how strong he was and the result was that he ended up throwing the girl down at his feet.

"Ooooophh!"

Esau not mean do that.

Anne's head hit a gravestone and there was a crack of ribs breaking against a sharp rock. She tried to cry out, but the splintered bones sent stabs of excruciating pain into her lungs and only the faintest whimper emerged from her lips.

Booteful his now. She 'ove Esau now.

Mercifully, her mind was a fading haze as Esau's weight crushed down upon her. Before she could be aware of anything, her vision erupted into pinwheels of red stars and black dots, and Anne passed out.

She never had any sensation that she was bleeding internally; nor did she have any further feeling of pain from her compound

fractures. As Esau moved to satisfy his need, there was no
further awareness for Anne, only a slowly dulling redness in
her mind, and then there was

 . . . nothing.
 . . . only a painless
 . . . dark and quiet
 . . . nothing.

10

She had passed the eye of the storm, and the wind and rain had
settled into a gentle drizzle. On a rusty sign Dianna saw the
words Fenwick, Vermont Population 2573.

Fenwick was a remote town in southern Vermont. The
buildings were a collage of architectural styles: a Gothic
municipal building, a federal farmhouse, a cluster of post–
World War II tract homes, and a charming storybook chapel in
need of paint. Only one traffic light marked the center of town,
an intersection lined with an assortment of sooty brick buildings. Altogether, Fenwick appeared run-down and somehow
lifeless, a place that had once seen vibrant times but now was
only half a ghost town, its strength dissipated.

This place has to have had a mill, Dianna thought, as she
approached a two-lane trestle bridge. Sure enough, to her right
stood the crumbling shell of a onetime mill factory. It was a
long, low building that clung to the rocks at the edge of a small
river. Most of the mill's windows were broken, and a part of
the structure had been reclaimed by the raging torrents of the
annual spring floods.

Set in stone over a large entrance were worn carved letters
that announced, Wilkinson Mill. The building gave more of the
impression of a prison than a place of employment.

I wonder how many workers' lives were sweated away in
that dingy structure? she thought, as she remembered her
history—slave wages, child labor, eighteen-hour days, lethal
working conditions. Interesting, how our concept of this part of
New England has almost totally changed—from land of
sweatshop to land of vacation, land of weekend haven.

A few miles ahead Dianna came to a sign that gave directions to The Briars, a colonial tavern that had sheltered travelers for over two hundred years. She had made the reservation from a pay phone near the Vermont state line. An ex-boyfriend had recommended the place as having the best chef in North America, and there were stables a mile down the road.

She turned off the road through a gate, then suddenly stepped on the brake, coming to a skidding stop in the gravel of the entrance driveway.

The Briars was gone and all that remained was a flat, smoldering ruin. There was the flashing light of a Fire Chief's car, and two firemen had their heads together in a solemn conference off to the side, near a collapsed section of foundation. One old man, his yellow slicker smeared with soot and ash, picked his way through the still-smoking debris. In a half daze he kicked at a smoldering timber with a blackened boot.

A sign on a post swayed gently in the breeze, its fresh paint untouched by the smoke or flames.

WELCOME TO THE BRIARS
Since 1856
Enjoy your stay

Dianna's first thought was, Well, I guess this means I won't be checking in. A wave of sadness came over her that such an old, unique building could have burned. She remembered the picture of the inn in her guidebook. What a shame, what an irreplaceable loss. A thing of history and beauty gone forever.

Then, as Dianna put the Honda in reverse and backed out of the drive, the realization hit her like a slap in the face—I could have been in there. I could have been inside that building—in the dining room, or taking a bath, or asleep in my bed.

Near death strikes twice. Very shaken up, she wondered, Will the third time be the charm?

Dianna took out her guide to New England and checked for the nearest place on the list. Only six miles away was the Peabody.

PEABODY INN
CLOSED FOR RENOVATION

Inside the old hotel a shadow moved. Dianna pulled up in front and grabbed her travel guide and a felt beret to keep off the light rain. Inside the building a wiry old man, puffing on a pipe, was down on his knees repairing a section of the floor.

"Excuse me? Sir . . . ," she said, stepping through the front door.

"What?" The man responded in a thick New England dialect, obviously resenting her intrusion.

"You wouldn't happen to have a room?" she asked.

"Lady, you got a problem, you can't read English? Didn't you see the sign out front?"

"Yes, well, I . . ."

"The sign reads 'Closed,' don't it?"

"I'm sorry, but you see, I had a reservation at The Briars. . . ."

"Place just burned down."

No kidding, moron, thought Dianna. "Yes, I know, but I saw a light in your window. . . ."

"The light don't say nothin' about havin' a room."

This guy is truly an asshole, she thought, losing her patience. He must spend his winter nights thinking up cryptic ways to put down strangers.

Her LaBianca mouth took charge. "Lights don't *speak* in the city either. Lights do sometimes suggest the presence of a human being with intelligence, and I thought that I might just find a decent person in here who could suggest a place in the area where a lady might find a room."

Dianna was pleased to see that the man was struck speechless for a solid fifteen seconds.

Then he turned sullen. "We have dinner here on Sundays but no rooms till June."

Dianna checked her guidebook. "How about McGuire's?"

"Went out of business three years ago. Your book's out of date."

"The Finley Hotel?"

"Not open."

"Wilkinson Inn?"

The man stopped working, thought about this one for a minute, and grinned a mean grin. "Pretty place."

Then he seemed to have a change of heart and checked

himself. "I don't know if they rent rooms this time of year. They got some of them new hotels 'round Rutland. You'd better look up there."

"How far is the Wilkinson Inn?" she persisted.

As he cradled the bowl of his pipe, Dianna noticed that the tips of two fingers were missing from his left hand. It probably happened working in the mill, she thought.

"I'd suggest you try one of them ski places over in West Dover."

"Could you please tell me how to get to the Wilkinson . . ."

"Up the road 'bout eight mile." He pointed north with his disfigured hand. The two middle fingers were short by an inch. Dianna suppressed a laugh; the man was inadvertently giving her the "horns," the Italian cuckold gesture that her father sometimes used.

Careful, Dianna, she thought to herself. Don't get yourself into more trouble.

While returning to the car, Dianna felt a chill in the air that promised a very cold night. The rain was beginning to let up, but the moisture was rising off the cold land in little clouds of soupy fog. The weather forced her decision to try the Wilkinson. Dianna had no intention of driving on these twisting roads in fog. Besides, the inn was close, and in her guidebook it was listed as having stables and trails on the premises.

Horses had once been a passion for Dianna, an all-consuming love that had shaped her every waking moment, as well as the substance of most of her dreams. Her equestrian "affair" had ended the summer of her junior year in high school, when she had taken a terrible fall. Since then Dianna had been on a horse only a couple of times.

But a touch of the old hunger had come back, and she had a longing to be on a horse. A little easy riding, she thought, would be great.

The truck incident and the burned inn had taken a toll and left Dianna drained. She kept yawning and found herself feeling an impulse to pull over for a short nap. The trip had taken such gruesome turns. Dianna ached to be inside, somewhere warm and safe, settled in for the night.

About five miles out of town Dianna passed a board nailed to a tree with an arrow pointing down a rutted road. On it in crude lettering was the word "Bread." A bakery in the forest? thought Dianna. That's strange.

Just a short distance farther a small yellowed sign reflected her headlight beams and just kept Dianna from missing the turnoff.

THE WILKINSON INN, EST. 1936
FINE FOOD, LIQUORS
STABLES TO LET
HORSES FOR HIRE

The last line of the sign was amended with the hand-printed words "IN SEASON."

Two oversized stone columns flanked the entrance of the drive to the inn. A thick, rusty chain, which could be padlocked across the road, hung from one column. It doesn't look that good, Dianna admitted to herself. But she had to find something, and she knew from a previous trip that in New England an establishment that called itself an inn was required to have rooms to rent.

She was running low on gas and decided she had better give it a try. If I don't stop soon, I'll end up nodding off and driving into a tree.

The gravel road, barely more than a car's width, lay covered in a blanket of wet leaves. There was no rain now, only occasional drips from the trees.

The forest around the drive was reclaiming its territory, and now and then a low-hanging wet branch flapped against the roof of the car. Dianna had bounced along the dark lane for what seemed forty-five minutes when she started to get worried.

Finally, she stopped and was about to turn around to go back when she noticed a pair of approaching headlights. Even after she had driven off the road in order to make room, there was just enough space for the two cars to pass. Dianna rolled down her window and waved. The oncoming car slowed and stopped beside her. She could see two men in the front seat, and what she took to be another couple necking in the rear.

"Is this the way to the Wilkinson Inn?"

"Straight ahead, you can't miss it," said the driver. "You better hurry. The kitchen closes if there's nobody around."

Well, it can't be that bad, she thought. The food's got to be pretty good to make people trek all the way out here. After another mile she came to a wooden bridge that spanned a racing stream. Beyond the trees, the road divided into two drives that encircled a large expanse of pasture. The land sloped upward away from the bridge, and on a rise where the two drives met was the Wilkinson Inn.

11

It stood massive and square, a fortress of heavy, cut stone. Two single-story wings flanked the central structure. The effect was splendid. The rays of light streaming out from the windows caught the slight dusting of fog and gave an aura of importance, a primitive majesty to the dark grounds.

The effect made her stop the car. The wind hushed and died down. Dianna sat for a moment in silence.

So, she thought, is this the site of my next adventure? It would take a fine painter, a Titian or a Turner, to do it justice—an artist who is a master at capturing dramatic light. The perspective should be from a low angle looking up, and the windows should be done in brilliant tones of white-yellow splashed against a dark stone background.

The middle section of the structure must be the original house, she reasoned. It's got to date back to the 1700's. Driving closer, she saw that the windows had keystones of marble with leaded glass. An enclosed porch had obviously been added in the building's more recent past. The porch jutted out from the center section and almost circled the original structure.

Lights beamed from the many windows on the main floor and from behind the curtains in one upstairs window.

A battered horse van and a BMW 320i sports car were the only vehicles in the lot. Dianna pulled in next to the BMW, grabbed her purse, got out, and stretched. The pungent, wonderfully familiar smell of horses came on the breeze and brought back a rush of old memories. To her left as she faced the inn Dianna saw the pump of an old well and not far away in the darkness the outline of a barn.

Whoever ran the inn had money to keep it up. The grounds were well tended and the buildings cared for. Yet there was an aura of disuse about the place, like a summer vacation home that had stood untouched for the winter.

As she headed for the front door Dianna heard a rustle in the leaves behind her. She stopped walking and listened. . . .

There was only silence. She continued on her way. The sound came again, as though there were someone running through the leaves behind her. She whirled around. Her heart leapt into her throat.

Something wet and hairy touched her wrist. She quickly pulled her hand away and looked down to see a German shepherd jumping up on its hind legs, its dripping tongue hanging out.

"Easy boy, easy now."

But the dog only panted and crouched down.

"You want to play, do you?"

The dog woofed.

"Why didn't you 'woof' before you jumped on me?"

There was no one behind the front desk. After a moment Dianna rang the bell. She stood in a small foyer that served as the lobby of the inn. The interior decor was appropriate to the architecture of the building: rough-hewn floorboards, dark paneling, walls cluttered with old prints. A portrait behind the front desk bore the name Oscar Wilkinson and the dates 1803–1864. Only the chrome pay phone on her left seemed anachronistic.

A beefy woman in a scruffy waitress uniform walked in, rubbing her hands with a towel. She had a wide-eyed fearful look that changed to weariness the second she saw Dianna.

"Kitchen's closed."

"I was really interested in a room."

"Got no rooms to let."

"You mean they're all full?"

"We ain't got no rooms."

Dianna's instincts were strangely mixed, almost torn. On the one hand, a part of her wanted to turn and walk out the door, even run to the car; on the other hand, she was exhausted from driving for almost six hours, and she wasn't sure where else she could go or if she would be able to stay awake to get there.

Dianna cranked up her toughest I'm-from-New-York-and-do-what-I-say-or-you-die voice. "You call this place an inn, don't you?"

The woman nodded nervously and Dianna continued. "Then, by law you are required to have available lodging. I would like a room."

The lady was taken aback by this bit of knowledge. Dianna had seen Arthur pull the same routine on an innkeeper in the Berkshires.

An eyebrow curled, and the heavyset woman asked, "Are you a friend of that magazine writer?"

Leading question, Dianna thought. The right answer gets me a bed for the night. Figuring she had nothing to lose, she answered, "Let's just say it's possible."

Still, the lady seemed on the verge of saying no. She mulled the decision over in her mind once more, then shrugged in a kind of sarcastic—or, Dianna thought, was it an ironic?—manner.

"All right, suit yourself."

"Thank you. I appreciate it. Well, should I sign or anything?"

"You got to. Like you say, it's the law," remarked the woman, pulling out a ragged book. As she signed, Dianna glanced at the last entry. "Dennis Conwell" was printed in neat, even letters.

"Come on."

As Dianna followed up the creaking staircase, she studied the woman. Her arms were as big as most women's thighs, with only a trace of fattiness. She was tall, five-nine or five-ten, with broad shoulders and hips that, as Dianna's mother used to say, were as wide as the Hudson. It was clear this woman had done hard physical labor all of her life. She took the stairs with a brisk waddle as her bulk shifted from one step to the next.

The staircase rose toward the rear of the house. At the top of the long flight, the woman made a 180-degree turn that led them back toward the front of the inn, which faced south. Four doors opened onto the floor.

"You've only got four rooms in the whole inn?"

"That's right. You get the last one."

The big woman stopped outside the room that took up the

southwest corner of the inn and pulled open a sturdy door that crackled with the sound of rusty hinges.

Grayed sheets, which the woman proceeded to gather and deposit in the hall, covered the furniture. The effect was unsettling and ghostly. The bath, to Dianna's right as she walked in, and a closet to her left formed a short entranceway. Then the room widened into a spacious, high-ceilinged area. A large double window with leaded panes looked out over the front yard of the inn. Another similar window faced the side. Dianna walked toward it thinking, I should be able to see the barn from here. Yes, she could just make it out through old panels of distorted glass.

"I'll hav'ta get clean sheets. No one's slept here for a year."

The woman waddled out, leaving Dianna to contemplate the oddly decorated room. On the inside wall, opposite the double windows, stood a heavy fieldstone fireplace, with a cast-iron ring stuffed with cord wood and an old, rusty fire set. On the mantel was a box of kitchen matches. An unusual assortment of lamps, mostly from the forties, lit the room. Against the same wall in the far corner was a desk in a style that Dianna could only describe as 1958-ugly. The charming pegged utility table that served as a nightstand was probably a hundred years old.

Dianna pulled off the sheets that covered the bed. It was an awesome maple structure with four towering posts, as thick as Dianna's waist, that spiraled to the ceiling. She thought, This is just the kind of thing you would expect to find in the estate of one of the old robber barons. On the carved headboard blank-eyed cupids fired arrows at each other across the mattress.

The woman returned with clean sheets.

Dianna gestured to the bed. "That's almost four feet off the ground. How do you get up there?"

"You got a stool under the corner post."

"No phone?" asked Dianna, looking around the room.

"Pay phone's down in the lobby. That's the only one we got."

"Hmmm." Not having a phone could have distinct advantages, thought Dianna.

A ragged bobcat head jutted out from the front wall beside the double windows. Around it was a set of four hunting prints.

A portrait of a gentleman hung over the mantel. A brass plaque on the frame read, The Great Philanthropist, Mr. Thomas Wilkinson.

"Is this the man who built the inn?"

"Nope, but his great grandfather did."

"What philanthropy was Mr. Thomas noted for?"

"He sold whiskey to the Indians, committed adultery, built churches, and traded in slaves."

"Nice."

"He *is* remembered for a duel he fought with Andrew Jackson in 1797. Used those pistols there." She pointed to a brace of dueling pistols in a glass case.

"I take it he didn't kill Jackson."

"Nope. Jackson's pistol didn't go off, and Mr. Thomas's return shot missed. Some folks that were there said Mr. Thomas acted like a true gentleman and dropped his aim. Others said he was too drunk to shoot straight."

"Lucky for the nation. Whose portrait is that in the foyer?"

"Oscar Samuel Wilkinson, Thomas's grandson."

The answers are so pat, Dianna thought, like the woman has given them a thousand times and expects to be rattling them off for all of eternity.

She continued. "He's the one built the mill in Fenwick and brought indentured workers over from Ireland and England. Ran the mill for twenty-five years, till a group of workers got fed up and took up arms over the poor conditions. They came one night, dragged him out of *this* bed, and hung him on the old sugar maple out back."

"Sweets for the sweet."

"Come again."

"Well, I'm glad I'm not a part of that family."

"I'm Miss Agnes *Wilkinson* . . . if you need anything. 'Night. Pleasant dreams."

Nice move, Dianna, she thought. The LaBianca mouth strikes again. Why do I always have to say what I'm thinking?

Agnes marched out of the room. Dianna quickly shut the door and turned the key in the heavy lock. She looked around the room and thought, This is what I get for going adventuring.

As Dianna filled the large prewar enamel bathtub with scalding water, she thought, You could have a ménage à trois in this thing, and in comfort. Not that Dianna was into that, but she could think of a couple of men, including the wretch Arthur, she would like to go one-on-one with in the old tub. Ah well, can't have everything.

Dianna examined herself in the mirror on the inside of the bathroom door. Not bad, she thought. Despite the office work, she managed to keep "the bod" in shape through aerobics and occasional jogging. Dianna stood five-foot-five and her eyes were a whitish light blue, just like her mother's. Her dark brown hair, complexion, and nicely rounded figure were from her father's Northern Italian side. The combination of Dianna's tan skin color and her sparkling silver-blue eyes was striking and evoked a lot of compliments.

She was just a touch on the busty side, with unusually full nipples, to an extent that sometimes gave her grief. Once, when Dianna made an appearance in the office in T-shirt sans bra, she caused such comment and distraction that getting work done that day became almost impossible.

"Body-to-die-for, great mind, what more could anyone want?" she quipped to herself.

After bathing and washing her hair Dianna took a closer look around the room. She thought, Granted, the furniture doesn't match, and the bed is a museum monstrosity, but somehow the effect is pleasing.

On a shelf near the bed was a selection of books, evidently left for the pleasure of guests: a yellowed copy of what must have been a first edition paperback of *Gone with the Wind*, a Gideon Bible, a *Reader's Digest* volume of condensed books, and a medical tome titled *Curiosities and Anomalies of Medicine, 1901*. A stack of faded magazines lay nearby, including a *TV Screen* and . . . This is odd, thought Dianna—a mutilated copy of *Penthouse*. She picked up the magazine and thumbed through the pages of exploitive photographs. Several pictures had been cut or torn out, and the pages were wrinkled.

Whoever had gotten their hands on this must have been one hot-blooded letch, she thought. Dianna giggled to herself as she wondered whether he'd left his name and address.

With the aid of the three-legged milking stool, she climbed onto the huge bed. It was much softer than her mattress in the city and seemed to absorb her and rearrange its stuffing to fit her contours. I'd sell my soul for a bed like this, she thought.

She got a chill when she remembered the story of the Wilkinson ancestor being dragged out of bed and taken to the maple tree out back. Well, she thought with a smile, shaking off the feeling, I might have had a worse fate. I could have had to go into the office tomorrow.

She fell into a restless sleep, her hands still busy clutching and turning her steering wheel.

12

At three-thirty in the morning the frantic barking of the German shepherd broke the quiet of the country darkness. The hinges of the front door of the inn squeaked as the door was opened. Then came a crash as the door was slammed shut, followed by a tinkling of broken glass.

Dianna slept on, the sounds reverberating on the edge of her consciousness.

Agnes Wilkinson spoke in a loud whisper, "Jacques? Jacques?!"

Heavy footsteps echoed in the foyer with the dull thud of a chair being knocked over. Another voice, male, fighting to take control, spoke, *"Qu'est-ce qu'il fait maintenant, le bete!"*

Then guttural sounds came from downstairs, utterances like speech but not like any language ever spoken, sounds similar to those produced by a deaf man—throaty masculine tones, uncontrolled, as if the speaker had a limited awareness of the nature of the sounds being produced.

"Garr-gah. Oooohag. Gragggg."

Agnes's voice made an inaudible reply, and the French Canadian commanded menacingly, *"Allez-y bete, allez-y bete!"*

A struggle was taking place in the foyer. Agnes and the man whispered harshly to each other in French.

Then came the third voice in response—cacophonous and strident, as if the air from the speaker's diaphragm beat uncontrollably against the vocal cords.

"Gaaagafag. Eeeee-haaaa. Neeeda."

It was a sound that could have been the result of an overwhelming speech impediment or some crippling injury to the brain. Yet the vocalizations emerged free, unencumbered by the necessity of pronunciation—a most natural, unnatural sound. Then the voice suddenly changed and became pleading, grotesquely childlike.

"Eeeeee-haa. Neeeeeda. Peeeeeeze!"

Agnes made a soothing reply followed by a firm "No."

Out of the babble of demented sounds came one distinguishable word, spoken with intense pleading urgency:

"Booo-tee-ful."

Then from anger and frustration the disjointed gibberish rose in volume and pitch.

"Boo-tee-ful. Boo-tee-ful. 'Ove boo-tee-ful!"

There was the crack of a chair being smashed to splinters against a wall.

The door to the room across from Dianna opened with a click. The sound of unoiled wheels moved down the hall to the top of the staircase.

A fourth voice now spoke inaudibly in guarded whispers, taking charge of the situation. At first this voice was harsh and authoritative, then calming and gentle. It was a woman's voice, old, yet strong of will.

With a whimper, the demented speaker begged with the elongated syllables of a spoiled three-year-old:

"Booooo-teeee-fuuul."

There was the crackling of cellophane and the sounds of lips smacking and chewing.

After a bit the creaking of wheels returned along the hall and into the front room.

The storm door slammed shut. Outside, away from the house there came a cry that resembled a timber wolf or a small elephant. The inhuman voice rose in a wail, a drawn-out moan filled with hunger and sadness.

"Gaaaaar-ga-oooohga-OOOOGA!"

Dianna lunged up in bed, startled, half-awake. Did I hear something? she thought. Voices, doors slamming, a dog's cry? What was it?

She listened. . . . No sound, only the German shepherd

barking in the distance. It's really nothing, she thought. There's nothing to hear. It's just a dream, the result of a strange environment and a different bed.

After a few moments of silence Dianna drifted back into her dreamless sleep.

PART II

A kanji that can be translated as "the way."

A human life . . .
A candle in the wind
Frost on the tile.

Chinese proverb

13

She rose early, still accustomed to her schedule in the city. Dianna vaguely remembered waking the night before, but the blue sky outside the window took her attention. In fifteen minutes she was dressed and on her way out the front door for a tour of the grounds.

A light brushing of high clouds, a slight chill in the air, just a trace of a breeze, it was perfect Vermont weather.

The quiet was broken by the nasal call of Agnes as she summoned a flock of geese for their morning feed. "Here, goose (honk), goose (honk), goose (honk)!"

The gaggle of fat birds disappeared at a fast waddle around to the back of the building. What Dianna had taken to be a barn to the west of the inn turned out to be a stable, painted equestrian red with a white trim on its doors and windows.

She decided to save the pleasure of visiting the barn until the last, giving herself a carrot, a little delight to look forward to. Setting an easy pace, she jogged away from the stable, to the east, along a leaf- and gravel-covered bridle path. She noticed a square garage on a fieldstone foundation sitting behind the inn not too far from the barn. That must have been converted from an icehouse, Dianna surmised. There was a building like that on her grandfather Dupre's estate that had been one of her favorite haunts during her childhood days in Delaware.

There were steps leading down below the ground to a wooden door and a grimy dark window that peeked out, toward the inn and the maple tree, from the rock at the base of the building.

• • •

Smell a booteful! See her! She booteful. She smell better than any booteful Esau smell.

Booteful different. Why?

That smell. Esau 'ove smell. Esau know that smell. Smell of Esau's dreams. Smell like 'ove. So good. Better than good. Smell best.

Smell make Esau big. But more. Smell make Esau feel warm. Make Esau feel safe. Booteful is best booteful. Best booteful for Esau in all big place. Make Esau feel home.

Esau want out.

Esau want booteful.

Esau must get out.

She Esau's.

MUST GET OUT!

Esau must take what is his.

As Dianna lost sight of the inn behind her, she could tell that the large estate had once been farmed. Stone fences, now overgrown and obsolete, stretched aimlessly into the forest.

Seeing the decay of the stone fences made her sad. It had taken so much labor to clear the land and so many hours of painstaking work had been spent to stone-by-stone fit odd-shaped pieces of rock into a wall that would stand without using mortar, a flattop pasture fence that meshed like a crossword puzzle or a fine handmade quilt.

Despite the abuse of time, the craft of the workmen was still there to be seen. It had taken a lifetime to learn how to build the stone fences, and now they were useless, their art fading into oblivion as the stones settled a little more each day into the bed of the forest.

Dianna was beginning to breathe hard from the walking, harder than she had expected to. It must be the slightly higher altitude, she reasoned. The trail curved, heading north. Knowing that most bridle paths circle back to their original point, she assumed that by staying on the trail she would eventually return to the inn.

Five years ago, Dianna thought, I would have been acting like a total WAP (Westchester American Princess—pronounced prin-*cess*). I would have been complaining about everything, bothered that it wasn't summer, that there were no leaves on the trees, that it was too cold, ad infinitum. Now I'm grinning like a fool, looking for something beautiful. She knew she had Takahashi to thank.

Dianna was still troubled by her last Za-zen session. Why had the Roshi seemed so distant and concerned? To be uncertain and disconcerted was so unlike him. He was such a rock—focused, confident, smooth as a mirror pond.

A bend in the trail took her to a site overlooking a breathtaking view of the mountains. On the site stood a family cemetery, going to seed, with a low iron fence around it that partitioned the area off from the encroaching forest.

In the center a tall marble column topped with a cross proclaimed "WILKINSON." In all, there were about two dozen weather-beaten stones and markers. Dianna ambled among the graves, looking at the inscriptions. The oldest she could find read, Sarah Adams Wilkinson, 1672–1703, She sleeps now in the bosom of the Lord. Facing the mountains was a small mausoleum. Walking toward it Dianna mused, It's got a nice view; I wonder if it's rent-stabilized. On the arch above the door was inscribed Oscar Samuel Wilkinson, on the bronze door in raised relief MAY   REST HIS SOUL. The word "GOD" had been gouged out of the stone. Probably an editorial comment by one of Oscar Wilkinson's irate mill workers, Dianna thought.

Three fairly recent graves formed a group by themselves. The first gravestone read, Michael Oscar Wilkinson; Husband, Father; 1929–1964. Next to it was another marker, reading, Karen Tate Wilkinson; Wife, Mother; 1934–1955; She died so that her son could live. Beside her grave was a third stone, Esau Michael Wilkinson, Loving Son, 1955–1966. By the dates, and the epitaph on Karen Tate's stone, Dianna could tell that the woman had died giving birth to Esau.

Long-withered wreaths lay on the father's and mother's graves. How peculiar, Dianna thought, no one put anything, not even a small wreath or a flower, on Esau's grave.

She took a moment to savor the view that stretched north over the mountaintops, and then she moved on.

The bridle path was indeed a complete circle bringing Dianna to the stable. The low and long building had a set of double doors at each end, and inside were rows of stalls that faced each other across a central aisle. In the stalls were two distinct categories of horses: thoroughbreds and the kind of work-weary mounts a stable might be lucky to rent by the hour. Dianna counted three thoroughbreds, probably being boarded for the winter. They stood in modernized stalls with automatic watering troughs. The assortment of saddle horses were a sad lot, who for the most part only stared at Dianna with dull eyes.

Just as she was finishing her tour of the stable, Dianna was taken completely by surprise as she almost walked into a man fumbling with a lock on a harness-room door. When he saw Dianna he casually let his hands drop from his padlock.

"Hello," he said.

"Good morning. It's much easier when you use a key, you know," quipped Dianna.

"I was just curious to see what kind of equipment they have. I'm Dennis Conwell. You don't work here, do you?"

"No, I'm a guest. Dianna LaBianca."

"That's your Honda I saw parked out front?"

"Yes, it is. And you must be the man from the magazine."

"Well, actually I'm here ah . . . writing for the travel section of the *Boston Herald*. I'm working on an article about a preseason tour of southern New England. You know, where to stay, where to dine, that sort of thing."

Dianna studied the man. He was approximately thirty-five, of average height. Dianna got a kick out of rating men in the same way she rated the reviews of Broadway shows: pan to mixed to rave. She looked at Dennis with her critic's cap on.

He was dressed casually but conservatively, like a stockbroker on a vacation. Everything about him said banker or prep school. She glanced down at his feet expecting to see something like a pair of penny loafers, but what she saw was Sperry Topsiders, which confirmed her first impression beyond a doubt. There was also a look of the outdoors about him, as though he skied or played a lot of tennis. Mixed, leaning to rave, she decided, handing down her review.

"Do you ride?" she asked, wondering why he had been interested in the tackle room.

"No, I don't. I don't know that much about horses really, only that my readers often like the opportunity to ride. I just wanted to check up on their equipment. What about you?" New England vowel sounds colored a good deal of his speech.

"There was a time when I rode a lot."

"I would love to give it a try. Say, you don't know whose initials are ESA, do you?"

"No. Why do you ask?"

"Someone's written them all over the barn. ESA. It's everywhere."

"Maybe the graffiti people from New York take their summers here."

Dennis laughed. "Maybe. You're up from the city?"

"Yes."

They started walking together toward the inn. "My home is Boston, but I spend a fair amount of time in Manhattan. Have you had breakfast?"

"No," said Dianna.

"Mind if I join you?"

"Why not."

"Is it *Miss* LaBianca?"

"*Ms*. LaBianca."

He smiled. "I guess I asked for that."

The German shepherd playfully ran out to greet them. Suddenly the dog jumped up and snatched Dianna's knitted scarf out of her hand and darted away.

Dianna started to chase him. "You rotten dog, give me back that scarf. Come here. Here, boy, come here."

The more Dianna chased the dog the more he ran away, dragging the scarf through the grass.

Dennis yelled after her, "Relax. He wants you to chase him." Dennis picked up a stick and waved it in the air. "Here, boy, here, boy."

The dog dropped the scarf and started to bark at the raised stick. Dennis tossed it into the pasture, and while the shepherd raced after the thrown stick, Dennis went to retrieve Dianna's scarf. "It's okay," he said, "if you don't mind a little dog saliva. That animal's a kleptomaniac; he tried to run off with my attaché case when I checked in. He chewed up the handle pretty good."

"I see," said Dianna. "A mugger dog. Vermont is not usually their natural habitat."

At the front desk Agnes stood sorting through receipts. She looked at the couple out of the corner of her eye as if she were thinking, I know what you two were up to last night.

Dianna put a little assertiveness in her voice. "Miss Agnes,

I've decided to stay for a week. That is, if the room is not booked up."

Agnes, obviously distressed, glanced back and forth between Dennis and Dianna. "It's a little early in the season. . . . I don't do maid service 'cept for Fridays and weekends. You'll have to make your own bed. Restaurant's only open Thursday and Friday nights and weekends. Other evenings, you'll have to go out and get your own meals."

"That's fine."

"Give me three days in advance."

"I will. Are the horses available for riding?"

"Not till June."

"I'm an experienced rider."

"Come back in June."

"Look, Miss Wilkinson, I know somebody's got to ride those nags every once in a while or they'll start throwing your customers in the dirt. I could save you some trouble."

"Feed 'em in the mornin'?"

Dianna hesitated. She knew all too well the hours this entailed. "Well . . . sure."

Agnes obviously wanted to sleep in, and the concept was beginning to appeal to her. "English or Western?"

"Both. Mostly English."

"I'll talk to Jacques."

Dennis said, "Miss Wilkinson, can we still get breakfast?"

"If you want it."

They chose a table in one of the small, enclosed porches at the front of the inn, with a view of the greenhouse and the grounds. Agnes came and recited the menu from memory. She recommended "Jacques's special egg casserole." They both decided to try it.

"Why is she acting like we know each other better than we do?" Dennis said.

"To tell you the truth, when I got here last night Agnes didn't want to give me a room. She asked if I knew a writer from some magazine. I was desperate, so I said I might. It did the trick. She changed her mind and gave me the room."

Dennis smiled. "That's the power of the press. Everyone here is terrified of getting a bad write-up. I'll back your story."

A heavyset, olive-complexioned man came in, bearing bread and fresh butter. His hands were meaty and rough, and he had a small mustache. He plopped the dishes on the table, gave Dianna the eye, and left without speaking a word.

"Jacques," said Dennis, "is the chef and does just about everything else around here. He's Canadian."

"Does he live in the inn?"

"I think he shares the room opposite mine with Miss Agnes. I gather they are . . . an item."

"Ah, I see," said Dianna. "Which room is yours?"

"I'm in the back of the inn on the west side."

"Then you're on the same side I am?"

"That's right."

"So who's in the other front room?"

"I don't know, but I've seen lights on," said Dennis.

The breakfast was divine. The casserole turned out to be a delightful combination of fresh eggs and sharp Vermont cheddar cheese with a blend of exotic spices. A basket of hearty biscuits arrived straight from the oven, accompanied by a mason jar of homemade crab-apple jam. On the side, Jacques served pear halves filled with sour cherries and orange slices. There was creamy butter and thick slices of hickory-smoked bacon cooked in maple syrup. A heady aroma wafted up from individual pots of dark, rich coffee on the table.

Dianna said, "Jacques can come cook for me anytime."

"I suppose they'd better have good food, with only four rooms to rent. People usually come here to eat, not to stay."

The twosome made polite conversation and exchanged the standard information. Dianna discovered that Dennis had grown up in Cape Ann, Massachusetts, and was single. He seemed reluctant to talk about his job. The more she got to know Dennis, the less he fit Dianna's conception of a journalist.

He dressed the wrong way—too conservatively—his clothes were a little too expensive, and he didn't have the aura or the focused sensitivities of any of the writers that she knew. Maybe it's just the difference between a Boston newspaperman and the ones I know in New York, she thought. She admitted that a person had to be a little strange just to live in Manhattan in the first place.

"How about you, what do you do?" asked Dennis.

Dianna hadn't gotten over her dislike of answering the question. "I'm an assistant producer. I work for Sy Field;

maybe you've heard of him. He produced *Chronicles for Living* and *Celebrations and Other Songs*."

"Oh, that's interesting. Funny, I would have guessed you were an actress. I don't know, there's something about you . . ."

Oh, great, thought Dianna, he has to rub salt in the wound. "Well, I used to be an actress. It just . . . it all got to be too much for me. It was a drag, making the rounds, carrying a portfolio of pictures, padding my resume. It turned out to be an enormous bore. The only work I ever seemed to do was to look for work. Most of my competition were idiots. One out of five of them had a brain in her head. But every single one of them could read a sweet ingenue role or a page of inane advertising copy just as well as I could."

"Did you study acting?" he asked.

"Oh, sure, but what good are four years of academic theater when it comes to selling toilet tissue or kitchen cleanser? I never had the credits to get into episodic television; they always told me I was too offbeat for the soaps. Hey, look, I made the right choice."

"Things have a way of working out for the best," said Dennis.

I hope so, she thought.

Dennis poured cream in his coffee as he said, "Look, I've got to check out some other places in the area this afternoon, but if you're free this evening, why don't we have dinner together? There's a French restaurant over in Newfane."

She looked at him and thought to herself, Dianna, you really didn't come here to be alone, did you? But then, she admitted, you never really go anywhere to be *alone*. Quit kidding yourself. Come on, it's a front, isn't it—a mask? You really go places to *possibly* be alone, but always with the *possibility* of . . . ? How else could there be adventures?

Even before her mind was rationally made up, she heard herself saying, "I'd like that. If anyone would know a good restaurant around here, you would."

He stared at her blankly. "Why do you say that?"

"Because it's your job, isn't it?"

"Of course, but you see, I've just started in this area, you know." Dennis looked down as he stirred his coffee and said, "How about if I pick you up around seven or so?"

14

The dog had been in the family since Esau could remember. Pumpkin had grown up with Esau, and the dog had never been afraid of him, never barked at him, and never been unkind to him. They had played together. They had shared food and shared smells that only the two of them understood.

The dog had been his only friend.

One day Esau's nose had found Pumpkin under the porch, where the old dog had crawled the day before to die. Pumpkin had had a fight with a German shepherd that had just been brought to the inn. The new dog was a two-year-old and Pumpkin was a geriatric, almost nineteen. Esau knew who had hurt his friend, for the smell of the German shepherd was all over Pumpkin.

The scent of Pumpkin as he lay still was all wrong, sick and strange, and Esau couldn't understand why the dog didn't move, why he wouldn't wake up and play.

Goody, Anges, and Jacques had taken Esau with them to the cemetery and let him watch as they put the dog in the ground, and the concept of death slowly took on a cold and very real meaning for Esau. After they covered Pumpkin with dirt, Esau had sat down on the fresh grave.

Goody pointed to a stone marker and said, "Dada."

Esau looked at the stone and the grass-covered plot of earth and asked, "Dada?"

Goody nodded, pointed again, and firmly repeated, "Dada. Dada dead. Pumpkin dead. Dada dead."

Esau sat there for a long time, his hand on his head, a confused ape staring at the place where Goody had said Dada was. Then he made the connection. It hit him like a club. He remembered his father lying still in the parking lot, as still as Pumpkin had been under the porch.

He pointed and asked, "Dada?"

Goody nodded and said, "Yes, Dada. Dada dead."

Esau suddenly knew where his father was, where his father had been all this time. He hadn't been away at the baseball game.

Esau moved away from Pumpkin's grave to the stone and the mound where Goody had pointed. His fingers touched the marker. He put his arms on the slightly raised mound where she had said Dada was.

Esau sat down on his father's grave. He stayed there for hours not moving, his hands occasionally patting the earth as his father had once patted his shoulders. At one time he lay down and spread his arms across the grave, embracing the mound.

When they tried to get him to leave, he wouldn't, and so they locked his chain around the monolithic family marker and let him stay. Esau remained there through the night, not moving from his place on the grave until the sun rose the next morning.

From that night, Esau understood the word "dead," and the cemetery took on a new meaning for him—it became the place of the dead stones.

15

After breakfast, back in her room, Dianna set up the laptop, laid out the play script and the list of changes to be made, then arranged neat piles of disks, notepaper, and pencils. Her first order of business was to scratch out *Remembered Jewels*.

She gazed out the window as she tried to think of a better title. Slightly to her left and west of the inn she could see the stable. At her right stood the old pump and the gnarled sugar maple. Which branch did they lynch Sir Thomas from? she wondered. How about *Hangin' Around* for a title? she joked to herself. Without giving the question any more thought, she plunged into her typing.

During her first six months in the office, Dianna had made a conscious effort to become indispensable to the FM. Dianna's fingers paused on the keyboard as she made a face and thought, Indispensable, what a wretched word. On the one hand, being indispensable was positive, reassuring, because it meant that her services were of irreplaceable value to her employer. On the other hand, she detested the implied concept of "service." Dianna didn't like the idea of being a servant to any person or organization.

What let her hold her head up on the job was the fact that she was still working toward an ideal, albeit a long-range one. If she could eventually become her own boss, a power-wielding producer in this field that she loved, well, that was worth compromise in many forms, be it learning the ignoble art of the Touch System or kissing the FM's butt through hard work, loyalty, and deserved flattery.

Beginning with the title page, she inserted her boss's

changes and stopped to make several small rewrites of her own as she went along. Kronenberger would have a seizure if he knew it was me, the lowly assistant producer, doing the revisions, Dianna thought. Even many of the improvements listed on the yellow pad had evolved from her suggestions.

Someday, Dianna thought. Someday they won't only be suggestions, they'll be demands, and the multitude will rush to comply, eager to do my bidding.

Dennis arrived promptly at seven. He took Dianna on a shortcut over winding backroads through the mountains. He pushed the 320i hard through the turns, staying in low gears and revving the engine mercilessly near the red line on his tachometer.

It was the kind of driving that made Dianna nervous. Even in high school, she had always hated it when her immature dates had wanted to show off their expensive cars. She started to say something about the speed but checked herself because Dennis seemed to be in complete control of the car.

The glove compartment held a selection of disks for the CD player. She sorted through the collection of mostly top ten and rock albums, decided against his one show album, *Shōgun: the Musical*, and opted for his long classical disk of Bach cantatas.

A stag lurched out of the trees at the edge of the road and leapt across the path of the BMW, causing Dennis to swerve and brake hard, throwing Dianna forward against her seat belt. With two quick bounds, the fear-crazed animal disappeared into the forest on the other side of the road.

Dennis and Dianna caught their breaths.

"That was a thirteen-pointer," said Dennis as he drove on. "He would be quite a catch."

"You don't hunt, do you?"

"Not deer. Only duck."

"You mean you actually shoot and kill harmless little ducks?" said Dianna.

"Adult ducks and only in season."

"It's still disgusting."

"I always eat them."

"That is no excuse."

"You had bacon this morning with breakfast, didn't you? Someone killed that animal just so you could eat it."

"That's different."

"Is a duck a more noble animal than a hog?"

"But you are killing primarily for sport, for entertainment."

"Only partially. But unless you're a vegetarian, *you* are being hypocritical."

"But *you* are deriving pleasure from killing."

"I am deriving satisfaction from the knowledge that I have the skill to bag my own dinner, at least once in a while—as human beings have been doing since the dawn of man, excuse me, perhaps the dawn of 'persons' would be a more appropriate thing to say."

"But at least domestic animals are killed quickly and humanely, not shot at and often left wounded to die in the bushes. We are supposed to be civilized human beings—not terrorizers of defenseless little creatures."

"Do you eat veal?"

"Well, yes, occasionally."

"Then you'd better stop. How do you think those cute little calves feel as they are led to the slaughter?"

He's got more fire than I thought, Dianna mused, starting to like him.

She glanced over at Dennis engrossed in his driving as he took a hard turn. He's so god-awful, smugly all-American, she thought. His feet are securely on the ground. He's part of the *real* world, not the illusions of the "great white way." He and I are light-years apart. With that thought, Dianna realized that the person she had described was very unwriterlike and decided to pry a bit at dinner.

Newfane was an enchanting little town. Five or six white colonial buildings, set well apart on a groomed tract of lawn, formed a square in the center of the village. Shops, inns, and restaurants, all nicely restored, framed the area.

Conspicuously placed on the walls of the restaurant where Dianna and Dennis ate were eight-by-ten photographs of various show business personalities that had eaten there. "I can't escape," she commented to herself. Dennis didn't seem to be in the least impressed by the restaurateur's collection of headshots. Maybe there's hope for him, she thought.

After ordering, they discussed politics and show business. He still evaded the subject of his own work. This, she realized, was also a very unwriterlike trait. Most of the authors she had dealt with never seemed to shut up about either their accomplishments or their problems.

Dianna wondered if perhaps Dennis didn't like his job. But whatever the reasons for his gentle ego, she had to admit he was a refreshing change. There was no sensation of having to compete with him. Usually, when talking with someone from a theater crowd, it was a constant game of one-upmanship. Dennis put her at ease and made her feel comfortable because he was (and she realized she had almost forgotten what it was like) a person who actually listened.

When the wine came, Dennis poured. "Are you sure you want a glass? There must be twenty or thirty different cultures of bacteria that are responsible for fermentation somewhere in this bottle. One sip of wine, and you'll be killing thousands of tiny organisms."

"A bacterium is not a duck."

"But a duck is not a deer or a chicken or a lamb?"

They lifted their glasses, and Dianna said, "Death to bacteria."

"I'll drink to that."

Dianna tossed out the question she had been holding back. "Why do you drive so fast?"

"Why not? I enjoy it."

"But why? Were you trying to impress me?"

He smiled. "No. I drive like that all the time, even when I'm alone. It's something I do purely for myself. It feels good. It's exciting. Don't you ever do things with an element of personal risk?"

"I have 'adventures' that do involve risk, but it is more of a personal risk than a physical one. I do occasionally take the subway and even walk unescorted down Broadway, and that can take courage, believe me. But I only do those things when I have to, and in the course of my risk-taking I am not endangering anyone else."

"Haven't you ever wanted to sail-kite or skydive?"

"Never had even the slightest urge. Besides, I might get too close to the sun. My wings would melt."

Dennis laughed and said, "But you ride. What about jumping?"

The question caught Dianna unaware. Jumping was an issue that brought back painful memories and pushed one of her most sensitive buttons.

". . . I used to do some jumping, but I don't anymore." Dianna sensed Dennis's disappointment at her answers.

He continued. "I guess with me, I feel that if I'm not willing to take a chance, that if I don't have the courage to risk my life, then I don't deserve to live. I don't have a right to life. . . . At least that's what my analyst feels, and I must say I agree."

"Sounds like you're compensating for a case of masculine insecurity." Dianna bit her tongue, wondering if Dennis could take that kind of stiff comeback. She was about to apologize, then thought, Hell with it; it's what I feel.

"My analyst says that, too. And I think you have a point. I may have to prove something to myself. But I don't think it's quite that simple. I think there's more to it. Didn't you get a rush from riding or jumping? Horses are pretty dangerous, aren't they?"

The question brought back a memory that was hard to face, but Dianna didn't let it show. "Yes." She urgently wanted to get off the subject. "Are you afraid when you drive?"

"Yes, and that's part of the fun of it." Dennis was getting miffed at her persistent line of questioning. "Look, the bottom line is I like it. I enjoy it. My heart beats faster. It's a high."

He continued. "Maybe at times it's a little selfish, but so what? What's wrong with going for it? What's wrong with living a little on the edge? What's wrong with trying to get an honest high, with being a little scared shitless and turned on at the same time? It's my own moment of getting off—of personal triumph. Look, Dianna, each time I come through it is great. Each time I survive I feel a little younger."

Here's the modern samurai, thought Dianna. His attitude reminded her of Roshi Takahashi's explanation of the cherry blossom as a symbol of the bloodthirsty warriors. It seemed such a contradiction to her that the samurai would take the delicate and fragile cherry blossom as an emblem. What was his point? she asked herself. Ah, yes—the flower was both beautiful yet at any moment ready to fall.

What was it about the swaggering of the samurai and Dennis's arguments that made her angry? Their whole point of view seems so senseless, so careless, so selfish. The thought screamed in her mind, Men! Stuff the samurai, and their aggressive, pointless ways. It is so wrong that any human being should have a thirst for blood.

The meal was carefully prepared and expertly served. But for all the expense and ambience, it could not top the home-cooked tastefulness of the morning's breakfast. If all the food at the Wilkinson is that good, Dianna thought, I won't fit into my Honda.

Dennis broke the long silence. "Do you always travel alone to strange places? I mean, I'm glad you do but . . ."

"All my life," said Dianna.

"Really?"

"Is there something wrong with a woman traveling alone?" she remarked coolly.

"My guess is you're compensating for your feminine insecurity."

Dianna felt the truth in the comment. "A hit, a palpable hit. But I'm also overreacting. In my family it was never possible to be alone. We took togetherness much too far."

"You're Catholic, aren't you?"

"I went to parochial school for twelve years, and my family is about as Catholic as you can get."

"If you had a choice, would you have done it differently?"

"I don't know. Maybe. I think so. Sometime I think half my time is spent trying to overcome a lot of Catholic hang-ups."

"Divorce and no birth control?"

"Not quite that bad but close. How did you know I was Catholic?"

"That statue in your car . . . though it did look kind of weird."

Dianna didn't feel like getting into her Zen right now with Dennis. It usually drove her crazy when she tried to explain the philosophy. The subject was always so difficult to get across. Most of the time when Dianna had tried to talk to people about enlightenment and meditation and things like koans, she met with nodding heads and blank looks, or people who started babbling about gurus or chanting or yin and yang when in reality they hadn't taken the time to study anything about it.

For now, keep the whole thing simple. Leave it at Catholic, she thought.

"How long have you been a writer?" she asked.

Dennis hesitated. "I guess I don't seem very much like I'm a member of the press, do I?"

Dianna had the strange and certain feeling that Dennis was going to confide in her and admit that he wasn't really a writer but had another occupation—was an agent for the FBI or something odd like that. But he hesitated again, then said in a quiet confidential tone, "I guess there's no point in trying to fool you. I'll be the first to admit, I don't intend to be a writer. I'm only doing this job for another year—it's part of a broad-based, hands-on training program. My family owns a publishing company, and I guess you could say, I'm paying my dues. I was really an econ major. I'm learning a lot doing this, but I won't try to kid you, my head is into management."

It made sense, Dianna admitted, and answered a lot of questions.

She found herself liking Dennis. He was warm, strong, reliable, and undoubtedly popular, like his CDs. But she had yet to see any specialness about him. Dianna usually went for something unique, above average, out of the ordinary in a man. He had to be someone who might someday write a Pulitzer play or could dance like Baryshnikov. Arthur had a competitive urge that made him a killer in litigation, and at times the man was simply brilliant, with a knowledge that came from extensive reading and a near-photographic memory.

Dennis was intelligent; he had a cultivated charm. He had probably been president of his college fraternity. But there was nothing that tantalized her fancy, sparked her imagination, made her wet just talking to him.

Why, then, am I still attracted to him? she asked herself. If we were in New York, and had been introduced at a party, I don't know if we ever would have started a conversation. Is it the fact that we are together on neutral territory? Is it just the situation we're in, free spirits drawn together when away from the restrictions of their natural habitats, like a pair of teenagers at a summer camp?

"How long are you staying?" she asked.

"I've got to get back to Boston for work tomorrow morning."

Dianna suddenly thought of the huge bed in her room and toyed with the idea of sharing it with Dennis. What would it be like? Would she be missing something if she didn't? Or if she did, would she be wishing that she hadn't in the clear light of morning?

But she didn't know enough about Dennis, not yet. She wasn't sure of his sexual history. What if he was into drugs? Or bisexual? She sensed he was straight, and he certainly didn't seem like a person who would ever come near a shared needle, but how could you be sure these days? She wasn't about to start thinking of sharing bodily fluids.

What a pain this AIDS thing was. What a curse. But a girl had to be so careful. Making love had become such a risk, such a very serious business. Ah, for a return to the simpler times of the seventies.

On the trip back, Dennis took it easy with his driving. In a way she was disappointed. Not because he wasn't driving fast, but that he was one to give in so easily. Dianna LaBianca deserved worthy opponents.

As they drove past the mill in Fenwick, Dianna saw the family name set in stone over the entrance door. "I guess we should be privileged to be staying in the ancestral home of such a distinguished family."

"The locals around here have no love for the Wilkinson name, that's for sure. Whenever you mention the mill or the family that ran it, people treat you like you're talking about the plague. I've heard the Wilkinsons kept the place going with gestapo tactics."

At the traffic light, Dennis took Dianna by surprise when he leaned over and kissed her gently and promisingly.

She responded, thinking how the trip had already turned into an adventure with very interesting possibilities. But it was too easy; there had to be a catch.

The horse trailer was gone, and the inn appeared empty. The door to her room was slightly ajar. "I must have forgotten to lock it," Dianna said.

Dennis touched her arm. This is it, she thought, he's putting on his big move. "Say, Dianna, I've got a great bottle of white Bordeaux. How about a nightcap?"

I'm tempted, she thought. Christ, am I tempted. But it was

just too fast, and Dennis was just a little too smooth. Dianna liked to make a man work first—he had to prove that she meant something to him. And the more polished and slick the approach of someone who came on to her, the more she felt taken for granted, and the more she wanted to give him a hard time. Of course, she had been impulsive on occasions in the past, but the prize had been more irresistible and the world not such a troubled place.

"Dennis, I don't think so," she said, but added, "not tonight."

She could read the disappointment in his face. She kissed him gently but lingeringly. His response was encouraging— definitely heterosexual. She had the confidence to answer him with an open mouth and a touch of tongue. Then she pulled away. "Good night."

" 'Night, Dianna."

She entered the room and let out a cry of surprise. It was chaos—chairs overturned, her suitcase upside down on the floor, her manuscript littered everywhere. The covers were rumpled on the bed and the bedspread smudged.

"Dianna, are you all right?" Dennis asked. Entering quickly, he took in the room. "What happened to this place?"

She spoke her first thought. "I've been robbed."

Her clothes were strewn about. A tall lamp was overturned and the shade bent.

Dennis sniffed the air and said, "What is that smell? Some kind of strange scent in the air. It's odd. What is it?"

Dianna sniffed. "Yes, it does smell strange, like some kind of animal."

"Reminds me of a monkey house or a bear cage at the zoo, yet it's different," said Dennis. "Well, whoever the mugger was, we can track him down by following our noses."

"I can't believe this. You expect this in the city maybe, but not here," said Dianna as she looked over her things.

The front door slammed downstairs.

"Did you have any cash or jewelry in the room?" asked Dennis.

"A little cash," Dianna said, looking in a corner pocket of her suitcase, "but nothing seems to be missing."

Dennis went to the door. "Miss Wilkinson, would you come up here for a minute?"

The heavy woman stopped at the doorway. Her mouth dropped open in fear. She wiped her hands on her dress and glanced around the room nervously.

"It's the dog, that mangy dog. I'll fix it up. I'm terribly sorry." Then Agnes turned and bolted down the stairs at a speed that seemed impossible for a woman of her bulk. From outside they heard her call, "Jacques! Jacques!"

"The dog?" Dennis said in disbelief.

Dianna examined a skirt that lay in a heap on the bed. "I think she's right; it looks like this has been chewed on. It's all wet with saliva."

Outside, a truck door slammed and the dog started to bark. Jacques shouted something in unintelligible French.

"Well, there's no real damage done, I guess," said Dianna. "I can't believe a dog would do this."

Dennis seemed lost in thought and looked around the room for a moment. Then he smiled. "Well, they probably left a door open and that mutt just snuck in looking for things to chew on. I wouldn't worry about it."

The explanation seemed a little odd to Dianna but Dennis's acceptance of everything made her relax.

"Listen," he said, "I'm planning to come out this way next weekend. And I'd love to be able to see you then."

"That would be nice."

Dennis picked up a lamp. "Let me help you with this mess."

"No, don't worry about it, I can manage. Now that I've really looked, there's not that much out of place."

"You're sure you're okay?"

"I'm fine. It was just a little upsetting to think that I might have been robbed."

"Well, good night again." He stopped at the door. "Take care of yourself."

It's nice that he's so concerned, thought Dianna. "Don't worry about me." And she kissed him again, a quick good-night.

Dianna was glad he would be back next weekend. It was something to look forward to, an excellent carrot.

Even though she was entirely conscious of the sham of her carrots, they seemed to work, drawing her right along. And, she had to admit, the trick always seemed to make the journey that little bit more pleasant.

Dianna opened the window to air out the room and started to straighten things up. Except for the lamp, there didn't seem to be any other physical damage. She went to the bathroom with a couple of wrinkled pages. The wastebasket had been upset, and her discarded yellow pages of notes were all over the floor.

There was an old baseball card from 1964 lying among the trash. Must have been in the bottom of the wastebasket, she thought, and threw it out. As she started to pick up the papers, she noticed that her small laundry bag, which had hung from a towel rack and had held a few items of dirty clothing, was missing.

She looked under the papers and then in the other room. The bag wasn't there. Probably just the kind of thing that crazy dog would take, she thought. She could imagine the German shepherd running around the front yard with a bra dangling from its mouth. Dianna shook her head and smiled.

16

Esau free. Esau in big place.

He ran along the bridle path toward the cemetery.

Esau happy. Happy.

Esau had craved her smell. He ached to play with the new booteful, but they wouldn't let him.

Esau had tricked them. When they had come to feed him, he had put a little stone in the lock of the inner door, and like before, it didn't fasten all the way. He waited until they were gone, then ran to find Dianna, but she wasn't there. Only the clothes that kept her warm, and her smell . . . everywhere.

He carried a pair of her underwear in his hand. He had taken it for the booteful's smell. Her best smell. The smell that made him grow big.

Esau wanted so much to play with Dianna in the way he had played with the straw-haired booteful.

Esau grinned and remembered how he had lost his bigness within the warmth of that booteful.

Later he had tried everything to make the straw-haired booteful wake up and see him and be his friend, shaking her, yelling at her, picking her up, but she wouldn't move. Her eyes had been open but strange, like the hard marbles he used to play with when he was a little boy. He thought at first that the booteful was just very tired and had gone to sleep. But then her warmth had left and her flesh had felt cold. So very cold.

Then it dawned on him what had happened. She had become dead, she had become like Pumpkin. Like Dada. Esau had become sad because she would probably have to go into a hole in the place of the dead stones and be covered up with dirt.

Esau lumbered into the cemetery and sat down on his father's grave and remembered his Dada and how he had loved him. He rocked back and forth, kneading the garment in his fingers. He rubbed it over the dead stone that marked his father's grave and said, "Booteful, booteful, 'ove booteful."

Esau rose and sniffed the air. *Dog after Esau. Dog and Man.*

Esau hated the French Canadian. The fear and loathing between the two males was intense. Jacques was often cruel and didn't hesitate to use force or inflict pain to control Esau.

Good if Jacques dead. Esau want Jacques in hole.

A rumble came from Esau's stomach. It would be morning soon, and he would have to go back before too long.

Esau hungry. Eat soon. But later. Now free.

He sniffed the stolen pair of underwear carefully, with an intense concentration, as a monkey would sniff a strange bit of tempting food. His keen nose drew in and savored the bootful's smell.

"Ahhhhhaaaaaga-gaaaaaa!"

Esau happy. Happy.

17

The next morning, Dianna's typing was interrupted by the sound of Jacques and Agnes loading several motley stable horses into the rear of the horse van. Dianna threw on a jean jacket and headed outside. "Need any help?" she asked.

"Not likely," piped Miss Wilkinson.

"Where are you taking them?"

"Got a cousin owns a summer camp in Portage."

"That's up in northern Maine, isn't it?"

"Yep."

"So, you only board them here in the winter?"

"Yep. We have to drive all eight of these nags up there by the week after next. You still want to ride?"

"Yes, I do."

"Saddle up that mare in number five."

The mare was a gentle old roan, obviously the perfect choice for a novice rider. Her worn stable blanket was stitched with the name Pickles. Dianna carefully bridled the horse and put on a heavy western saddle from the rack outside the stall. It had been a full ten years since she had been near a horse, but Pickles didn't seem to care about Dianna's nervousness.

"Steady now. Be a good girl."

She found she had to slap the reins and use almost every muscle in her legs to get the nag moving. Finally, Pickles gave in to the idea of being ridden and stepped off with a lurch of assurance. Dianna headed the horse out onto the oval drive. She put the animal into a trot, then a canter, and finally through a couple of easy turns, before returning to Miss Wilkinson.

"Well, you can ride all right, but you're used to riding

English, aren't you?" Agnes checked over the stirrups and saddle adjustments.

"If Goody's around, I guess you can ride, but only when she's here." Jacques climbed onto the cab of the horse van and started the engine.

Dianna led Pickles over to them and said, "Wait a minute. Who's Goody?"

Jacques looked at Agnes, then at Dianna, but didn't reply.

Dianna asked, "Is Goody here?"

"Oh, she's here," Agnes said, as she entered the cab of the truck. Jacques gunned the engine and the two drove off.

Dianna looked after the truck, then glanced back at the house, wondering who Goody was. Pickles started and took a few paces sideways. Dianna could feel the animal's restlessness. "Come on, Pickles. Let's put you in your stall." But to Dianna's surprise, Pickles didn't want to go back. "You want to run, do you?" Dianna said to the animal. "You're not lazy, just stubborn."

Dianna firmly reined her toward the barn, and Pickles went along obediently. "Oh, hell with it, Pickles, let's have a little fun."

At first she stayed in the oval drive in front of the inn, but then she decided to try the bridle path she had walked the day before. Dianna felt uneasy and glanced at the windows in the inn. With the distinct impression that someone was watching her, she urged the horse forward. The tendons on the inside of her knees were aching already. It's been so long, she thought. I'm going to feel it in my legs in the morning.

The old animal moved reluctantly into stride, but Dianna drove her into a gallop, exhilarated by the horse's strength and the wind on her face. As Pickles quickly tired and fell off the pace, Dianna slowed her to a walk. At the Wilkinson plot she paused by the overlook to take in the view. Dianna's legs were already tightening up from the unaccustomed activity, so she dismounted, stretched, and massaged the muscles by rubbing her hand down her thighs.

She had a quick flash of Dennis's hand on her thigh. She always felt sensual after a ride, not completely turned on, just comfortably awakened. Some of her friends from high school used to have orgasms riding, but it had never worked for Dianna. Well, nobody's perfect.

A patch of color caught her eye on the ground in front of her. It was a torn bit of her undies, entirely out of place amidst the earthen colors. The pattern of the material identified it as the one she had left in the laundry bag. She picked it up and looked around for the bag and other pieces of the clothing.

"Crazy dog," she said.

Back in the barn, Dianna gave Pickles what must have been the first brushing the animal had had since birth. After returning her to her stall, Dianna went back to the inn. She felt hungry and decided to drive to Fenwick for an early lunch. As she climbed the stairs to her room, a door at the end of the hall slowly began to open.

Dianna hadn't been aware that there was a door in that part of the wall. It had a metal finish, and there was no handle. As Dianna watched, her fingers clutching the banister, the door completed its mechanical motion and opened with a thunk.

Out rolled a gray-haired woman in a squeaking wheelchair with bicycle tires. This could only be Goody, Dianna realized.

"Good morning," the lady said as she wheeled herself over. "I'm obliged to tell you the elevator is not for the use of guests. I'm afraid our insurance company doesn't permit it. You must be the friend of that magazine writer."

"I'm Dianna LaBianca, and I am only a recent acquaintance of Mr. Conwell."

"Is that so?"

This joke is getting a little old, Dianna thought.

She studied the ancient woman's face. It was crisscrossed with lines, wrinkles upon wrinkles. Yet the face was very much alive. Her two eyes, two dark crystals, were in the process of picking Dianna apart. The woman's silver hair was stringy and sparse. Her ears were pierced and held beautifully wrought silver earrings. From her jewelry, clothing, and the way she sat proud and erect in the wheelchair, Dianna could tell that Goody was a woman of taste. Probably quite an elegant lady in her day, Dianna thought—but then she still seems to be having "her day," doesn't she?

"I watched you riding Pickles," the elderly woman commented.

"I wouldn't have ridden so long, but I thought she needed a workout," Dianna said, feeling a little guilty for keeping the horse out.

"You ride with style."

"Thank you, but I think my lower anatomy is going to be doing some complaining."

There was an aura about the old woman. She was imposing, almost noble. She had a larger-than-life tragic quality and a grandness that Dianna would have expected to find in a character from a classical play—a Portia, a Lady Macbeth, a Mother Courage.

"I trust my granddaughter told you the kitchen is closed."

Agnes is her granddaughter? thought Dianna. My God, Goody must be two hundred years old.

"I'm only eighty-six, if that's what you're thinking."

This lady is sharp as a pin, thought Dianna. "I was wondering where I could find a good place to get breakfast."

"Try O'Connor's in Fenwick. Go to the light, turn left, two blocks."

"Thank you."

"I'm sorry, but with Jacques and Agnes away we won't be serving till Thursday. However, if you will be in this evening, I would enjoy the pleasure of your company at dinner."

"I'd love to, thank you."

"I warn you, though, I don't intend to make a habit of it."

Dianna smiled. "I understand."

"Six o'clock sharp," Goody quipped and wheeled herself quickly off toward the back of the inn.

18

The rest of the afternoon Dianna spent at the laptop. She had committed herself to getting the script done the first week, leaving a second week of play—for a carrot reward. By the time I'm finished, she thought, I'll be bored to death of this place, and I'll go farther north, maybe to the coast of Maine.

The inn was working out well. It gave her just the right amount of privacy for work, stables to break the monotony, and an ideal setting for solitary meditation. What is it that makes me want to be alone, at least some of the time? she wondered.

My meditation is a thing of aloneness. I don't have a gang of friends I spend hours "hanging out" with. Even my affair, she thought a little bitterly, is the perfect choice for an "unpeopled" home life. I live in the crowded madness of the city, but walking in step with a company of rush-hour commuters provides about as much personal contact as a cell in solitary.

Her need for aloneness often took her to places where she could feel apart from society, like her family's summer house in Bridgehampton, which often sat empty, or the solitude and quiet of the Zendo, or a late night screening of some obscure film in a near-empty theater.

. . . Then there was the aloneness of being on stage. A way to be in front of people and yet have the protection and isolation of a character to hide behind. A way to flaunt aloneness. I am definitely eccentric, she admitted.

Dianna had a feeling that Goody was a fanatic for punctuality, so she kept herself on schedule and was dressed and downstairs for dinner promptly at six. Sure enough, as Dianna reached the bottom step, Goody, with a tray on her lap, rolled her wheelchair into the dining room.

"Can I be of help?" asked Dianna.

"Yes. Sit down and stop thinking that I am an invalid. I require no assistance. Mind if I say grace?"

"No," said Dianna.

Goody deftly set out the contents of her tray on the table and bowed her head.

Dianna followed suit.

"Lord, we thank Thee for this bounteous harvest that Thou hast so freely given us from the flesh of Thy body. Bless our seed and watch over them and bless our loved ones lost. In Thy name, amen."

Dianna raised her head and at the last word crossed herself. She noticed that Goody had seen the motion and almost as an apology said, "I was raised Catholic."

"Is that so? Well, in that case, I'm sure you will die Catholic."

Dianna smiled to herself, thinking, Well, that's one way of looking at it. "I don't know if I *will* die Catholic," she said. "I find the Christianity female guilt thing a little hard to deal with."

"What 'Christianity female guilt thing'?" asked Goody, with an obvious edge of distaste in her tone.

Dianna wondered if she had gotten herself onto theological thin ice with the woman. "Well, it's the placing of the blame for the sins of the world on women. . . . The serpent is the seducer, but it was Eve who picked the apple and gave it to Adam. As a result, all women share an inherent guilt. It's not an idea that is very common in other religions and mythologies."

"Well, I never before stopped to think about it, but I'd say, dearie, that you've got a point. We've had our share of preachers around here who didn't know the first thing about a woman. Unless she was lying on her back."

The comment took Dianna by surprise and made her smile. She thought, This lady's got a lot of spirit.

The dinner was hearty but rather bland, like British hotel food. Jacques was obviously the one in the inn who knew how to cook. They ate for a time in silence.

"Mrs. . . . um . . . I'm sorry, I don't believe you ever told me your last name."

"It's Mrs. Wilkinson, my dear," Goody said matter-of-factly. Surprise registered on Dianna's face. "You seem surprised. Why is that?"

"I just took it for granted that you were born a Wilkinson. Pardon me for saying so, but your features even around the eyes . . . you bear a strong resemblance to some of the Wilkinson family portraits."

Goody smiled a bitter little smile, as if Dianna's observation made sense to her. "No, young lady. I married Harold Wilkinson sixty-seven years ago. My maiden name is Proctor."

Yet the resemblance is so strong, Dianna thought. She wanted to ask if Goody could be a distant relation of the Wilkinsons, or if there had been a previous intermixing of the family's bloodlines. But Dianna checked her LaBianca mouth—if it was true, it could be a delicate subject.

"My family came from around Boston," the elderly lady remarked. "They say that married couples grow to look alike after so many years together. I believe that. You see, I was only nineteen when I married Harold, and his family, the Wilkinsons, had a profound effect on me. Perhaps it had something to do with their being entrenched in this house and this soil for so many generations.

"The Wilkinsons have grown their roots deep into the earth here, you know. They gave so much time to the working of the soil, put so much of themselves into making their home here, and so much of their blood and so many of their dead have gone into the ground, that they have made it their own. The force of the Wilkinson personality exudes from this land, and that force is irresistible, overpowering.

"I know. I was devoured by it. I became a Wilkinson as much as if I had been born one. And it was more than appearance. My blood became Wilkinson blood, their joys mine, their sorrows mine. . . ."

Goody drifted off in thought for a moment, then remarked, "If you have liberated views, I'm sure you're outraged at my history. But times were different then. I spoke my vows even before the twenties."

"I find it hard to believe that the change in a person could be so overwhelming."

"Well, believe it, and I was quite strong, my dear. As strong-willed as you are."

"The stronger the box, the harder to get out of it," said Dianna.

"Beg pardon?" said Goody.

"I study a little Eastern philosophy, and my teacher says that all of the money, the physical possessions, the desires of the world are like a box around a person. This box keeps us from finding our true selves. To find enlightenment, my teacher says, all you have to do is get out the box. The more you have, the harder it is to give it up—the stronger the box, the harder to get out of it."

"Sounds like a lot of horse manure to me," said Goody, and she popped a bite of food in her mouth.

That's what I get for trying to talk about Zen, thought Dianna, and she attempted to get the conversation moving again. "Do a lot of Wilkinsons still live in this area?"

Goody paused, then said, "The only direct descendant is Agnes, and she is childless. But there's hardly a soul in Fenwick that isn't one or two parts Wilkinson.

"But a lot of us have moved away. It's because there isn't much work to be found in Fenwick, not since the mill closed. The last bolt of cloth was shipped out many a year ago. Trucks used to cover the roads. . . ."

The woman began to ramble on, and Dianna got the impression that on occasion, Goody's age might slow down her thinking.

". . . Most of the young people have moved away," said the old woman.

"Family is important. Never forget that," said Goody. "It's all you have in the end, if you think about it. Family. Daughters. Sons. Your bloodline. Bloodline children. That's about all there is in this world."

For a moment Dianna wondered if the woman was all there. It seemed that there just might be one card missing from Goody's deck of fifty-two.

The old woman continued, "Children are the building blocks of this earth and must be looked after . . . no matter what the price." Then Goody seemed to recover and stared out the window, lost in melancholy.

Well, whatever, thought Dianna, she is one remarkable woman—in her late eighties, intelligent, and active. I'll be lucky if I'm still inhaling and exhaling when I'm her age.

Yet there was something unexplained about Goody, a quality dark and secret—an aura of tragedy. Dianna thought, She's like a Hedda Gabler, but a Hedda who didn't go through with her suicide. Goody seemed a woman who had chosen instead to live her life with some untenable situation. Maybe, she thought, it's got something to do with losing the use of her legs. Or Goody could have been paralyzed since birth—that would explain it.

Dianna needed a way to find out more and said, "You seem to know horses. Did you ride?"

"You mean before my accident? Yes. All of us Wilkinsons used to ride. English, of course. But I was always a bit of a rebel and loved to sneak out on a western saddle whenever I could. Riding was my greatest joy. That's how I was injured. A . . . well, my horse was suddenly frightened, and I was thrown. But we mustn't let a little thing like that stop us, must we?"

The pay phone rang, and Goody hurriedly wheeled over to the desk and answered it. "Wilkinson Inn. . . . What's the matter, doesn't he want to work? . . . Well, who else can I get? How about your other boy? . . . Good-bye." She hung up, then dialed a number. "Operator? Is this Elizabeth? . . . Oh, Alice, good evening. Could you switch me over to Elizabeth? . . . Hello, Liz? This is Goody. Can one of your boys come over and do some work for me? . . . What about the Adams boys? . . . Well, thanks anyway. Liz, if you think of someone, ring me up. Good-bye."

Goody wheeled back to the table. "My stable boy just made the varsity band or some such nonsense, and I can't seem to find a replacement."

"Could I be of help?"

"I can feed and water them myself, but if you could put them out to run tomorrow, I would appreciate it."

"I'd love to."

"The real problem is the stalls."

"You let me ride, and you've got a stable boy."

"We have a bargain." Goody started to clean off the table, and Dianna almost offered to help but checked herself.

"You're learning," the old woman said, placing the dishes on a tray in her lap. A second later she returned with dessert. "There's a nice run out the southeast up to Bread and back."

"Oh, yes, I saw a sign for Bread, somewhere," said Dianna. "What is it?"

"Used to be a religious commune till their spiritual leader, or whatever he was, left town with the Chief of Police's wife, and the commune's bank account in his pocket. . . . 'Bout two miles away as the crow flies."

"I'm not a big fan of those cults. If you look into it, you usually find that the operation is nothing more than somebody's power trip. The few communes I've seen have been really creepy."

"Last summer a couple of local boys burned the place to the ground. Best thing they could have done."

"Do you own the inn?" asked Dianna.

"Well, let's say for all practical purposes I do. I'm the executor of the estate."

"You seem to do an excellent job."

"It's interesting on occasion. Other times it's a lot like eternal damnation."

As Goody cleared away the cups and saucers, she locked Dianna's eyes in a hard stare. "By the way, I wouldn't go out walking at night. It's remarkably easy to get lost. Keep in mind the temperature up here can drop forty degrees in an hour, and there's no one around but myself to go looking for you. Good night."

Before going to bed that evening, Dianna went out on the front porch to meditate. She set herself up on her small cushion and looked out across the serene, starlit grounds. She tried to focus her eyes on nothing, on a mountain in the distance, as her Roshi had taught her.

Ten breaths counting, ten more breaths, ten more. Try to find that space between breaths where the in changes to the out. Lose yourself there. Try to get hold of the space. But don't try. Try to find it, but don't think of it. Try to understand, but don't reason. There is no problem to solve. Just count, just breathe, just go on.

Something in your mind, a thought? Throw it out. Just be. Concentrate on "mu." Concentrate on nothing. Don't concentrate.

Dianna inhaled the clean air through her nostrils and felt wonderfully peaceful and contentedly alone.

19

The next morning, Dianna skipped breakfast, worked on the manuscript a double shift from seven until three, and managed to forge her way through three-quarters of Kronenberger's first act. When she was ready to collect her carrot, she quit for the day and headed for the stable.

Her body was a collection of minor aches and pains from the short ride of the day before, but her taste for horses had been whetted, and Dianna was anxious to be at it again. The German shepherd, whom Goody had referred to as Lancelot, met her on the way and made a halfhearted attempt at her windbreaker, but Dianna was onto his tricks and kept the jacket out of reach.

As she neared the stable, Goody was wheeling down the row of stalls with a feed bag on her lap. "Hello, Mrs. Wilkinson. How are you?"

"As fit as a Stradivarius. I've got the whole stable fed and watered. Do you think you could let them out to run? And, if you don't mind, could you do a few of the stables?"

"I'd be glad to."

"Just bridle the palomino swayback in number three and walk him out. He's their leader. The others would gladly follow him anywhere, even to their just reward. If you have any problems, I'll be in my room."

As Goody vigorously pushed herself toward the inn Dianna called out, "Mrs. Wilkinson, is it all right if I take out one of the English mounts?"

"Please do. Give the gelding a turn. But watch him. He's a touch skittish."

After turning out the stable horses, Dianna took a helmet and saddle from the rack and went to Crumpet's stall. The horse was nervous as Dianna opened the gate.

"Hello, Crumpet. Easy, boy, easy. Hello. How are you today, Crumpet?"

Her banter calmed the animal. She knew she would have to handle the high-strung gelding with special care. As Dianna hoisted the light saddle onto the curve of the thoroughbred's back, she thought, if ever there was beauty in nature, God or Buddha certainly put it in horseflesh.

Crumpet was fast and muscular and rode well, though he tended to be a little headstrong. Dianna knew she had lost her seat and didn't feel at all at home in the English saddle, but she had no problem managing the animal and was surprised how much of her technique had stayed with her.

The trail Dianna took proved to be a lot more difficult than she had expected. In places it was steep and narrow. I'm on an expert trail, she thought. She held the gelding to a trot over the unfamiliar territory, wishing she had picked an easier route. Then she saw a jump ahead. It was low, only three feet or so. The gelding obviously knew the trail, because he started to pick up speed to make the hurdle. Dianna reined the animal in.

The day of her fall—the day she had given up jumping—was still vivid in her memory. It had happened over ten years ago, while she was following the lead of Lydia Bass, her tyrannical riding instructor. They were on an extremely difficult Olympic training trail, and Dianna's mount was an unpredictable young mare. Miss Bass had set an unrelenting pace, pressing Dianna and her mount hard. At a high fence with a tricky downhill approach, the young mare, who was beginning to tire, balked. Dianna was thrown over the animal's mane, struck the fence, and landed on her head twelve feet below.

Paramedics had rushed her away in an ambulance, with a broken arm and a cracked vertebra in her lower neck. If she had landed with a little more force or at a slightly different angle, she would have been dead or paralyzed for life.

Sweat trickled down her chin strap. Dianna's breathing was rushed and deep, and for a moment she felt faint. Little black dots danced on the surface of her eyeballs, then a wave of red flashed across her eyes and she had to put her head down on the gelding's mane to keep from passing out.

With the hurdle before her, Dianna said, "Easy, Crumpet" and thought, I'm just not up to this. She led the animal past the obstacle and pressed on.

After walking Crumpet around three more jumps, Dianna was feeling like a total fool. She stopped before the next rail, determined to give it a try.

Crumpet was ready. He bowed his head, anxious to make the attempt.

Dianna stared at the wooden post. It was only three feet high. It had a clear approach with level ground on the far side.

She just sat still, looking at the jump. Again her forehead was perspiring; her hands trembled at the reins. Crumpet felt her nervousness and sauntered sideways.

After a few moments, she dismounted, thoroughly depressed and humiliated.

She walked the horse around. That's the last time I take this path, she thought.

A turn ahead brought Dianna onto the highway, and once back in the saddle, she was quickly at the entrance drive. Knowing there were no jumps, Dianna drove Crumpet back to the inn at a wild gallop.

20

Wednesday went quickly and pleasantly, divided between working and riding. Dianna rose early, forced herself to type until she was ready to throw the laptop at the wall, then went out and rode until she and her mount were ready to drop.

She knew she was working harder than if she had been in the office, but there were no hassles and she was her own taskmaster—or taskmistress, as she preferred to label herself. Since Monday, Dianna had slept like a baby, eaten like a stable horse, gone jogging once, and had at least two sessions of meditation a day. She was losing weight and felt in better shape than she had since high school.

Dianna went for lunch at a local restaurant, but after just one meal by herself her dining-alone quotient was thoroughly filled. That night she again had supper with Mrs. Wilkinson. Dianna had come to like the old woman, with her brusque ways and boundless energy. Mrs. Wilkinson seemed to genuinely appreciate Dianna's help with the stable work, and would have been at a loss without Dianna to do some of the more mobile tasks.

The old lady was quite a sight pushing herself in the wheelchair down the rows of stalls, with a bucket perched on her lap, whistling some obscure Sousa march. That morning, Goody had wheeled over to Dianna and handed her a small stack of ten and twenty dollar bills.

"What's this?" asked Dianna, looking at the bundle of cash.

"That's your advance for the room. Can't ask a guest to be doing the work of a stable hand."

Later, when Dianna had gone to get the old swayback to lead

the saddle horses out for their exercise, the ancient beast seemed as calm and geriatric as ever. Just as Dianna entered the stall, a bridle in hand, she heard a strange, muffled cry in the distance. Goody wheeled through the barn and out the door at a breakneck speed.

In the next stall the palomino's ears perked up, and his eyes bulged out of his head. All the other horses suddenly grew restless. They whinnied and pranced in their stalls. The old horse beside Dianna summoned up an unexpected burst of energy and reared up at her. Caught by surprise, Dianna almost fell as she dodged out the gate of the stall. The horse reared again, then kicked with his hind legs, knocking two boards out of the outside barn wall.

"Whoa, whoa, boy!" Dianna shouted.

Then, as suddenly as it had come, the old horse's reserve of energy gave out. The palomino paced from side to side in the stall, eying Dianna nervously. All the horses were restless and upset. What kind of sound could have caused all that? wondered Dianna.

She cautiously went outside and looked over the grounds, half expecting to see a mountain lion or some other kind of creature, but everything appeared normal.

Goody wheeled out from the direction of the icehouse. Her face looked dangerously red, and she was completely out of breath. "Sounded like a wolf, or maybe just somebody's dog gone wild. I was afraid it was after the geese. We still see bear up here."

"Bears up here?" said Dianna.

"Yes, ma'am, we sure do, from time to time. You'd best stay in after dark, you hear me?"

Dianna nodded soberly.

"Garrhhh!"
Esau want out! Esau want out to play!
NOW!
Since seeing Dianna that morning, Esau had gone half insane in the stone cellar. All through the day he caught glimpses and little teasing aromas of the booteful, which sifted in through the cracks around his window and set him on fire.
Booteful so close. So near.
"Garr-ooooh-gahhh!"

She was there just out of his reach and her presence was driving him wild and the warm spring weather only made things worse.

Want booteful! Need booteful.

"Peeeeza. Garrhhh!"

Need her so much.

The walls of his prison were creeping in on him. The icehouse cellar was becoming smaller and more cruel with each day she was out there.

Esau often broke things and could throw loud, raging tantrums. Goody had done everything possible to make sure that any noise in the icehouse could not be heard on the grounds. The old woman had had a single stone removed from the wall, creating a feeding slot, so that even if guests were present on the grounds, Esau's meals could be quietly delivered.

Esau had pushed open the small swinging door that covered the slot and had bellowed at the top of his lungs. His voice was muffled by a soundproofed outer door, but Esau had put everything he had into the cry and still the sound had been enough to startle Dianna and the horses in the barn.

Goody, please let Esau out. NOW.

"Kaggaragarh!"

All day all night Esau big. Esau always need the good feeling.

The days were bad, but the nights were worse. He lay sleepless in the darkness, touching himself until his skin was raw and his muscle ached.

Dianna's meditation that night was one of those magical moments, extraordinary and highly emotional in its perfection.

She had had an experience like it once before. It was one afternoon at the Zendo. She was sitting with her mind focused on her *hara*—that place below the pit of her stomach, behind her diaphragm muscle, the place that her Roshi taught was her center, her body's home-for-the-soul. At first her *hara* became warm, then she had a feeling that she was losing her identity, and her mind seemed to divorce itself from her body and drift upward into the room.

That night on the porch of the inn, it was windy, and the

gusts set up a kind of rhythm in the trees. Dianna felt lost within herself, very whole and complete, centered, as if the world and all that existed was in a circle around her, and she was both its heart and its extremities. It was the same feeling Dianna had experienced before in the Zendo, but that had been only a slight foreshadowing of what she felt on this night.

She sat there in the wind with tears running down her face, tears of wonderment and joy.

21

By Thursday Dianna felt at home and quite content in the barn. Her head was so into horses that she was enjoying even the shoveling out of the stables. The thoroughbreds were all becoming old friends with distinct personalities that demanded special handling. Early that evening Jacques and Agnes returned from Maine and reopened the dining room.

By the time Dianna appeared downstairs for dinner, the lobby was almost full of people waiting for tables. The attendance is surprising, thought Dianna, considering that it's so early in the season. Obviously, it's a tribute to Jacques's culinary art. Grabbing a free weekly tabloid that purported to tell all that was happening in southern Vermont, she took a table by herself in the corner.

Jacques came over and recited the menu. Dianna opted for a Duck Montmorency and ordered a half bottle of a fine wine. Several minutes later, when Jacques brought an appetizer, he quietly said in his husky French Canadian accent, "I see zat you are all a-lone zis evening."

"It does appear that way," Dianna said.

"It eez beautiful to ride at night in zee moonlight. Perhaps a little later . . . ?"

Dianna thought, There's no mistaking this guy's intention. I know *whom* he would like to be riding in the moonlight. "Thank you, Jacques, but no. The moon is not out tonight. It's cloudy."

"Well, perhaps zee moon will shine another time. Enjoy your dinner."

Loyalty and devotion and men, why do the three so rarely coexist? she thought. What is it in the Homo sapiens male that so rarely allows him to be faithful to a female?

Dianna remembered Arthur and his wife Connie. She had met her once—petulant, spoiled, full of an exaggerated self-worth, a professional shopper. But despite Dianna's opinion of the woman, she felt guilty for being a party to Arthur's infidelity. And though Dianna knew it was somewhat of a rationalization, at least she wasn't cheating on anyone but herself. What is it with men like Arthur and Jacques? Why can't they love and be true?

What was it that Yul Brynner sang to Anna as the king in *The King and I*? Dianna couldn't recall the exact lyric but the song was sung to support his chauvinistic point of view. Yes, she remembered, didn't it begin with an analogy of a girl to a flower—about how she, the flower, was supposed to keep her honey just to be given to one man, the honey bee. The man was described as flitting about from flower to flower gathering all the honey he can.

Dianna had always hated the punch line of the lyric which used faulty logic to try and make a point about out how the honey bee was by his very nature free to do his flitting, but how absurd would be to think of a flower that flitted from one bee to another bee to another.

How absurd, how illogical. How old-fashioned. How unforgivably male.

But Dianna chuckled to herself. Those words were written almost forty years ago. Today there was a difference, a just and modern twist—today the bee could be male or female. And there were a lot of females she knew, herself included, who were out there being bees. Most were discreet and secret but very busy bees nevertheless.

As Dianna sipped her wine and read the newspaper, she noticed, in the corner of the back page, a small picture of a young woman. Beneath the photo, in bold type, were the words "STILL MISSING. Anne Spencer Caufield. A former resident of the communal living group at 'Bread.' Last seen in the vicinity of Fenwick. Anyone with information as to the whereabouts of Anne please contact . . ." A phone number and a post office box in Boston were listed. At the end of the ad was the word "Reward."

Jacques served the main course and remarked, "I think eet eez clearing up. I can see zee stars."

"Please," said Dianna, looking him in the eye, "accept a polite 'no.' . . ."

The French Canadian frowned and returned to the kitchen.

22

By Friday morning Dianna was completely at ease in the saddle, though she still avoided jumping. And praise be to the Virgin, with the exception of minor corrections that she could do in a couple of hours, the draft of the manuscript was finished. The problem now was ennui.

To hell with aloneness. Dianna was hungry for companionship. She missed her friends at the office, she missed Arthur, she missed the sea of faces at the theater. She was even starting to speculate how Jacques would be in bed, and Dianna knew if that was happening, it was definitely time to think about moving on to more eligible pastures.

But Dennis was returning this weekend. Though he was not necessarily the perfect Stanley to her Blanche, she did have a warm memory of his handsome face, and his lips were tender, and she felt a rise when she thought of being with him. That last good night kiss had stayed with her and tickled her imagination. Dianna decided to give him until Saturday morning to make an appearance, and if he didn't show up, she'd be off to Maine.

While Goody was preoccupied, Dianna had snuck a glance at the front desk to check on Dennis's reservation. She had found the register, but his name wasn't entered. However, there was a slip of paper that said, "Change room three." Dianna was optimistic that he would appear.

The day had begun with a long ride, and later she made an unsuccessful attempt at taking a nap. By five-thirty Dianna found herself sitting on the porch trying to read a magazine.

Who am I fooling? she thought. I've put myself in the best

seat in the house to see whether or not Dennis shows up.
Dianna had refused to let herself make dinner plans until the
last minute.

Two hours later, losing patience, she stood up and headed
for the door. This is ridiculous, she thought, me sitting here on
the edge of my chair like a teenybopper. Just as her appetite
was about to push her into the dining room for something to
snack on, the 320i came up the drive.

As Dennis got out of the car and came up the drive, he
looked better than she had remembered, though Dianna admitted to herself that the overdose of hormones she felt surging
into her bloodstream might just be affecting her objectivity.

Her first impulse was to drag him up to her room, rip off his
clothes, and have her way with him. Instead she responded
with a reserved kiss and a calm acceptance of an invitation for
dinner at the inn.

I must act this way because I'm Catholic, she thought.

One portion of the dinner conversation was obligatory and
seemed to Dianna almost embarrassingly obvious. But they
braved it with sincere faces, and Dianna quickly realized that
Dennis genuinely wanted answers to certain very important
questions. And as each of their sexual histories unfolded, they
both seemed satisfied. Dennis had lived with one woman for
the majority of the last several years and, more importantly,
seemed concerned and conscientious. His questions about the
character of Arthur hit a little close to home, but at the same
time the fact that Dennis was so careful was most reassuring.

Though they were both much hungrier for each other than
they were for dinner, they spent a hour over their food trying
to give one another a cool and casual impression and then
wasted another fifteen minutes in the lobby looking through the
local paper for a film they could both tolerate. Finally, they
compromised on a foreign spy thriller.

The film didn't start until nine-thirty, so Dennis asked
Dianna up for a drink, and she had to check herself to keep
from sounding too agreeable. Her heart was beating fast as they
stood outside his door, and Dennis's fingers trembled as he
fumbled with the key in the lock.

There was a moment at the door when she was sure he was
about to kiss her and she knew she would respond if he did, but
Dennis let the moment pass and they moved into his room. A

tall canopy bed covered with a hand-embroidered comforter dominated the space. The consciousness of being alone to-gether, so close to such a romantic and inviting bed, had an effect on both of them.

The walls of the room were decorated entirely with old portraits in dark oil. Above the fireplace was a portrait of a woman. Below the painting was the name Ruth Sarah Wilkinson.

"You know, in college," said Dianna, "I had an acting professor who loved to assign portraits as exercises. You had to study the painting and try to become the character, to understand how she lived, how she dealt with other people and her environment, and so on."

Dennis joined her beside the painting, standing close, their shoulders touching.

"I don't think I'd like becoming that woman," he said. "She looks like she'd slit her grandmother's throat and not bat an eye."

"The artist was good," Dianna said. "Look at the features, brittle, almost mean, look at that cold half smile . . . and the eyes. My professor always said the essence of the person was in the eyes."

Ruth Wilkinson had round, fat eyes, dull and bottomless, that looked as if they would never miss an opportunity for cruelty.

As Dianna stared into those murky brown orbs, she felt just the touch of a chill tingle up her spine and ripple across her shoulders. She felt alone and pressed herself closer to Dennis.

He turned her and kissed her, softly and gently. Dianna responded. Their bodies locked in an embrace, holding, wanting, then clutching.

He undressed her slowly, to the point where she wanted to scream with desire. His hands caressed her firmly and rhythmically. When he slipped off her bra, he drew in a breath at the sight of her nipples. "Jesus." He bent down and ran his tongue and lips over her breasts until the tips were like plump, inch-long stones. His fingertips caressed the inside of her thighs.

Her heartbeat raced; her breathing came fast. "Dennis," she said, looking him in the eyes, "make love to me."

She allowed herself to be taken to Dennis's bed. He sat her on the edge of the mattress, but just her weight caused the hundred-year-old bedsprings to squeak and groan. The couple laughed quietly together.

"That would give the folks downstairs something to talk about," Dianna said.

Dennis took a patchwork quilt, spread it on the rug, and drew Dianna down beside him on the floor. She reached over and into her purse, then turned back to offer him a package of condoms just as he took a condom from his trouser pocket. They laughed together.

Their lovemaking was explosive at first, then smooth and easy.

Later they opened Dennis's bottle of wine and made love throughout the night.

23

Dennis awoke first the next morning and began to gently caress Dianna. After opening her eyes and realizing his pleasant intention, she slipped out of bed and headed for the bathroom door, where she paused a second, blew him a coy kiss, and said, "See you for breakfast, Mr. Conwell." Not that Dianna didn't like to make love in the morning, but she wanted to check Dennis's impulse, put it on hold, so that he would be thinking about her, and wanting to make love to her, for at least a good part of the day.

Riding turned out to be a lot of laughs and a hell of a lot of fun. Dennis had never been on a horse before but proved to be a good sport about the whole thing. He was quite a sight bouncing along and hanging on for dear life.

Dianna atoned for her morning tease in a remote and secluded clearing. After they had ridden for a couple of hours, and Dennis was obviously in need of a rest, Dianna suggested they dismount and let the horses cool off. She tied their mounts to a sapling, and as Dennis, in mild agony, began to rub the muscles on the inside of his thighs, Dianna came up behind him and put her hands around his waist.

She whispered, "Let me do that," and her fingers slipped around to the front of his jeans and down over his thighs. Her hands began slowly working their way upward, seeking a response.

A little later Dianna took the blankets off the horses and laid them over a bed of pine needles.

As they undressed, Dianna was excited but nervous. Being outdoors had more of an effect on her than she would have thought, and she had an image in her mind that they were a primitive couple, a nomadic twosome on the run, hunted by some predatory tribe. For her, it gave the lovemaking a paranoia, as if they were being watched and had to find a completion before they were discovered and taken captive.

Bare bottoms white in the sunlight, the scent of sweat mingling with pine. Coming out in the open air.

How sweet to be alive.

Later they went for a drive and Dennis made stops at two different inns. He told Dianna that he was doing some canvassing for a magazine article. At the second hotel, Dianna was able to watch him through a bay window. She thought it odd that Dennis took out what looked like a brochure or picture and showed it to the clerk at the desk. The clerk looked it over and shook his head. Dennis said something in reply and left.

That night they had an Italian dinner at a romantic little place not far from Fenwick. Afterward, when they were both wonderfully full and mellow, Dennis said, "Miss LaBianca, would you care to come up to my room?"

Dianna answered in a Southern accent, "Why, sir, what for?"

"I . . . uh . . . I have a wonderful ceiling I would like to show you."

"A ceiling! My, my, my."

"And a bottle of champagne."

"No, thank you, but I don't believe I will. I feel certain that my lily-white skin and my delicate constitution would never stand the strain and exertion of bein' in your little ol' room tonight."

Dennis smiled, enjoying her mock refusal. He was getting used to her occasional game playing and knew that he'd better be ready at any moment for her to pull something like this.

"However," she continued, "if you care to, you and your bottle of champagne are cordially invited to appear in my room this evening. But you'll have to promise to be a gentleman."

"You're doing what's-her-name from *Streetcar Named Desire*!" Dennis said, catching on to her game.

"Very good."

He tried to do a Brando imitation, and failed miserably. "I'll rip my best T-shirt and come over."

Dianna laughed at his bad impression and responded, "You're an animal, that's what you are."

It was the bed in her room, Dianna realized, that had led to her invitation. She wanted to make love in that weird, magnificent, cupid-infested bed.

As they walked from the car to the inn, through the gaggle of honking geese, Dennis spotted the German shepherd. "Look out, here comes Lancelot. Hold onto your purse."

Dianna gripped her shoulder bag and swung it around behind her. But then she looked down and saw that the German shepherd was sexually aroused and didn't have the least interest in her purse. He pawed his way up Dianna's arm and started humping away.

Dennis tried to pull the dog off her, but Lancelot only barked menacingly at him and continued at Dianna, nipping at her shoulder and arm. Dianna laughed nervously and managed to push the animal away. Dennis stayed between the dog and Dianna as they ran for the inn. Undaunted, Lancelot kept trying to get at her, barking and making pelvic undulations.

"The dog's got taste," said Dennis, and they laughed together.

Dianna struck a pose in the safety of the front door and said with a Southern drawl, "That's merely the effect I have on every male."

Dianna wanted to make the moment that Dennis entered her room special and dramatic, an event that he would take with him back to Boston, a memory that hopefully would stay in his head long enough for him to make that next and most important call.

She was starting to like Dennis. He had become, in her thinking, a "candidate," someone who she felt she could someday care for, a man who had the potential to become a permanent part of her life. Her feelings at this point were only in the "could" stage, but meeting a candidate was not something that happened very often. And Dianna wanted to motivate him to think of her in a long-term way.

She undressed and draped the bedspread around herself suggestively. Keep him guessing, on his toes, a little off balance, always expecting something exciting. It was fun, and after all, it did give her an element of control.

Dennis knocked, rather loudly she thought, and Dianna posed in the soft glow of a lamp. For a moment she had an apparition, a flash, that some stranger was behind the door, but she shook off the notion and coyly said, "Come in."

Dennis appeared with two glasses and wine. One look at Dianna, and his mouth fell open. He hurriedly closed the door behind him and turned the large brass key in the heavy, cast-iron lock.

As he entered the room, Dianna let the bedspread slide down from around her neck to the top of her breasts. Dennis leaned back against the door, watching her, savoring the moment.

Then, slowly, a fraction of an inch at a time, Dianna lowered the spread, first across her left breast, letting the fabric hang from her hard nipple for a moment before she nudged it off. Then, in one steady move she took the bedspread down to her navel, revealing her right breast. Dennis's eyes were filled with wanting.

Ever so slowly, Dianna continued the motion until her improvised garment was just below her waist. Then she opened the front of the spread and stretched out her arms to him. Her stance legs apart, she reached out to him, offering all he could want of her.

Dennis moved quickly to her, and she enveloped his hot embrace in the bedspread.

Dianna didn't give him time to get all his clothes off. She drew him down onto the floor with his shirt pulled up and his trousers down around his knees and took him inside her.

They made love in the folds of her fabric cocoon.

Her coming with Dennis was good. As the kneading shock waves rolled up and down her stomach, down and into the muscles of her thighs, a worldless feeling seemed to take her over. Everything seemed to stop, all thought, all existence. There was no passing of time. She smiled to herself and thought, Maybe this is the way to attain satori. Nah, then everybody would be studying Zen.

She felt him get even harder and knew that he was about to come. "Yes, come on. Let it go. Yes, do it with me."

Hard. Fine. Intense. Making love can be so good, she thought, as the non-moment floated on.

Thank you, God, for orgasms. What a gift, what a wonderful gift.

"Yes! Yes! That's it, give it to me. Do it!" she commanded, moving against his thrusts. "Come on. More. Come baby. Do it for me. Yes, come for me!"

The following morning Dennis said he had some business to take care of and left Dianna to enjoy her daily ride alone. She suspected the real reason for his declining her company had a lot to do with the pain he was certainly feeling from his last ride. Dianna decided to take Crumpet out toward the southeast on the trail that Goody had recommended.

Dianna was getting to know and like the way the gelding handled. Confident and relaxed in the saddle, she reined up before a low jump.

I've got to try this, she told herself. Immediately her hands began shaking, and sweat formed on her brow. "Concentrate, focus," Dianna told herself as she tried to ignore her body's signals and put her mind on the jump.

Her heels lightly touched the animal's flanks. The well-trained horse shot forward. For just an instant Dianna wanted to rein up, even to jump off. Her stomach tightened up in a hard knot. A few feet away from the hurdle, she closed her eyes.

When she felt Crumpet's hooves settle into stride again, she looked back. The rail was up, she was in the saddle, and all her bones were intact. Dianna broke out in a grin. Feeling pleased, with a touch of her old courage back, she took several more little jumps of two or three feet. I have been redeemed for not jumping earlier in the week, she thought.

As Dianna climbed up along the unfamiliar trail, she came upon the ruins of the burnt-out religious commune Bread. Through the trees, she thought she saw a sparkle of metal and caught a glimpse of a car driving away down the gravel access road. Dianna couldn't be sure because the foliage was so dense, but she got the impression it was Dennis's 320i.

She mentioned it to him when they were together that night. It was their last dinner before Dennis was due to go back to Boston.

He looked at her and said, "No, it wasn't me. Must have been another BMW."

"Who would go out there?"

"Wealthy hunters, real estate agents—there are a lot of people with 320i's in Vermont." Dennis changed the subject. "So, Dianna, have you made plans for the coming week?"

"I think I'll drive to New Hampshire. I've got a good friend from school who works for a TV station near Dartmouth."

I wonder, should I let him know whether my friend is a lady or a man? It was, in fact, a woman. They had been roommates their sophomore year at college, but Dianna decided not to tell Dennis, to see if he would ask. It could be a way to find out if he was really interested. It would be revealing to see the way Dennis handled the situation.

"Why don't you come to Boston?"

Aha, I think Ms. LaBianca has made an impression. "I promised myself I would get up to Dartmouth, but if things work out, I could stop in Boston on my way back to New York sometime next weekend."

"How about Friday?"

"Let me see what my friend wants to do." That invitation earns him my best behavior, she thought. "Suzy's my roommate from college. We survived Theater together." Dianna was pleased that Dennis looked just the slightest bit relieved. "Why don't you give me your number, and I'll call you by Thursday or Friday at the latest."

"You promise?"

"You have my most solemn word as a lady."

"Great."

Dennis wandered over to the window and looked out, suddenly serious. "Dianna, I've got a confession to make."

A sudden déjà vu flashed in Dianna's mind, of her first night with Arthur. "Dear God, please don't tell me you're married."

"No."

"Engaged? . . . You have an unmentionable infectious disease?"

"No, nothing like that. It's nothing to do with my social life. I'm quite unattached. It's not anything that would affect the two of us. . . . No, look, it's better if I don't tell you here." With this comment Dennis looked out at the grounds of the inn. "I'll tell you when we see each other again."

"You're sure?"

"Positive. It's nothing. Just forget about it."

"Oh, come on. You're not just going to drop this?"

"Believe me, it doesn't really matter. It's nothing that would affect the two of us directly."

Dianna smiled. "That is totally unethical. I am consumed with curiosity."

"Well, good. Now you know what you put me through. It's tough to take a dose of your own medicine, isn't it?" he asked with a knowing smile.

"Are you suggesting that 'little ol' me' is elusive and unpredictable?"

"No kidding. But I'll catch up. . . . So, if you're curious, you'll just have to come and see me on Friday to find out the details of my little secret."

The night was long and wonderful, fueled with the knowledge that they would soon part. It heightened the passion—made the loving hot, the wanting deeper, and the moments of coming together all the more explosive.

A very tired Dennis left Dianna at four in the morning to drive back to Boston.

Esau hate man. Man try to take booteful. He try take her away.

Want make man dead.

From the shadows of his cellar, Esau watched them through the window. He saw them kiss and hug good-bye, and watched her wave after Dennis as he drove away.

But booteful not go. She stay.

She stay to be with Esau.

24

Monday morning, Dianna slept till eleven and went for a final ride on Lady Ann. As she walked from the stables to the inn, feeling exhilarated and confident, ready to pack and check out, the German shepherd came up to her with something in his mouth. It was a thick green wallet. Dianna stopped and stared. What on earth would a dog be doing with a woman's wallet?

Something cried out at Dianna from the dark corners of her mind, Walk away! Get in the car and go to Maine! Leave the wallet alone! Don't stop! Don't get involved!

Images and information clicked together in her subconscious, like random pieces of data that suddenly fall into a pattern of significance.

A lump rose in her throat. Goose bumps broke out on her arms and legs. Dianna had a crazy and frightening notion, a wild insight about whose wallet it was. She turned to walk into the inn but couldn't seem to take another step. Beads of perspiration grew on her forehead.

Could she just turn her back and walk away from this situation? No, it simply wasn't something she could ever do. With a determined look, Dianna faced Lancelot.

She tried to entice the playful animal. "Here, boy, here."

But this time the dog was wise to her tricks and only pranced back and forth, shaking his head from side to side, almost as if saying "no." The dog's eyes and teeth, as they held the wallet, seemed locked in a mad grimace. Dianna tried chasing Lancelot, but he kept dodging away from her at the last possible moment.

She threw sticks, rocks, and even an old can, but the dog

held on to the wallet with clenched teeth. Finally, Dianna turned and pretended to walk away. The shepherd followed, growling and running at her feet to force her to stay in the game. When she didn't stop, he barked several times, and the wallet dropped on the grass.

She grabbed a rotting stick from under a bush and gave it a toss.

As Lancelot raced after it, Dianna picked up the wallet and headed for the inn. Soon the animal lost interest in the crumbling stick and came after her, barking and trying to retrieve the wallet. Then, with a sudden mood change, the dog became turned on and began jumping on her, humping her legs.

Dianna escaped into the lobby of the inn and was relieved to find that none of the Wilkinson clan was about. She went straight to her room and shut the door behind her.

The wallet was covered with teeth marks and had mold growing on the leather. Inside was sixteen dollars in bills and a small amount of change in a snap pocket. There was an old ID card from the graduate school of the University of Massachusetts, and pressed inside the leather pocket was a withered flower. A plastic foldout that should have held about twenty photographs was ripped, and only ten remained. Amongst them was a driver's license in the name of Miss Anne Spencer Caufield.

That's the missing young woman, Dianna realized.

There were many pictures of Anne. She was a pretty girl with long, brown hair. The pictures showed her dressed in patched jeans and tie-dyed tops with slogans printed on them like "No Nukes" and "Save the Whales."

One of the snapshots almost made Dianna drop the wallet.

There, smiling at her in the photo, was Dennis. Several years younger then he was now, but it was definitely Dennis. Dianna hurriedly flipped through the remaining photos. There were two more shots of him. One was apparently taken around the time he was in high school, and the other was a family grouping taken at a college graduation. Dennis, wearing a mortar board and gown, stood between two people who were undoubtedly his parents. To the left stood a very young Anne.

Anne is Dennis's sister, Dianna realized. She looked at the driver's license again. Miss Anne Spencer *Caufield*.

But Dennis's last name was . . . What was Dennis's last name? Her mind raced. Conway . . . Conwell. That was it! Dennis Conwell.

But why would they have different names? Wait, Dennis and Anne could be half brother and sister, or maybe one was adopted? Not likely, she thought; the family resemblances were too strong.

Maybe Dennis's last name isn't Conwell after all.

Why would Dennis use a phony name?

What was he doing here anyway? Could it have been Dennis's BMW that I saw by the commune? He said it wasn't, but if he lied to me about his name, he could easily have lied about that, too.

A rush of questions flooded her mind.

What was Dennis doing that first day when I caught him snooping in the harness room?

And when I saw Dennis showing that hotel clerk something, could it have been a picture of Anne?

Was Dennis here to search for his missing sister? That would explain a lot of things.

But then why was he using an alias?

Dianna had to think about this one for a bit. But then she came up with a possible explanation: Dennis probably felt he stood a better chance of finding out the truth if people didn't know that he was Anne's brother.

Of course, that was Dennis's secret—the one he wouldn't tell me until I visited him in Boston. He isn't Dennis Conwell, he's Dennis Caufield and he's probably not a writer. Yes, my instincts were right, he's no writer. He only came out here to try and find his sister, Anne.

Why didn't Dennis tell me about it? He probably felt he didn't know me well enough to let me in on his secret. Or he could have thought it would upset me if he told me about his sister. After all, I am staying alone in a place just a couple of miles from where she disappeared.

Dianna clutched her stomach as the fear welled up inside her. The question pounded in her brain: What had happened to Anne?

Dianna knew that having the wallet could, without question, involve her in a deadly situation. It could draw her into a case of murder, or a cover-up, and someone might be ready to kill again if they knew she had the billfold.

Why wasn't there a phone in the room? She could call home, Dennis, the police, anyone.

Quivering, Dianna looked at the wallet in her hands and thought, I've got to get rid of this. Should I destroy it? No, it might be a clue to finding Anne, but I can't leave it where it can be seen.

She stuffed the moldy green billfold into her suitcase, under a pile of clothes.

Dianna whispered aloud, "What happened to Anne?"

25

It was a sound like a guttural moan, coming from outside in the yard, that brought Dianna to the window. The cry seemed to be both a threat and a call to battle—a call that made the German shepherd growl and bark an answer. As she neared the window, Dianna froze in mid-motion.

Through the leaded panes she saw a sight that drove every consideration of Anne Spencer Caufield from her mind.

At first she thought it was an optical illusion caused by the distortion of the leaded glass. She pressed her face to the windowpane and realized that what she was looking at really was a human being—a male person, of living form and substance.

The immense bulk of the grotesque human made the German shepherd seem like a half-sized, stuffed toy. Dianna's eyes were riveted on the creature as if she were looking at pictures of some terrible disaster—disgusting pictures that held a person's attention because of the sheer horror of their content.

From somewhere in the distance, Dianna vaguely heard a door slam out in the hall, then shouting voices and footsteps running down the stairs.

The dog and the monstrosity—the word was all that Dianna could think of at the moment—were faced off in a life-or-death struggle. Lancelot fought with a half erection dangling between his legs.

The dog snarled and circled, watching his enemy carefully with angry eyes, looking for a chance to leap for the neck.

An aura of finality, of impending, absolute resolution was in the air. The two seemed to share a long-standing hatred—a mutual need for vengeance that could only be satisfied through death.

Both males stopped, poised to strike, eyes focused on enemy eyes, every muscle taut with readiness.

Lancelot made the first attack, leaping for the man-creature's throat, but with a flick of a fist the hulking figure hit the dog on the side of the skull.

What seemed to be an effortless gesture proved a devastating backhand blow. The stunned animal was knocked in a ten-foot arc. He landed on the ground, got up slowly, staggering and shaking his head, trying in vain to stay on his feet.

The monstrosity moved in on the helpless dog, clamped an oversized hand around the animal's snout, and pulled the whimpering head upward with a jerk. Dianna could hear the soft crack of bone.

The victor smiled, tossed the carcass aside, and threw his misshapen shoulders back in triumph. Then, with a slow turn of his twisted neck, he looked directly up at Dianna.

Through the wavelike distortions of the leaded glass, their eyes locked.

The message conveyed from the creature's eyes was unmistakable. Dianna had seen that look countless times before on many men in all sorts of situations. Even Arthur had had a touch of the same look the first time they met. It was the identical message, one as old as the human race, this time imparted in the most direct manner possible, with no mask of civilized deportment or sense of fair play. It was communicated with raw purpose and with animal-like single-mindedness.

The glistening, squinting eyes sent a personalized message of utter determination:

I am going to fuck you.

Dianna whirled in panic to grab her keys. Her singular thought was to get to the car and escape.

To her surprise, standing in the doorway, blocking the only escape from her room, was Agnes. In her hand was a large butcher knife. The heavy woman eyed Dianna wearily and commanded, "Step back if you please."

Dianna retreated a few paces into the room. Taking the weighty brass key out of the inside of the lock, Agnes stepped back out to the hall and said, "If you keep quiet, you won't get hurt." The woman slammed the door shut. As Dianna ran to it she heard the click of the lock turning. She threw her weight against the door. It was as solid as a wall of granite.

She paced in the room, whispering to herself, "My God, my God. What is going on here? What was that thing I saw?"

Outside there were shouts in French, then came harsh words from Agnes and a quiet command from Goody. Dianna went to the window and saw Jacques walking from around the front of the inn, dragging a long length of strong chain. From the opposite direction, Dianna heard an inhuman, high-pitched whine, almost a scream.

She ran with full force into the door and beat her fists against it, but she quickly realized it was pointless. As Agnes had said, the door was unusually sturdy, more like the front door to a fortress—made of solid oak reinforced with metal plate and secured with a lock and hinges of heavy steel. On the inside were thick metal bars at top and bottom, which Dianna slid home. She thought, If I can't get out, at least they can't get in.

Dianna wandered the room, in a daze of unreality, a walking coma. Her head churned with confusion.

Where am I? Who am I? What am I doing here? This is not happening.

Why am I locked in this room? Was it the wallet? No, I don't think anyone could know I have the wallet.

Was it because I saw that monster in the yard? What is that man-thing? Is it really human?

Dianna remembered the look the creature had given her. She had felt something else in that look, more than just the message of consuming lust; it had been a deeper communication on some other plane. The message had come to Dianna on a nonverbal level, especially from his body language, both his swagger and his expressions.

There was a certainty in the mind of the man-thing, an almost spiritual knowledge, instinctual yet absolute, that he was somehow bound to her and she to him. The man-thing believed their destinies were intertwined like two vines growing in circles around the same sapling. They would somehow be forged or wedded together.

The thought made Dianna's body react almost violently. A spasm attacked the flesh of her back, like a chill but more gripping, more consuming. It moved up toward her neck in a crawl, as a slow wave would move, twisting and turning her skin, pulling at it with a nauseating electrical kind of twitch.

The inn quieted except for the sound of the clanking of chain. Dianna had a flash image that they were going to lock her in leg irons, and she went to the window.

Jacques was dragging the long length of chain slowly across the lawn. The heavy links turned as it followed behind him, like a serpent crawling through the grass. There was the thick ring of a metal shackle bolted to one end, and Dianna could see that the loop of steel was much too big for her foot.

She knew whom the shackle was meant for.

Jacques took a large padlock and fastened the chain to itself around the sugar maple. Now that Dianna looked more carefully, she could see a cross-hatching of scar marks all over the bark at the base of the old tree.

Another hour passed. Dianna sat on the edge of the bed in shock, her eyes fixed on a point on the wall. Her mind was swirling and unfocused, her thoughts a jumble of confusion.

26

Keys rattled outside the door, and the lock turned, but the bars held fast. There was a soft knock and the sound of Goody's voice, "Dianna. . . . Miss LaBianca. . . . Open the door."

Thoughts raced through Dianna's mind: What should I do? Should I open the door or stay in the security of the room? What do they want? If I let them in they could . . . do what? On the other hand if I keep the door locked . . . ?

"Dianna, if you don't draw the latch, we will have to break the door down. You don't want us to do that, do you?"

What's the point? Bars wouldn't keep anyone out for long. She drew the long sliders back. Goody wheeled herself in, followed by Jacques and Agnes. From the grimness of their expressions, Dianna wasn't sure she had made the right decision. She backed away into a corner.

Goody said, "Dearie, what is your real name?"

Dianna stared at her and said, "Pardon?"

"I said, what is your real name? It surely isn't LaBianca, just like Mr. Conwell is not, nor has he ever been, Mr. Conwell."

So Dennis *was* using a phony name, Dianna realized. "I don't know anything about Mr. Conwell. I just met him."

"Don't lie to me. He's Dennis Caufield, and he's up here looking for his sister who disappeared from that commune last September."

Dianna almost blurted out, "Anne," but caught herself. Somehow Anne's disappearance has something to do with these people and the creature I saw in the yard, she thought. And they're all hiding something. "I had no idea that Dennis even had a sister."

118

"She's lying," said Agnes.

"Go through her things," Goody commanded.

Dianna inadvertently glanced at the suitcase that held Anne's billfold and shouted, "No, you have no right!"

Minutes later her captors were holding the green wallet. They were obviously shaken by the discovery.

"Where did you find this?" Goody demanded.

Dianna looked away. "The dog had it."

Agnes hissed, "She knows everything."

"No," Dianna blurted out, "I heard about all this for the first time just now."

Goody continued, "We know all about Mr. Caufield. He's been showing pictures of his sister in every store and motel in the area since the police stopped their investigation. How long have you two been lovers?"

". . . I just met him last weekend."

Jacques laughed and shook his head.

Another high-pitched scream was heard from behind the house. They all seemed to hold their breaths and listen anxiously.

"What is that thing?" asked Dianna.

Goody looked at Jacques and Agnes. "Now that you have had the rare privilege of seeing him, I might as well enlighten you. He is my grandson, Esau Wilkinson," she smiled with a bitter irony, "the last man-child in the illustrious line of Wilkinsons."

Dianna said, "He is not . . . not . . ."

"Normal?" Goody finished the statement. "No, he has many deformities: a hunchback, a pituitary imbalance that has made him almost a giant, the brain of a six-year-old child, and besides all of that, he is ugly—birthmarked and almost completely covered with body hair. No, Esau is not in any sense what you would consider a normal person."

"Why did he kill the German shepherd?"

"He's hated the German shepherd for years, and besides, I think he decided that Lancelot was his rival."

"A rival?"

"Yes," Goody continued. "Esau unfortunately is quite 'normal' in one respect. He lusts after the opposite sex. Esau saw the dog as his rival for you."

Dianna's knees buckled under her.

27

The thought obliterated all sense of being. Dianna felt paralyzed kneeling there before the trio. Time stopped as she
wrestled with the concept that this thing lusted after her. It
wants you . . . you . . . you . . . you . . . you. The
loathsome idea kept coming back at her like a train on a
Möbius strip.

Finally she spoke, "I saw a grave for Esau Wilkinson."

"Yes, well, Esau is legally dead. You see, Esau has brought
this family little but grief. His mother died from the rigors of
giving him birth. His father wanted no part of the deformed
baby and it was left for me to name him. He had come from the
womb covered with hair, and so I called him Esau.

"He killed my son, his father, when he was nine. They were
at a baseball game together when Esau took up a bat and
fractured his father's skull. After that, the state wanted to put
Esau in an institution, but we arranged to have him 'pass away'
in a boating accident. Esau would have never survived in an
institution."

"I don't know anything about any of this," Dianna protested. "I never saw Dennis before this weekend. You've got to
believe me."

"She must have put two and two together by now," said
Agnes, near hysteria. "They'll get us for it. We'll all go down
together. Maybe she's found the body."

"Hold your tongue!" shouted Goody.

Dianna broke down in tears. "Dennis is a stranger. I don't
have anything to do with Anne or any of this. Please believe
me."

"You're lying," said Goody. "But even if you are not, it doesn't make any difference now. The problem is that you're a very bright woman. And my granddaughter has a point—you must have made the necessary deductions by now."

Goody exchanged a look with Agnes, who took a rag and a brown bottle from an apron pocket.

The old woman continued, "Esau escaped from his cellar one night and came across Anne Caufield on the southwest trail. Esau desired her. But in the process, Anne resisted, and he killed her—quite unintentionally—but nevertheless he killed her. You have observed that he is not the gentlest of men. It all makes no difference now. I'm sorry, I liked you. . . ."

"What are you going to do?" Dianna asked.

Goody nodded to Jacques. He grabbed Dianna.

Agnes poured some of the contents of the bottle on the rag.

Goody said, "Just giving you a little nap, my dear, a little nap."

Dianna screamed as Jacques forced her down on the bed. The French Canadian pinned her arms while Agnes placed the rag over her face. Dianna fought back, trying to hold her breath. On the rag she could smell the foul odor that had filled her room the night it was ransacked.

Goody said, "Lock the chain across the front drive and run her car into the horse trailer."

The last words Dianna heard as she went under were "put her belongings . . . " and "accident. . . ."

PART III

A character that forms the suffix of many Japanese arts, disciplines, and philosophies. As in Shodo—calligraphy; Bushido—the code of the Samurai; Iaido and Kyudo—martial arts of the sword and the bow.

The messenger of death enters
And all business stops.

A beautiful bird
Is the only kind we cage.

Chinese proverbs

28

I exist. I am. I breathe. I live. This was the stream of Dianna's thoughts as consciousness returned to her.

She lay on her back on the floor of a damp stone cellar. Her hands were tied behind her, and strips of duct tape covered her mouth. Straw was piled deep on the floor, and in her nostrils was the same familiar, hideous, zoo-animal stench that she had smelled in her room the time the "dog" had ransacked it. The difference was that now the smell was omnipresent, over-whelming.

One greasy window let in the barest glow of light. Dianna gagged and nearly choked to death because of the tape that cut off any breathing through her mouth.

After sitting up, she discovered that the only way to get around was by hopping. Dianna managed, after a couple of falls, to reach the window. There were bars on the inside of the wall opening, and there was a separation of two feet from the wall to the small dirty window itself. She could look out only if she stood on a bench. Beyond the several layers of glass, Dianna could see the side of the inn. I'm in the icehouse, she realized, in the large square pit below the surface of the earth.

Through the window, she saw that her car was gone from the space where she had parked it in the driveway. And there, chained to the sugar maple tree in the backyard, was a lump that reminded Dianna of a rhino sleeping on the grass. Esau. He was curled up in a ball with his back to the icehouse.

Dianna slumped to the floor. What are they going to do with me? It was a hard question to face in the hopeless gloom and disgusting stench of the filthy cell. But Dianna thought she knew the answer: "*Finito la* LaBianca."

She remembered hearing the word "accident" before passing out.

What time is it? She twisted around to look at her watch—four forty-five. She had been unconscious for almost four hours. Her mind raced. When will they try to kill me? Probably under the cover of darkness, probably tonight. "Put out the light, and then put out the light."

How? Put me in my car and push it into a ravine? Shoot me? Poison me? Throw me into a lake? There are a thousand different possible ways they could kill me. And my body could be disposed of anywhere in this country. I could disappear without leaving so much as a ripple on a pond.

She felt helpless, depressed from the aftereffects of the sleeping drug and from the damp and fetid environment. A part of her wished that she had never awakened from her enforced nap.

Dianna looked around the cellar and suddenly realized, My God, I'm in that thing's home. This is where Esau lives. She noticed a light cord. By grabbing it between her chin and her shoulder, she managed to turn on the light. There were ancient rugs torn and rotting on the stone walls, covered with patches of green mold. Decaying straw was strewn across the floor and gave the cell even more of the feeling of a kennel.

Something about the environment struck a spark of rage and kindled a determination. Dianna felt insulted that she had been thrown into the cagelike cell with no just reason. She thought, there has to be something I can do, some action I can take.

First Dianna examined the door. It was solid welded steel, very strong and with a large dead-bolt lock. When she peeked through a crack in the metal frame, she realized that the icehouse actually had two doors. A few feet away from the inside door was an outer door that let in a little light around the cracks in its frame. The inside of the outer door was covered with thick soundproofing insulation.

The inner door looked as if it had been broken once before and repaired. But, Dianna knew, if it could contain the room's usual occupant, there was no way that she would ever get it open. As she shuffled through the rancid straw, she saw Esau's wrinkled porno magazines, ragged baseball cards, his collection of toilet articles, and, stuck up on nails, his pictures of handsome men.

Dianna searched for something to cut the bonds and free her hands and came across Esau's assortment of cologne bottles on the shelf. She tipped them down, shattering one on the stone floor. Rolling on her back and picking up a shard of glass, Dianna tried to use it like a knife. But her hands were tied in such a way that she couldn't bring the glass to bear on the heavy rope.

She looked everywhere on the wall for a stone with a sharp edge, but there was none. Then the modern frame of the inner door caught her attention. The jam was sheet metal, and its edge was sharp. Dianna feverishly began rubbing the rope against the metal.

The work was tiring. Her head was pounding as if she were suffering from a massive hangover, and her feet and ankles ached because the bonds cut off her circulation. Still, she worked until her muscles cramped, waited until she could move again, and then pressed on.

The tape made it almost impossible to breathe, especially when her exertion caused her to be short of breath. Dianna hopped to a nail on the wall that held a few of Esau's pictures, put her face up to it, and pushed the head of the nail through the tape and into her mouth. Catching the nail head on the tape, she pulled back. It felt as if she were inch by inch tearing off her own face, but finally the tape came off with a painful jerk and dangled from the nail.

There in front of her, on the top of the stack of pictures pinned to the wall, was a familiar face. Taking the tape off of the nail with her mouth, Dianna uncovered a snapshot of Anne. It had to be one of the missing photos from the plastic pockets of Anne's wallet.

Suddenly shaken by the thought that someone was coming for her at the very moment, Dianna hopped to the window and looked out. But no one was in sight. The interior lights of the inn were on now, and an outside light partially illuminated the backyard.

Esau was awake. He lay stretched out on his stomach at the end of his chain, trying to get his fingers around a water spigot that protruded from the ground.

Dianna started back to the door but stopped beside the pull

cord. She realized that the light might draw attention, and
taking the cord in her mouth, she clicked it off.

Back at the door edge, she wondered, What could I
accomplish if I do free my hands? I still can't get out.

Maybe I could hide behind the door and hit whoever comes
in over the head with something. At least I'd have some
chance.

Even if I do get out, what could I do? How long would I last
in the woods? I'd have to get to the road and then wave
somebody down.

She felt the rope loosening and wriggled her hands free.
Dianna had to keep herself from crying out as the blood seeped
back to her fingers and brought a sensation of fire-tingling
pain. She untied the lashes on her feet and returned to the
bench and the window.

Esau had managed to reach the water faucet and was pulling
on the pipe, yanking it out of the ground, using all the strength
of his legs and arms. Mother of God, he's trying to get free,
thought Dianna. He's got some plan, and he's going to use the
pipe to break loose.

Dianna frantically combed every inch of the cellar: the
stones around the door, the beams of the ceiling. There was no
sign of a weakness or any means of possible escape.

She stopped, fascinated by a muddy handprint on one of the
fieldstones. Dianna placed her own palm upon it. From heel to
fingertips her hand was less than half of the print on the wall.

Pulling on each of the bars, she hoped to find that one of
them could be worked loose, but each steel bar seemed solidly
implanted in the stone.

Glancing outside, Dianna saw Esau standing next to the tree.
He had broken off the section of the pipe and had stuck it
through the chain that was padlocked around the maple. There
was a little fountain of water coming from the earth where he
had broken off the pipe. If he can break that chain, thought
Dianna, his next stop is going to be the cellar.

As Esau yanked on the end of the long pipe, it bent in the
middle with a loud creak. A light blinked off on the second
floor, and Jacques came out the back door of the inn. He saw
the pipe in Esau's hand, went back inside, and returned with a
chocolate bar. At the sight of the candy, Esau dropped the pipe
and ran to the end of his chain, gesturing for the chocolate.

Jacques threw it on the grass behind the tree, and Esau went for it. Jacques eyed Esau and examined the padlock that held the chain around the trunk.

Agnes opened a window upstairs and shouted to Jacques, "Is everything all right?"

Jacques answered, *"Oui,"* and Agnes closed the window.

While Dianna watched, Esau lost patience trying to open the candy wrapper. He glanced in Dianna's direction at the ice-house and it struck her that he had remembered something more desirable than candy. As Jacques bent to check the links of chain, Esau suddenly hit him with full force from behind, slamming the French Canadian's head into the tree trunk. Jacques, caught completely unaware, fell unconscious on the grass.

Dianna watched in stunned silence. Esau began to jump up and down on Jacques like a demented chimpanzee, his three-hundred-plus pounds of bulk slamming again and again into the fallen man, crushing the life from his body. Dianna gagged and croaked the words, "Holy Virgin, bless his soul." But she couldn't look away.

Esau fumbled in Jacques's pockets, and Dianna saw the glint of metal as he found a ring of keys. One at a time he tried each key on his leg shackles. This kind of small motor skill was obviously difficult for him, and he kept dropping the key ring as he turned it over in his clumsy hands. After much fumbling he found the one that fit, and the shackles fell to the ground.

Dianna backed away from the window, convinced that Esau was coming for her. She became hysterical, screaming with total abandon, then realized that no one could hear. Even if they did, what good would it do?

She needed a weapon, but there was nothing. A bench, a board from a shelf, some bottles, straw on the floor—no possible means of defending herself.

Dianna heard the outer door open and close and gasped as the inner door shook with a terrible thud. Huge fists beat on the metal. Dianna circled the cellar like a trapped animal.

The pounding stopped. Dianna ran to the window. With one hand Esau was dragging the iron pipe like a matchstick toward the icehouse.

Agnes ran out the back door and saw the body of Jacques. She fell to her knees in the grass beside him and gently turned

Jacques around to face her. A heart's pump of blood came spurting out of his mouth. Agnes screamed.

Esau only glanced in Agnes's direction, continuing on a determined path toward the icehouse. Dianna started yelling uncontrollably, "Goody, Goody! Please stop him, Goody. Goody, stop him, Goody!"

The pounding on the door began again. The pipe beat against the metal frame, a loud hit then a soft hit, and the deafening noise reverberated off the walls of the rock cellar. The sound fell into a rhythm like the amplified faltering pulse of a person in the spasms of a coronary attack.

Dianna searched the room, frantically looking for something to shore up the door. She dragged the bench over to the entrance and wedged it under the dead-bolt lock. She knew it couldn't be much more than a worthless gesture, but at least it was something.

Then suddenly there was silence. Dianna heard a movement behind her and turned quickly. Esau's face pressed against the glass of the little window; his two eyes stared at her. She jumped back. The face disappeared.

A second later a fieldstone came through the opening, smashing the glass to smithereens. Esau appeared at the window frame, trying to pull himself through. The broken glass cut his fingers. Angrily, he grabbed the window casement and jerked it out of the rock foundation. When he had forced himself into the tight square, his bulk filled up the entire opening.

His fat, brown eyes leered at her huddled in the far corner. He pushed his arm in between the bars and groped for her, his body straining against the steel rods. His fingers reached out for her, his face pleaded.

Esau said one word, "Booteful."

A voice spoke from behind him, sharp and commanding. "That will be quite enough."

It was Goody, wheeling across the grass. In her lap was the set of keys for the chain. Esau turned away from the window and whimpered. Goody rolled right up to him for the confrontation. They were an unlikely pair of adversaries. As she locked eyes with Esau, the shrunken elderly woman in her wheelchair was dwarfed by his slouching bulk.

Moving quietly, trying to overhear and watch from a corner

of the window, Dianna inched in as close as she could get to the conversation. Anything said or done could affect her.

Dianna was surprised to see Esau cowering before Goody. He lowered and ducked his head with the behavior of a subservient dog. He whined—a pleading whine, very nasal, like the sound of a spoiled child trying to get a parent to buy an expensive toy.

"No!" said Goody. "Come here."

But Esau ignored her, repeating his groveling motions and strident pleading.

Across the yard, Agnes lifted the motionless figure of Jacques. His bloody mouth fell open as if he were about to say something, but the lower jaw only dangled. His head and the front of his shirt were awash in blood. The French Canadian's eyes were crossed, and with his gaping mouth he looked like a comic-book goon. Agnes felt for a pulse, and when she found none, she put her ear to Jacques's blood-soaked chest.

Esau pointed a finger at the icehouse, toward Dianna, his whine rising to a stuttering wail that made him sound like a hungry Siamese cat.

"No! Bad!" shouted Goody, and she held out her palm toward Esau, facing upward. The small bony appendage shook slightly, as frail and fragile as a winter's leaf. Esau hesitatingly put forward his hand, facing down, and set it for a second atop Goody's. Then he jerked it back as if he was afraid of leaving it there.

"Esau!" said Goody, thrusting her palm forward.

Esau put out his hand once more, this time letting it rest on hers. His face was squinting with little spasms of anticipated pain. Goody grabbed onto Esau's muscular middle finger, and with her other hand she began pinching the sensitive vein-riddled skin on the underside of Esau's wrist. She pinched hard and repeatedly, causing him to grimace in pain.

Dianna couldn't help thinking of the absurdity of it all, and recalled a couplet from *The Mikado*:

> Let the punishment fit the crime
> The punishment fit the crime

Agnes closed both of Jacques's eyelids and rose slowly to face Goody. On one side of her face was a blot of smeared blood. When the heavyset woman had Goody's attention, she looked down at Jacques's motionless figure and shook her head in a helpless way, as if to say, "He's gone." Goody sighed a deep and troubled sigh, closed her eyes, and whispered a prayer.

She gestured for Agnes to bring the leg shackle and come over. The woman nodded in response and smeared her face with more blood as she tried to wipe the tears from her eyes. Agnes heaved the chain up and onto her shoulder and dragged it forward.

Dianna shifted her position, accidentally stepping on a shard from the broken window. There was a crunch of ground glass.

Goody and Esau turned but merely glanced in Dianna's direction. Goody was a little flushed, obviously deeply upset and concerned over Jacques's fate. Her mind seemed occasionally to wander off, away from Esau, as if she was trying to think her way out of the deadly predicament.

Goody took her anger out on Esau with more pinches on his wrist. "Bad, bad, bad, *bad*!" Tears filled the man-thing's eyes.

Bad? thought Dianna with sarcasm. Yes, well, I would have to agree, murder *is* very bad.

Agnes came up close to Esau and thrust her face close to his. She gave him a look of disgust and loathing. In the look was a lifetime of hatred. No, thought Dianna, seven lifetimes of hatred. At that moment, if Agnes could have killed, she would have struck Esau down on the spot.

Dianna got an understanding through Agnes's expression of what it must have been like for the simple hardworking woman to grow up with such a brother. He was a curse to Agnes, an undeserved but constant curse, a living millstone dropped around her neck by some cruel god.

Goody pointed for Agnes to put the shackle on Esau's ankle.

As Agnes bent to lock the chain, Esau protested. This time he did not act demure and babyish, but instead his voice was throaty and assertive, a garglelike growl. He was not bowing to their will, and in his tone was more than a hint of aggression.

Both Goody and Agnes were taken aback. Dianna was terrified as it became apparent that neither of these women had encountered this kind of behavior from Esau before. What if they aren't able to control him? she thought. If Esau turned on them, her cause would be lost.

Goody summoned up her most authoritative tone of voice. Her words were shrill, losing some of their effectiveness because of the high pitch.

"You will obey me or you will suffer the consequences!"

Esau started to obey but then hesitated. Goody and Agnes watched him, intent on every nuance of his behavior. Dianna could feel their fear—for all three women this was a moment of true crisis, a moment that could easily erupt into a hell of killing and death. Esau's hesitation lengthened, becoming a statement of defiance and rebellion that held Goody and Agnes, breathless and uncertain.

"You will do as I say, or you will never eat again!" commanded Goody.

Esau weighed this, obviously torn. He took a step toward Agnes and went into a crouch of readiness. A part of him seemed to be wondering what his life would be like without them, considering what would happen if he simply smashed in Agnes's face and picked up Goody's wheelchair and threw her against a tree. His eyes darted back and forth between Goody, Agnes, and the icehouse. But other emotions were also at war inside him.

Dianna thought, Agnes and Goody have to be the ones who take care of him and feed him. Esau can't possibly function very well on his own. He's got to grasp that fact.

Goody pulled out a candy bar. "Here, this is for you, as soon as you do as I ask."

Esau looked hungrily at the candy bar, his large eyes still red from tears. A series of gargles erupted from his stomach.

"And if you're a good boy, I'll see that you get some ice cream."

Great, thought Dianna, and maybe if he doesn't kill for a week, they'll throw him a testimonial dinner.

The tension went out of Esau's stance and Agnes bent to put on the leg shackle. Holding out the candy bar, Goody led Esau toward a large elm tree in another part of the backyard. Agnes wrapped the heavy chain once around the base of the elm, padlocked it onto itself, uttered a grunt of relief, and went into the inn.

As soon as the job was done, Goody gave Esau the candy. He ripped the package open and stuffed the bar whole in his mouth. Through a mush of chocolate, Esau asked, "Icca-cree-gam?"

As Goody wheeled off, Dianna shouted after her, "What are you going to do with me?" Goody only threw a glance in Dianna's direction, as if she were contemplating what to do with a patch of crabgrass in her lawn, and rolled off to the front of the inn.

Agnes came out a moment later with a bed sheet and laid it over Jacques's body. As she trudged back toward the inn, Dianna shouted again, "What's going to happen to me? . . . I'm talking to you!"

Agnes gave Dianna a look of hatred, and as she disappeared through the rear door of the inn, she turned and called out, "This is all your doing."

Esau came toward the icehouse window, as far as he could at the end of his chain. He leaned toward Dianna and whined longingly. Dianna dropped back from the window out of his sight.

She sat on the bench, trying to focus, attempting to second-guess what they might have planned for her. But even when she made an effort to calm herself through the rhythms of meditation, she couldn't focus. Her mind fixated on a image that kept recurring. She saw a pair of dark Wilkinson eyes, eyes that grew and grew until she was overwhelmed with a blackness like the void.

29

Dianna knew she needed to put herself in Goody's situation, into Goody's character, to best understand every possible course of action open for the Wilkinson matriarch. She kept going over her situation again and again, trying to view it from every angle.

It seemed that Goody really had only one of two alternatives. The first was to let Dianna go free, talk to the police, turn Esau over to them, and then tell the authorities about Anne's death, Jacques's death, Esau's sham death, and anything else that might relate. But the course of action didn't seem probable. It would make Agnes and Goody accessories to some very serious crimes.

Or—and, Dianna thought grimly, this is the most likely alternative—Goody could keep covering everything up, which meant burying Jacques and creating an alibi for his disappearance. This would present another problem, one they would soon have to get around to dealing with—the unpleasant business of disposing of their unwanted witness and guest.

Just after the sun set, several halogen yard fixtures flashed on, illuminating the rear of the inn in a wash of unearthly amber light. Goody gave Dianna a moment of hope when she wheeled out the back door of the inn. The old woman was warmly dressed, and on her lap she had a pile of blankets topped off with a half-gallon carton of ice cream. Goody put the ice cream in Esau's outstretched hands and threw him a ladle-sized serving spoon. Dianna supposed that at least some of the blankets were for her. But Goody dropped the entire pile beside Esau.

Then Agnes came around the corner of the inn from the direction of the barn. The blood and tears had dried on her face, giving her a resemblance to something from *Night of the Living Dead*. Dianna's heart sank—in Agnes's hand was a shovel. That meant a cover-up.

Dianna could well imagine the gist of their horrible and self-serving plan. First they would bury Jacques, then Agnes and Goody would concoct some plausible alibi—say, that they had caught Jacques dallying with a female guest and sent him packing back to Canada.

They would then kill Dianna LaBianca. How the two women would choose to commit murder, Dianna could only imagine.

Agnes began her digging in the grass at the base of the hanging tree. She outlined a shallow rectangular trench in the fork between two roots. Like two gnarled fingers, the roots arched upward and away from the base of the sugar maple and then poked their way down into the earth. The soil was soft and Agnes made steady progress.

Dianna knew that her being allowed to watch the disposal of the body was also not a good sign. It could only mean that it was not intended that she be among the living if anyone should come around to inquire about the disappearance of Chef Jacques.

Agnes's shovel struck a large underground root near the center of her excavation, which forced her to dig around it, to carve out a curving grave, narrower at the ends. It reminded Dianna of a hole for a giant dead banana.

As the pit grew ever so slowly deeper, a mere half shovel at a time, Dianna kept getting this persistent feeling that Agnes was digging a grave not for Jacques but for Dianna herself. She couldn't get the shape of the grave out of her mind and kept thinking that she was going to be the banana they buried.

Agitated, feeling a helpless desperation, Dianna paced Esau's lair, her nose welcoming the fresh air from the broken window. She checked her watch, but the hands had stopped moving, and when she tried to wind it, all she heard was a tiny grinding noise.

Her sense of time began to play tricks on her, and it seemed that the whole night had passed before Agnes finally threw her shovel down on the mound of freshly dug earth. The woman dragged Jacques's blanketed body to the grave side and rolled it over, flopping it into its bed of final sleep. Dianna felt relieved to see that there was not enough room in the grave for herself and Jacques.

Wormwood, wormwood, thought Dianna.

Goody joined Agnes a moment later, wheeling out of the house with a Bible in her lap. The two women had their profiles to Dianna at grave side, Agnes standing with bowed head, and Goody cradling her Bible in her supplicating hands.

Esau threw them an occasional glance, looking on with hardly a trace of interest. His tongue was busy, carefully licking clean the corners of his ice cream carton.

Watching the ghoulishly yellow-lit scene through the bars of the small rectangular window opening made Dianna feel like a voyeur, a Peeping Tom at a very private screening of some obscure and bizarre European horror film.

Goody opened her Bible at the ribbon bookmark and spoke, her words carrying across the yard and into the cellar-pit of the icehouse. She announced, "Revelations 21, verse 3," and read, "Behold, the tabernacle of God is with men, and he will dwell with them, and they shall be his people, and God himself shall be with them, and be their God. And God shall wipe away all tears from their eyes; and there shall be no more death, neither sorrow, nor crying, neither shall there be any more pain: for the former things are passed away. In the name of the Lord our savior, Amen."

Goody closed her book and looked heavenward. "Bless him, he was, in his way, a good man."

"Yes," echoed Agnes, "in his way he was."

The whole thing made Dianna wonder if they had it in their scheme to be equally "thoughtful" over her own burial site.

Both women threw in a handful of dirt, and Goody left Agnes to the job of covering over the body of her former lover.

While Agnes shoveled, Goody made several trips from the greenhouse, bringing wheelchair loads of potted sweet william plants. When the grave was covered over, Agnes set out a neat arrangement of the ground cover on the small mound of earth. Dianna had watched her mother plant sweet williams around their house in Scarsdale, and she knew that it was foolish to be planting anything this early in the season—one late frost could kill it.

As Goody made her last delivery and wheeled for the inn's

rear door, Dianna called out to her, "Mrs. Wilkinson, please talk to me. What is going to happen?"

Goody still tried to ignore her, but Dianna persisted. "Please, for God's sake, say something! I'm a human being!" Dianna shouted.

Goody stopped her progress and called back, "You hungry?"

Dianna shouted, "Yes!"

Goody wheeled into the inn.

An hour later, Agnes brought a bottle of water and a tray of cold cuts, cheese, and bread. The food went in the slot in the stone of the wall near the outer door. Dianna found a grimy little swinging door that opened onto the food slot from her side of the wall.

Stuffing her face with a chunk of cheese, Dianna called out the window, "Agnes. Agnes!"

But the woman didn't even bother to glance back in Dianna's direction.

A New England chill sent the temperature in the icehouse down into the low forties. Dianna shivered and she checked outside. Esau, seemingly content, was huddled under his blankets. The cold gave Dianna no choice. After scavenging the cellar, she found several ragged, decaying blankets and wrapped them around her shoulders.

Later the yard lights and the overhead bulb clicked off. Dianna tried the pull string, but the light wouldn't come on. They must have another switch, she thought, somewhere in the inn, a master switch, so that they can turn the lights out on Esau.

Dianna lay down on her wooden bench under her pile of stinking bedclothes and trembled in the frigid darkness.

30

The next morning, Goody ignored Esau's protests of hunger and made him go without breakfast. And how Goody went about it seemed pointlessly cruel. She wheeled out with a tray in her lap, filled with a large mound of eggs and toast. But Goody didn't give the tray to Esau. Instead, she set it down on the ground beyond his reach at the end of his chain.

Esau went wild stretching and grabbing and doing everything he could to get his fingers on the food. Dianna got a portion of the same breakfast shoved into her serving slot.

All morning long, Esau begged and pleaded and whined and screamed and threw roaring temper tantrums, but no one even bothered to glance at him from a window of the house. Dianna knew they had to have a reason for teasing him in such a cruel manner.

It's a fairy tale, she decided grimly, and they are going to feed me to him. He is the giant on the beanstalk, and they are priming him, teasing his hunger to the point that he will start singing "Fee, fi, fo, fum," tear me to pieces, and eat me up.

An hour or so later Goody came out the back door carrying a yardstick. She rolled directly for the icehouse.

Dianna tried a different approach. "Mrs. Wilkinson, be reasonable, you have to let me go. I can't stay here. There are people who are going to miss me and they will come looking for me."

Goody only seemed to be half listening and quickly took measurements of the size of the broken icehouse window. Another sign that does not bode well, thought Dianna.

Dianna kept on her rational tack. "You will get yourself and

Agnes into a lot of trouble if you try to keep me here. You could be liable for some very serious charges."

"Some things can't be helped. Some things are just God's will," declared the old lady, and she rolled away toward the barn.

"Goddamn, you let me out of here! I want out of here, this minute!" shouted Dianna.

Goody didn't offer the slightest response.

A little after midday, when Esau's food protests had dulled to only a few sporadic outbursts of whimpering, the horse van came around from the front of the house, with Agnes at the wheel. As Dianna watched, Agnes drove up on the grass and backed the vehicle around in a semicircle so that the tailgate faced Esau's tree. The woman opened the truck's rear double doors.

Goody came out of the house with a tray stacked high with hamburgers, potato chips, and a carton of ice cream. Esau sprang to life, crazed with hunger, sniffing the air, clawing toward the tray, and using his full repertoire of begging tones. The old woman rolled up to the edge of Esau's circle of reach, keeping just far enough away so that Esau could not get a finger on any of the eats.

After letting him have a good look and sniff of the tray, Goody handed it to Agnes, who made a show of setting it on the floor, deep in the back of the horse van, near a wooden wall that separated the truck cab from the horse compartments. She also included the cold breakfast tray of eggs and toast.

With the keys in hand, Goody rolled to Esau, who obediently raised his leg with the shackle. Goody opened the padlock, and he dashed straight for the food in the rear of the truck. A second later Agnes slammed the rear door of the horse van shut, turned the locking bar handle down, and snapped a heavy padlock on the hasp. Agnes and Goody breathed a deep sigh of relief.

Agnes reached in the passenger side of the truck and took out a rectangular piece of plywood, a hammer, and some nails.

Dianna immediately knew what the wood was for and started shouting. "You are not going to shut me in here. You can't do this to me. I have rights. You can't keep me locked in here against my will. You both will go to prison for life. This is kidnapping!"

The board shut out the light and the fresh air, and the hammer hitting the nails echoed in the cellar like ricocheting gunfire.

Dianna tried the light's pull cord. The bulb didn't go on.

When the pounding finally stopped, Dianna heard the creak of Goody's wheelchair fading away and she shouted, "Goddamn you! Goddamn you to hell!"

Agnes spoke from the other side of the window board. "City bitch."

A few minutes later, Dianna heard the engine of the horse van start up and listened as the sound of the truck moved away into the distance.

31

But for the luck of a horseshoe, Esau would have been safely imprisoned in his usual summer domicile in the northern reaches of Maine. Hidden on the grounds of a onetime Wilkinson estate near Portland was a 1950's vintage bomb shelter that Goody had fortified to hold Esau. The estate was now in the care of one of Goody's cousins, who, in exchange for a bit of monthly cash and a place to live, maintained the buildings and kept watch on Esau through the summer months.

Thirty minutes after leaving the inn, Esau had wolfed down the ice cream followed by the chips and burgers and half the eggs and toast. He was gathering straw to make himself a bed so that he could sleep through the familiar long journey he made twice a year. The worn horseshoe was in the corner under some straw. Esau picked it up and studied the rusty U of metal, dimly remembering one of his Dada's comments about horseshoes.

Lucky thing? Yes. Lucky thing.

Agnes sipped a cup of coffee and listened to a Vermont talk radio channel as she turned north onto the Interstate. The banging of metal on wood took her by surprise and made her put her foot down on the accelerator. She knew she had better get the van in a hurry to the next exit, which was a good twenty-five minutes farther on the four-lane highway.

Agnes would have preferred to make a U-turn, or even to pull over to the side for a few moments, but she could not risk the chance of being approached by the police. Esau's pounding would certainly draw attention, and it would be very hard for Agnes to explain who was locked in the back of her van.

Esau held the horseshoe in his hand like a pair of brass knuckles and was idly slamming his fist into the walls.

Esau, bang, bang, bang.

Agnes kept her speed to a few miles above the legal limit. She wasn't sure what Esau was up to, and she couldn't figure what it was he was using to bang with. If there was any chance of his getting out, she knew she had to turn around and get the truck back to the inn.

The side of the van was sheet metal and Agnes wasn't worried about Esau getting through, but the window partition at Agnes's back was only made of plywood and it shook with Esau's pounding.

The countryside was forested mountains, mostly deserted, with only an occasional country road crossing the Interstate on an overpass. Agnes needed to find a place she could pull off and not be bothered by any prying eyes.

With a pop, a knothole shot out of the wood above the headrest of the passenger seat and bounced off the glove compartment. Then there was another louder crunch, and the horseshoe and Esau's fist came through in a splintering of wood. He knocked out another hunk of the plywood and pressed his forehead, nose, and eyes through the opening into the cab.

Esau see! Good. See out. Fun.

Enormously pleased with himself, he kept his head thrust through the partition and happily watched the landscape go by.

Agnes stayed as far as possible over to the right side of the right lane, so that if anyone passed her they would not get a very good look into the cab of the van. Esau didn't make things easy. Each time he saw a car or a truck pass, he would pull out his head, put his arm and shoulder through the opening, and wave at the departing vehicle.

Hello car. Hello truck. Fun. Fun.

Agnes was most worried about passing semi trucks. With their oversized sideview mirrors and high cabs, they would get an excellent view of this very strange head protruding out of the wall of the horse van. Then there was the state police.

Agnes certainly wasn't going to be able to cover much distance with the present state of things.

Fortunately, traffic was light, and only an occasional car attempted to pass. Agnes tried to keep moving at a slightly faster pace than the semis, so they wouldn't try to go around her.

One trucker, who was making time, gunned ahead of her and got a glimpse of Esau. The trucker started to slow and keep pace with Agnes, throwing glances at the horse van.

Agnes braked hard to drop out of the trucker's line of vision and then changed into the lane directly behind the semi.

By the time she reached the first possible exit, Agnes was sweating like a horse. She took a cloverleaf onto a state highway that ran parallel to a railroad spur and the expanse of the Hudson River. The road was leading her toward several groupings of derelict factory buildings.

After getting strange looks from several oncoming vehicles, Agnes turned off onto a deserted access road that had once serviced a foundry at the river's edge. She headed toward the cover of a roofless brick factory that caught her eye, following an overgrown, potholed road through an abandoned yard of rust-covered, monolithic iron castings. Agnes bumped her way behind the isolated building and stopped out of sight of the road, not far from a crumbling riverside pier.

Esau peered out, eyes wide with concern.

Where Esau? New place. Strange. Esau no like strange place.

Agnes needed to find something to cover the break in the plywood in the back wall of the cab—boards, a piece of steel, anything that he couldn't pound through.

Spotting a pile of rusting scrap metal on a collapsing loading dock, she left the van engine running, grabbed her gloves, and climbed out of the cab, shutting the door behind her.

Esau watched her from his vantage point until she disappeared from sight behind the van.

Scared. Where Ag-ga go? Why Esau in strange place?

Agnes noticed a piece of sheet steel on the bottom of the scrap pile, a piece that looked about the size she needed. While she was preoccupied, clearing away the top of the junk pile to get to the steel plate, Esau's nervousness grew.

Bad place. Esau no want stay here. Where Ag-ga? Esau want go. Want go now.

He wasn't used to being in strange places, and he wasn't at all used to being in strange places alone.

Esau panicked. With a desperate burst of strength enchanced

by fear, he yanked the panel of the cab completely off of its mounting brackets.

Agnes, digging in the pile of scrap metal, didn't hear a thing.

Esau climbed into the cab of the van, and when he could look out and see Agnes, he immediately felt much better.

Car! Go.

"Garooom! Puka-puka-puka."

Car fun!

He almost went out to Agnes, but it had been years since he had been in the driver's seat of a vehicle, and he grinned as he scrunched behind the steering wheel and made noises like a child.

"Puka-puka. Voooomga!"

Wheel turn. Esau drive. Like Dada.

He bounced up and down in the seat and playfully turned the wheel back and forth . . . until his thumb hit the transmission shift lever and put the van into reverse gear.

Agnes was dragging the metal plate back to the truck when it started to creep backward. She dropped the steel, ran for the van, and managed to get a foot up on the passenger's side running board. There was Esau in the driver's seat, his face a wide-eyed mixture of terror and joy.

"Ahhh-gahhhh! Wooooowga! Goody Maaa-maaaa!"

Agnes desperately pulled at the door handle, but because she was standing on the running board, there wasn't enough room to allow her to open the door. She was about to try to smash the window when Esau's foot hit the gas pedal. The vehicle lurched backward, almost throwing Agnes into the dirt, but she just managed to keep a grip on the door handle and stay on the running board.

The van went in reverse out onto the rotten shipping pier, where barges had once docked to take the large castings down the Hudson to New York terminals and points beyond. Esau, trying hopelessly to take control, turned the steering wheel back and forth, putting the vehicle into a series of backward-moving S curves.

Agnes fought to keep her balance, her ten bloodless fingers clinging to the door handle.

As Esau was being thrown side to side he tried to brace himself in the seat with his feet. In doing so, his right foot tromped on the gas pedal, pressing it all the way to the floor.

The sudden rearward acceleration of the van threw Esau against the steering wheel, and the vehicle sped in reverse in a wide semicircle that took it in a path toward the side of the pier and a drop-off.

The surface of the Hudson River was twelve feet below. The water churned with soil brought down from the hills above, a brown torrent relentlessly moving its earthen cargo toward the sea.

As the van skirted the pier side at the apex of its arc, the passenger wheels rolled up and onto the splintered wooden toe rail that bordered the structure.

From her precarious perch on the running board, Agnes watched the vehicle as it swung toward the edge.

The van looked as if it was going over and into the river. In the split second, Agnes wasn't sure whether to hold on or jump.

She hadn't been anywhere near water in twenty-five years, and she certainly didn't want to end up at the bottom of a raging river with a horse van on top of her.

Agnes opted for land. To hell with it; the vehicle and Esau could go over by itself. But her decision came too late.

Trying carefully to minimize her impact, she let go of the door handle and attempted to step off. But Agnes hadn't taken into account the motion of the vehicle, and as her feet hit the pier deck, they went out from under her, and she went into a head-over-heels roll that sent her over the side of the pier and down toward the cold and racing water.

The van continued its arc, almost going over itself, but Esau was holding onto the steering wheel for balance, unintentionally holding it steady. With his foot still stamped down on the gas, the van continued to accelerate on its backward journey.

"Ahhhhhgaaaaaa-oooooooooga!"

It was going close to sixty miles an hour across the rotted decking of the pier when its tailgate smashed into a huge iron ship's bollard embedded in the dock's superstructure.

The vehicle slammed to a dead halt and Esau was thrown back against the headrest and seat. With a crunch, the planking of the pier gave way and the truck began to fall—down through the boards into the river.

Out! Esau get out now! No fun now.

• • •

Agnes hit the water with a muted splash and was surprised that she hardly felt the impact. Her torn, cheaply insulated work jacket helped to cushion her fall.

The cold sluiced under her clothing like a rain of icy knives, and her jacket insulation began quickly to suck in the river water like a hungry sponge.

Agnes remembered how to swim, but the cold was so intense, so total, so overpowering, it robbed the strength and the will from her body. She knew she had to move her arms, to try to swim, to make some motion, any gesture, to get to the shore, to stay alive. But the cold enveloped her, taking its toll on her body. She felt paralyzed, and her mind became so numb and her thinking so slow.

What did it matter?

The shore looked so far away. A thousand miles away—a lifetime away.

What did it matter?

The weight of the ice water in her jacket, in her shoes, on her brain, drew her down. The shock of the cold took so much out of her.

What did it matter?

The brown water closed over her eyes and nose. She couldn't breathe.

Her hair went with the current for a few seconds, then settled downward, disappearing from view.

There was a moment of panic, an inner struggle, a yielding, and one final thought:

What did it matter?

The rear wheels of the truck fell through the ancient planking, and the entire deck around the bollard began to give way. Esau felt the angle of the truck shift drastically. He knew something was very wrong, and he had already had too many unpleasant surprises behind the wheel.

Esau no want drive more! Must get out!

He pulled on the window crank, broke off the locking button, yanked on the armrest, but he couldn't discover the pull lever set into the flat surface of the door—the handle wasn't like the door handles of the cars he had known as a child.

There was the sound of cracking timbers, and the van gave

another shudder and fell over to one side as the left rear axle dropped below the level of the deck.

Esau put his fist through the windshield, and the plate glass shattered into a galaxy of tiny pieces. He scrambled out the window and onto the hood of the tilting vehicle. As Esau stepped onto the pier deck, there was a loud crack as the dock supports gave way and the van tipped sideways and fell through the dock into the brown water.

"Garhh-gaa?!"

Where truck? Truck gone?

Lowering himself on all fours, Esau peered down through the gaping hole where the truck had just fallen. Only one corner of the roof was now visible, breaking the smooth surface of the river into swirling rivulets of angry brown foam.

"Ag-ga!" he bellowed. "Ag-ga!"

Esau smelled the air, and he called her name again and again.

"Ag-ga!" he cried out. "Ag-ga!"

Esau had walked over every foot of the pier, searching for Agnes. He had leaned over the sides, looking underneath the structure, and had peered down into the tumbling river.

"Ag-ga! Ag-gaaaaa!"

When all his attempts continued to fail, Esau wandered over to an open door near the scrap pile where Agnes had found the metal plate, and entered the abandoned factory.

"Aag-gaa! Ag-ga!"

He shuffled through vaulting, ceilingless rooms, pressing on with his search between the dead assembly lines of rust-flaked machinery.

Where Esau? What this place? Why Esau here?

Where Ag-ga? Why she not here? Esau cold. Esau hungry. Where Ag-ga? She have to feed him soon. Esau need her come. When she come back and take Esau to other place?

He huddled down in a corner of the loading dock, his back to a sliding door. Every few seconds he would look toward the pier, nervously waiting for Agnes's return.

"Ag-ga! Aaaaag-gaaaaa!"

32

The small pinpricks of light around the edges of the foundation and the window frame were fading, letting Dianna know the day was almost over. She sat unmoving, huddled on the bench where she had been since morning, trying to keep warm under the pile of oily rags. In the blackness of the cellar, the warmth of the day's sun had no chance to reach her.

Dianna knew the basementlike structure was functioning exactly the way it was meant to—it was doing a very good job of keeping *in* the cold.

Her grandfather Dupre had had an icehouse on the grounds of his pre–Civil War Delaware river estate. The building had been redesigned and a floor built over its pit, creating an upstairs level, which was a guest quarters, and a well-stocked basement wine cellar. Grandfather loved to tell how in the "good old days" people were able to have ice in the hot summers, even though there were no ice factories or regular deliveries of ice by wagon.

A wealthy landowner would have winter ice cut from a frozen lake and carted to his icehouse. There the small blocks were neatly stacked into a large cubic mass. The excellent natural insulating properties of the earth, together with a dense covering of straw that was put on top of the ice, would keep the huge block frozen—even through the hot August months—providing an ample supply of cold ice for drinks and iceboxes.

She moved to the window and listened, attuned to every nuance of sound. Occasionally she could make out the honk of a goose, but there were no other noises, no doors opening or closing and no sounds of people or vehicles.

Something crawled up her arm, and as she slapped down on it, she recognized the feel of a tick. Dianna repressed an urge to scream and trapped the squirming hard-shelled insect in her palm with a thumb. When she tried to crush it with her fingernail, it only crawled away.

From then on, Dianna's skin itched constantly with insects real or imagined. She could feel a thousand tiny creatures crawling on her, nesting everywhere in her scalp and on her flesh.

Across the floor, in the blackness of her crypt, she could hear the scurry of little feet, and occasionally the straw near her would stir with life rustling in spurts of burrowing.

The pinpricks of light went out. Sitting on the bench, she kept her feet up off the floor and her knees drawn up to her chest. Dianna wanted to cry, but she could not.

Esau sat, nervous and fretting, until the sun went down.
"Ag-ga. Ag-ga?"
Esau cold. Esau alone. Where Ag-ga?
Periodically, he had risen and resumed his search, wandering over to the pier to check under the decking and whimper loudly or bellow down the length of the river. As the chill of the oncoming night set in and Agnes still was nowhere to be seen, his stomach spoke to him and his restlessness grew.
"Ag-ga?"
Esau hungry. Where Ag-ga? . . . Go home? Home that way.
Esau knew the direction back to the inn. It was as clear in his mind as an arrow and as correct as a needle on a compass. He had a homing instinct, like the seasonal guidance system of a swallow or the once-in-a-lifetime nesting drive of a great ocean turtle. It was a sensation in his head that felt to him like a pointer affixed to a spot between his eyebrows, a pointer that moved as he moved, always adjusting its aim to the direction of food, Goody, and his place of rest.
Go home? Esau want Goody. Want warm.
He might have stayed longer at the foundry, another day or so, but there was something else that drew him homeward, the booteful—she had whet his other appetite. Her face called him back.
Esau want booteful. Esau want go home. Esau afraid.

He didn't like the idea of setting out, and he didn't want to go back alone, for he feared people, especially men and boys, who had never been kind to him. Many times when he was little he had been set on by packs of children who threw stones to hurt him—or called him names that hurt even more.

Esau want home.

But the remembered scent of the booteful drew him out into the night. He left the foundry without a glance back. He leapt off the pier and onto the bank of the river. Loping with the rhythm of a timber wolf, he disappeared into the high rushes.

Home.

33

She meditated and counted breaths. She tried to think but could not.

In the black the hours crawled.

She had no hope. She could think of no plan and felt totally incapable of coming up with one—her lethargy was complete.

She kept trying to put on the light, but there was still no power. Strange, thought Dianna, that Goody hadn't thrown the master switch. There shouldn't be any harm in having the light on. Perhaps Goody had just forgotten.

The loss of those tiny points of sunlight had much more of an effect than she could have thought. Slowly her terror began to grow. Blackness upon blackness. Now, thought Dianna, I know what it's like to be blind.

She had a feeling of being pressed into a well of black ink, down under a liquid shroud of darkness that disoriented her and blocked not only her sight but her thinking. The thick black fog was everywhere—to her left, to her right, above her, and below her. It was there when her eyes were closed, and when she opened her eyes, there was no change. It drained her courage and made her question whether or not she was actually awake—or even alive.

Go. Run. Hide. Run. Go.

The land had unusual boundaries for Esau. Fences or hedges or No Trespassing signs did not matter in the least.

Road bad. Hide. Go.

But many other things frightened Esau—all roads were a danger, barriers to be crossed with great care only after a period of waiting and watching, when all was clear, when no people or cars were near, so that Esau would not be seen or hurt.

Men, children hurt Esau.

A town was dangerous, to be avoided.

Dark good. Trees good.

The darkness was his protection, his friend, and the trees and overgrown fields were comforting.

Not go home. Go wrong. Home there. That way.

Esau's first task was to cross the huge river he now followed, for its bank was forcing him to take a course different from the direction of his arrow. He wouldn't dare to try and swim. He had been in the goose pond many times in the summers, but he knew how cold the water was this time of year.

River scary. River bad. Make dead.

His instincts warned him. He could sense danger in the strange smell of the moving water.

He came to a long-abandoned railroad bridge—a spiderweb of delicate vaulting steel arches over two hundred feet above the Hudson's rolling waters.

Esau tore down a fence that blocked access to the bridge and began to work his way across slowly.

High. Too high. Esau never been this high. Esau fall. Esau dead.

The ground far below, he picked his way along the tall span, often in terror, sometimes crawling on hands and knees over the bridge's rotting railroad ties and narrow, riveted beams. He traveled half a mile in the air before reaching the opposite shore.

With his feet on the earth once again, he followed the arrow in his mind, making a beeline through plowed-under cornfields and muddy pastures.

He was sighted by a dairy farmer working in his barn, but before the frightened man could return with a deer rifle, Esau was well away over the dark fields.

For a while his journey took him south, moving alongside a highway.

Booteful. Esau smell a booteful. Esau find her.

The scent came to him like the heady breath of a sweet flower, filling him with a quivering desire. His nose took him toward an antique shop just off the highway.

• • •

Dianna was beginning to be defeated by the cellar's atmosphere of fatal gloom. Her mood was the cumulative result of her many dark, empty hours, the mildewed cryptlike air in the icehouse, her crawling skin, and the increasing activities of the night creatures. The rustle of the soft-footed rodents grew in volume, and their boldness brought them dancing ever closer to her ankles.

Dianna pulled up her feet and sat in a huddle, her arms around her knees, holding onto herself, afraid to even set a foot down upon the rock floor.

She began to feel that all things were conspiring against her. And her fears evoked images that crept up from the darkest corners of her mind—hideous mental pictures of herself dying awful prolonged deaths, being tortured by rodent creatures from the mind of Hieronymous Bosch.

She saw her face becoming a skull and felt her flesh shredding and dropping off her body in chunks that were quickly devoured by rats on the floor.

One fear that gripped her mind—one which she might have been able to cope with if she could have seen even a glimmer of light—was a grim certainty that negated everything her philosophies had taught her. She began to be convinced that . . .

Death was the end.

It was final.

And being dead was . . .

Simply and permanently . . .

Forever and ever . . .

Being dead.

34

Booteful smell good.

The porch room of the antique shop was crammed with furniture, and every inch of the place was filled with glass, china, old prints, and other collectibles. As Esau crept over to the side of the building, he saw a booteful come out onto the glassed-in front porch. She was young and had dark hair, and she began to close up for the night, opening an electrical box that held a series of switches. The neon sign on the rooftop of the store blinked out, followed by the yard light that lit the parking lot.

Esau want touch booteful.

From behind the cover of a clump of evergreens, Esau watched her turn around a sign in the front window to read Closed. Esau liked the look of the booteful. He came to the entrance and put his hand on the doorknob, giving it a rattle as he tried to turn it. The door was locked, but the sound drew the girl's attention.

Her name was Dierdre, and she was a pretty high school girl who worked a few nights a week in the shop. She peered into the darkness and called out, "I'm sorry, but we're closed."

Esau rattled the doorknob again. She moved over to the glass-paneled porch door and peered out into the darkness. Esau's face suddenly pressed up flat against a pane of glass.

The girl took one look at Esau, screamed, turned, and ran.

Esau jerked on the doorknob and it came away in his hand. He smashed the door with a fist and knocked out the entire center section of glass panels in the brittle old door. He stepped through the opening and into the porch.

Dierdre's screams continued, fading away into the back of the building.

A few seconds later the shop's owner, a white-haired old gentleman in his seventies, looked out onto the porch from within. The man was taken aback when he saw Esau; he stopped short and stammered, "Ah . . . ah . . . Excuse me, but you'll have to . . ."

Esau ignored the command and rushed past the frail man, pushing him aside and slamming his head backward into the wall. The store owner crumpled, unconscious, on the floor.

As Esau ran out the back door, he saw Dierdre gunning a car out of the parking lot. He watched her turn onto the highway and saw the taillights disappear in the distance.

Why booteful go?

Esau went back in the shop. He roamed through the rooms, looking for food, breaking a small fortune in furniture and china.

He smelled the old man, who was still slumped, unconscious. He could tell from the man's breathing that he was asleep, but Esau decided not to try to wake him up.

When he had been through every room and hadn't smelled anything to eat, he went out the front door and, following his arrow, sauntered away into the trees.

Food. Home. Booteful.

Dianna awoke the next morning with a few points of dull red light from the coming sun glowing through the foundation. There was no sound in the cellar or from the grounds, and her little dark world seemed still with a nervous silence.

Where was Goody? Was she ever going to come again? Or, thought Dianna, has the woman simply boarded me up in the icehouse to let me die a slow death of dehydration and starvation.

That would be the easy way for Goody, Dianna realized. Just leave the icehouse sealed up for a few weeks or a month, and let nature take its insidious course. Then Goody and Agnes would be saved the trouble of ever having to raise a finger to carry out the vile deed.

Dianna screamed for a half an hour in the direction of the plywood that covered her window. When her voice was reduced to a harsh rasp, she gave up and sat in silence.

• • •

The only way Dianna could tell time was by the change in the little dots of light. As the sun moved, the intensity of the dots on one side of the foundation began to darken, while they grew brighter on another side. As the morning passed there was no Goody and no food. Dianna calculated that she had gone more than thirty hours without food or water. Her hunger wasn't that bad, but her thirst was beginning to gnaw at her.

Dianna remembered having seen a discolored spot on the rocks, which could be a place where water was oozing in. For two hours she felt the cold stones from floor to ceiling. Finally her fingers located a moist spot near the floor between two fieldstones. There was a single bead of water clinging to the rock. Dianna tasted the moisture on her fingers. It was so brackish that she gave up her search.

How long can I last without water? she asked herself. A person can go for weeks without food, but water? Wasn't it something like three days without a drink before your body began to die?

35

When Esau's fist slammed into the plywood that covered her window, Dianna was almost relieved.

The man-thing's attack on the door and the cellar was relentless and went on for the rest of the day and into the night.

The dead bolt kept him from opening the inner door from outside. So, with the section of pipe and his fists, he beat on the inner door a thousand times. The noise of his assault on the metal was a deafening siege, crashing and banging and exploding in the room.

Later Esau tore away the section of plywood and once again pushed himself right up to the bars, pressing his cheeks against the steel, trying to get at her. Then he began to alternate between pounding on the bars with the pipe and going around to pound on the door.

At first, his attempts were terrifying and made Dianna feel she was a prisoner condemned to death, trapped in a cell as a one-man lynch mob tried to break down the bars. As the hours passed and Esau's attempts continued undaunted, however, her fear of the attack dulled. The pounding became only an emotional drain, and finally, as her exhaustion set in, the whole thing became just an annoying background noise, a static that refused to go away. Where was Goody? Where was Agnes? How had Esau gotten away from Agnes?

After enduring nine hours of Esau's attack on the cellar, Dianna dropped off into a deep sleep of fatigue.

When she next awoke, Dianna knew Esau's attempts to get in the cellar had continued for hours after her collapse. The evidence was readily apparent. The steel inner door had buckled inward, and one of the steel window bars had been bent to the side from some enormous effort. Dianna moved to the window to check the yard.

There was no sign of life on the grounds. A night-light burned near the door of the inn. And there were other lights on in the rooms of the house. Where is Goody, she wondered, and why had so many lights been left on?

Where was the creature? she thought. She crawled to the entrance and felt around it. The door was dented, and some of the stonework surrounding the frame was loose. Where was he?

One of the geese honked, signaling the approaching dawn. A shaft of light streaked in through the window and the cracks around the battered inner door frame. Dianna peeked out. Esau was lying in a heap on the grass a few feet from the outer door. He was so close she could hear his breathing. The pipe was still clutched in his hand. Dianna knew he must have tired himself out trying to break into the cellar.

Where was Agnes? How did Esau get away from her? Is she on her way here? Where is Goody? Goody must have gone somewhere, thought Dianna, because Goody would not have let Esau carry on the way he had. She must have left the inn sometime after Agnes left. In that case, when will Goody get back, and what will she do when she does return?

Will she try to cover up two more murders? Is it possible she could set me free, or will my head still be on the chopping block?

Dianna studied the spacing between the bent bar and the bar next to it and wondered whether she might be able to squeeze through the opening. Moving over to take a closer look, she tripped on the leg of the bench. There was a sharp clatter.

Dianna froze and listened. Dear God, please don't let him wake up.

Esau's heavy breathing remained regular.

Dianna's eyes measured the opening. Because of the bend in the middle bar, she thought her head just might fit through.

She hurried back to the bench and quietly carried it to the window. There were pieces of glass on the sill and drops of blood where Esau had cut his hands. She cleaned away some of the larger chunks of glass and began to put her head between the bars. She stopped.

Where am I going?

What will I do if I escape?

What chance would I have on foot? I probably can't outrun Esau.

Then she remembered the horses. *God, if I can only get on a horse.*

Again Dianna pulled herself up into the opening. By turning her head sideways, she could just manage to force it between the bars. But as she tried to push her way through the narrow slot, her shoulders became wedged between the steel rods, and she was stuck.

Dianna had a vision of Esau awakening and catching her in this helpless position halfway out the window—the very idea did wonders for her motivation. With fingernails clawing at the stone wall, arms straining against the bars, Dianna wriggled and twisted, and with a muffled grind of glass against stone, she was through.

Her clothing was shredded, and the broken bits of window had sliced and slivered her shoulders. One sleeve became damp with blood as she dropped to the grass and listened . . . still no sound.

Should I run or try to be quiet? she wondered.

Dianna compromised and walked quickly and as silently as she could. The flock of geese gathered near the back door of the inn, honked loudly, and approached her as she passed by.

At the far corner of the house she turned and checked behind her, toward the cellar. Still no sign of movement. Dianna glanced up at the inn, but there was no indication of activity inside either.

Where was Goody?

The geese were making even more noise now, flapping their wings and closing in around her. *Of course, they want to be fed,* she realized.

Dianna had to leave the cover of the house as she ran for the barn. After a mad dash, she threw herself against the high double doors—they didn't open. They were barred from the inside.

She ran to the side entrance. It was padlocked as well. Dianna thought, *Jesus, no, it's all locked.*

In desperation she ran to the outer double door at the far end of the barn—also barred from the inside. She could hear the horses moving in their stables.

What do I do now? Mother Mary, what do I do now?

Suddenly the horses whinnied.

The geese quieted down. She saw them scattering across the yard. Dianna knew exactly what the animals' disturbed behavior meant. A lump rose in her throat.

She was at the far side of the barn, away from the inn. Feeling oddly embarrassed, almost like a kid playing a game of hide and seek, she looked around the corner of the barn.

There was Esau moving hurriedly from around the back of the inn. He spotted Dianna at once and launched himself directly toward her.

For a half second Dianna stood clinging to her corner of the barn, just watching him close the distance. She felt caught, as if she were in a dream—paralyzed and unable to move while the terrible creature came closer and closer. Then she tore her fingers from the wood slats and bolted around the stable in the other direction, running as hard as she could.

But where? Where do I run?

She neared the end of the barn and looked back. Esau was turning the far corner, covering ground much faster than she.

Where? Back to the cellar? No, I'll never get through the bars in time.

The inn? Somewhere in the inn.

She sprinted for the front door and was frightened by the wheeze of her own breathing as she fought for air.

The door was locked. Dianna heard heavy steps behind her and tore around the far side of the house.

I'm slowing down—the thought came with a terrifying awareness. I can't run anymore.

She climbed the back steps and clawed at the doorknob. It turned.

Esau rounded the corner. Dianna bolted through the door with no time to lock it and heard Esau trip on the steps behind her.

What now? Get a weapon? Hide?

Her gasps for breath told her she wasn't going to be able to do another hundred-yard dash—that was certain. Dianna entered the dining room and for an instant considered the idea of going to the kitchen to get a knife or some kind of weapon, but she really wasn't sure where the kitchen was or what she would do with a knife if she found one.

She ran up the steps to the second floor.

A terrible stitch stabbed at her side below her rib cage. She could hear the thump of heavy footsteps from the dining room.

Dianna rushed into her room at the end of the hall, slammed the door shut behind her, and threw the two bars into place.

Seconds later Esau's heavy weight smashed against the door.

Dianna turned the key.

Esau kept throwing his body against the entrance.

She pressed her back to the solid oak of the door and spread her arms out over the threshold, her body absorbing the vibration from the repeated attacks.

36

Again and again Esau hit the oak with his shoulders, pounded it with his fists, and battered it with his feet and elbows. The onslaught at the door seemed endless, but the sturdy construction held.

After Oscar Samuel Wilkinson had been hanged by the mill workers, his surviving brother had rebuilt the house like a fortress. He vowed that he would never be surprised and dragged from his bed. The door to Dianna's room was cross-grained layers of oak, four-and-one-half inches thick, carefully fitted together and reinforced in many places with steel and sheet brass. The large hinges were hand-tempered steel, a little rusty but still strong. The iron key turned a sturdy lock above a weighty brass handle.

At both knee height and eye level the two solid steel bars were held in place by iron straps. The bars slid into recesses in the door frame. The weakest parts were six decorative panels on the top half of the door and four larger ones on the bottom.

Still panting from her chase, Dianna sat on the bed and eyed the door with dull terror. She realized that she was being saved by two things: the strong construction of the old door and the fact that it opened outward into the hall. All of Esau's efforts were forcing the door into the sturdy frame, so that the walls themselves were absorbing the shocks. The lock and the steel bars only kept the door from being opened, and they might not have held if Esau were inside the room, trying to get out.

Esau attempted everything he could think of: he clawed the panels with his nails and tried to get his fingers under the door; he yanked the handle with both hands.

Dianna cowered by the far wall of the room.

The pounding stopped for a few moments, and Esau returned with a hammer. He beat on the sheet brass and managed to get the claw of the tool under the thin metal. After pulling a piece of brass away from the wood, he took the hammer with both hands and attacked one of the panels. A piece of the panel split, opening up a small hole in the door, but the strength of the blow broke the head of the hammer off of the handle.

Esau worked at the opening, trying to enlarge it.

Dianna crossed to a leaded window and looked down. It was at least twenty-five feet to the ground, with nothing to break her fall. It would be easy to fracture a leg from this height.

In the meantime, Esau's pounding with what was left of the hammer handle had widened the hole to an irregular circle about three inches across. With a crack, the wooden hammer shaft split along the grain.

Esau pressed one bulbous eyeball against the hole. He was like an animal in one cage sizing up another strange species of animal that had just arrived in the adjoining cage. The eye gave Dianna the once-over.

His peeping orb moved slowly over the contours of her body, mentally undressing her. The blatant hunger of the disembodied eye sent a shiver up her spine, a mini-version of the shiver that had attacked her the day before.

She darted into the bathroom, out of the line of Esau's vision. After a moment she heard him slump to the floor of the hall, panting from his full-out exertion.

The filth of the cellar and the paranoia of having bugs all over her made Dianna strip off her clothing and pile it in the corner. She turned on the water to fill the tub and bent over the sink, drinking her fill of cold water.

Chilled, aching, fatigued, and ravenous, she slipped into the steaming water laced with a quarter of a bottle of shampoo. Dianna needed to relax, but she only felt uneasy. She kept thinking of *Psycho*. If anything, being in the bath seemed to make her more nervous. She couldn't help wondering whether Esau would suddenly break down the door and attack, catching her naked and completely defenseless.

She tried to calm herself, letting the sudsy, healing water focus her thinking and help her come to grips with the unreality of the situation. She thought, I cannot possibly be who I am, where I am, with that thing or man or animal or whatever it is waiting to get at me.

She pressed her head between her hands, as if the action would somehow ground her or give her body a substance or tangibility.

"Dianna." She spoke her own name. For the last day and a half in the darkness of the cellar she had been lost, she had almost forgotten who she was. Now she felt the need to place herself in her setting, and so she reminded herself of her label.

That's how her Roshi always referred to all words, as useless labels. "Man-made categories for man's faulty conception of the world."

"Dianna." Again she spoke her name. What does the label "Dianna" mean? she asked herself. An apartment, a Honda Acura, two closets of clothes? No, they were only possessions. Is "Dianna" revising scripts, counting tickets, going to the theater? Or is she eating, breathing, defecating, making love? Is that who "Dianna" is? she wondered. What will "Dianna" mean after I'm dead? A weathered headstone? A fading memory in the minds of a few relatives?

An idea slipped into her consciousness and gave her a little hope. Why not make friends with Esau? If I can win him to my side, he might let me out of here. Goody seemed able to control him. She had said that he possessed the mind of a six-year-old. An adult can reason with a six-year-old. If I can make Esau like me as a friend . . .

There had to be an advantage in befriending him. Dianna liked the concept. It appealed to her idealism. It seemed the rational, sensible way of solving the problem.

She needed a gift to give Esau, something that would demand another gift in return.

In a bathrobe, her hair up in a towel, Dianna went through her things. Her suitcases were where they had been left after Jacques and Agnes's searching. She thought about Esau's drab cellar home and tried to imagine what he could possibly want as a present.

Let's see, she thought, what do you get for the man who has nothing? She came across a small chrome case that she used to carry jewelry and took it with her to the door.

Esau sat, eyes closed, resting his head against the banister. The man-thing's size and unusual proportions made a power-

ful, intimidating impression. His torso was unnaturally long,
his legs short, and his neck like a small tree stump. He wasn't
wearing pants, only an indeterminable number of bedspreads
and blankets worn poncho-style. The ragged ends of the
makeshift garment hung down below Esau's knees. His feet
were bare and covered with dirty corns and calluses. They
looked hardened to Dianna, as tough as a pair of shoes.

Almost all of Esau's exposed body was covered with curly,
black hair. His clothing, face, and body were caked with
grime. Down around his ears the hair hung in a tangle of greasy
dreadlocks. The only apparent bald area was the skin on the
knotted, bright red splotch that covered most of Esau's face.
The huge deformity on his back throbbed under the filthy
blanket.

Her courage about to fail, Dianna thought, I've got to give
this a try.

"Esau. . . . Esau. . . ." Dianna spoke the name with a
strange duality. On the one hand it was like calling to a child;
on the other it had the feeling of addressing a wild animal while
sharing its den.

The head slowly lifted.

"I have a present, Esau."

Esau moved to the hole. Dianna inched back to a safe
distance. "Look, a present."

Esau stared at her, uncomprehending.

"This is for you, from me."

Esau tilted his head to the side and gave her a questioning
look. He grunted and moved closer.

Dianna put the jewelry box through the hole. His fingers
awkwardly grabbed for it. As Dianna let go, the box almost
slipped out of Esau's clumsy grasp.

"A present for Esau from Dianna." Though she tried to
sound as calm and friendly as possible, her voice cracked. "It's
a gift, a toy."

At the word "toy" Esau's eyes lit up, and he smiled at her.
"T-O-Y," he said with difficulty. His expression was open and
warm.

For the first time Dianna recognized in Esau a glimmer of
humanity, a quality that had been heretofore masked by his
repulsiveness.

Esau looked at her, eyes wide with puppy love.

There's hope, Dianna thought.

Esau whined quietly and sighed like a contented baby. He held the case to his cheek and nodded his head quickly. He pressed his eye to the hole and sighed again. Then Esau said, "Booteful."

Well, he is definitely not interested in my mind, thought Dianna. "Now, Esau, you have to bring a toy for me."

Esau looked at her with his questioning expression. The look was similar to the one a dog gives its master when the command is beyond the animal's understanding.

She repeated, "You must bring a toy for me, a toy for the booteful."

Esau nodded, made a number of incomprehensible sounds, then looked lost.

Dianna took the key from the lock and held it up. "Keys. Booteful wants keys for toy. Trade. Make a trade for the keys. And hopefully the keys to the barn," she said to herself under her breath.

She mimed a key opening a lock and pointed toward the back of the house. After about five minutes of explanation, Esau finally got the idea. He ran down the stairs, and Dianna heard the back door slam.

I hope he can remember where the keys are, she thought. If I can get into the barn, I can get on a horse.

Esau returned a moment later with Jacques's key ring. He began to push it through the hole in the door, but as Dianna reached for the keys his face lit up with a silly grin, and he pulled them away. Esau smiled at her and shook his head. He grabbed the door handle, rattled it, then held up the keys. He repeated this action several times.

I don't believe it, thought Dianna. He wants me to open the door in exchange for the keys. He's a lot smarter than I thought. "No," said Dianna firmly.

Esau made a pouting face and turned the handle again.

"Boo-tee-ful, peeeeeza."

"No, absolutely not," Dianna said, mustering up her best schoolteacher voice.

His face lit up once more, and he ran down the hall into Jacques and Agnes's room. Dianna heard the sound of drawers being pulled out and furniture being turned over. I wonder what he's up to now.

She thought, How incongruous it was to see tenderness in Esau's face. In spite of everything, I was touched when he smiled at the sight of the toy.

Esau returned with a handful of magazines. Dianna caught a glimpse of some of the covers. They were all pornographic. Esau awkwardly turned the pages of one until he came to a picture of a nude couple posed in the throes of mutual orgasm.

Esau pointed to himself and the man and then to Dianna and the woman. "Booteful . . . Eeee-saaaau," he said, and looked at Dianna.

"No," said Dianna. "Not on our first date."

Then he held up the keys and made gyrating motions with his pelvis.

Suddenly the situation didn't seem in the least bit humorous to her. "No, absolutely no. No, no, no!" Dianna shouted, growing hysterical.

She backed a few feet away from the hole and glanced around at the suitcase, trying to think whether there was anything else she could give as a gift. A second after Dianna turned, Esau's finger reached through the hole in the door and caught a handful of her hair. Dianna shrieked and tried to pull away, but Esau now had a fistful of her hair out through the hole, and he snapped her head toward him with a hard jerk.

Dianna almost lost consciousness as her forehead hit the hard oak of the panel. Esau eased his grip for a moment, and she managed to turn sideways to the door. As he pulled a second time, Dianna pushed away with all her strength. She could hear as well as feel the hair rip out of her scalp.

When the force holding her gave way, Dianna tumbled to the floor and crawled to the center of the room. Her head was bleeding where a patch of skin had been torn out.

The searing pain from Dianna's scalp produced one clear, dominant emotion—hatred. Strike back, hurt Esau. Maim him. Kill him.

But she checked herself and thought, Wait a minute, Dianna. You're above that kind of unthinking vengeance—Esau is not responsible for his actions. He probably doesn't even understand what he is doing.

The pain brought an agony of tears to her eyes. One thing she had learned with certainty: she could never let herself trust the man-thing again. He may have the mind of a six-year-old, but he has demonstrated both cunning and brutality.

There had to be a way to deal intelligently with the situation. Dianna was not ready to give up completely on Esau's humanity. She tried to rationalize away her anger.

After all, she thought, hadn't she always been the one for settling things by talking them out? It was how she had been brought up. It was the lesson of her years. It was the lesson of her sex.

Though her head pounded in agony, and blood ran down her neck onto her blouse, she was convinced and determined that she should work things out in some kind of calm, intelligent manner.

"Esau," she said through the hole in the door.

The eye appeared, and Dianna backed away a little.

"Esau, it's wrong for you to keep me in here. Do you understand that?"

There was no response from the eye.

She continued, "You killed Jacques. He's dead. Does that mean anything to you?"

The eye only stared at her.

"Esau, you have to give me the keys, and you have to let me go home. I could get help for you."

Nothing.

"I know that you like me, and . . ." Dianna trailed off as the eye began to wander lustfully up and down her anatomy. "If you do the things I say—get the keys and let me go out—I will promise to be your friend."

God, do I sound like an asshole, she thought. "Now give me the keys."

The eye disappeared. A second later the key ring was dangling just outside the hole. Dianna moved toward the door and started to reach through but checked herself. If she put her hand into the hole, it would be simple for Esau to grab it. "Give me the keys," she said.

Esau's huge fist moved the keys closer to the opening.

"Hand them through to me." Dianna tried to instill as much authority in her voice as she could muster.

Esau's grime-blackened thumb dangled the keys nearer— just inside the hole.

Dianna stepped closer, poised to snatch them with as fast a

move as possible in order to avoid getting caught. Esau watched her unblinkingly through the gouged-out opening.

It was a trap, she knew. He was baiting her as cleverly as a trout fisherman bobs a fly on the surface of a stream. But she needed the keys.

Dianna lowered her arm and turned as if to walk away. Then, thinking she had put him off guard, she swirled and snatched at the key ring.

Just as she had a hold on them, Esau's thumb closed on the ring, and with eye-blinking speed, he jerked her whole arm out through the jagged hole and clamped a hand around her wrist.

Dianna's shoulder was slammed against the door, and the pain that shot through her shoulder socket made her certain that her arm would be torn off.

The keys dropped to the floor out in the hall. Esau held her fast and wiggled the door handle.

Oh, no, she thought, he wants me to let him in. If I don't, he'll rip off my arm.

Esau tugged harder on the arm to let her know that he meant business.

She was about to reach for the knob when she yelled, "What do you want, Esau? I don't understand!"

The pressure on the arm eased. "If you want me to open the door I've got to use both hands."

Esau thought about this for a moment, then smiled as if to say, "You're playing a little game with me, and I'm on to you." Then he put his weight against the door and pulled on her wrist.

Dianna screamed, expecting her arm to pop out of its socket. The pain made her more desperate.

"I can't open the door with only one hand."

The pressure let up, and she felt her arm being slowly pushed back through the hole until Esau's fingers that held her wrist were resting on the bottom of the opening. He peered in at her.

Seizing the opportunity, Dianna dug her teeth into Esau's index finger.

Esau yelled in agony and yanked his hand away, slamming Dianna's head against the door. In spite of the mutual pain, neither would let go.

Dianna's teeth drew blood, but Esau's two fingers held her

wrist in an unbreakable grip. She bit down with all the strength she could muster, and once again Esau jerked her head back against the door.

But this time the impact only caused her teeth to sink even deeper, near to the bone of the finger.

Dianna was at the point of losing consciousness when the pain in Esau's finger became too much, and he finally relaxed his grip.

She tore her hand from his grasp and fell away from the door into the safety of the room.

37

How could I be so stupid? Dianna asked herself. Using kindness and gentle words could have gotten me killed.

The splinters and cuts in her arm, along with the hammering pain in her head, gave her thinking a sharp, focused clarity. One thing was very certain: there would be no talking, no friendship; no quarter would be given. If "Dianna" was to continue to be a label—one that would survive in this time—she was going to have to start playing a more ruthless game.

But how far will I be able to go? Dianna wondered with considerable anxiety.

For a second there I wanted to kill him. If I had been able to press a button and murder Esau, I might have done it.

She asked herself, if it ever came down to a him-or-me situation, could I kill? Could I take a life, even to save my own? Would I be able to live with myself if I did?

Dianna cautiously went to the door hole and looked out. Esau was fast asleep on the floor, clutching a wad of locks of her hair. It was pressed to his nose, as if he had been savoring its special perfume.

Dianna paced the room. The stuffed bobcat head seemed to follow her steps, its glass eyes feigning life. She returned its gaze, thinking, You didn't survive, did you? You finished second, and now you're only a wall decoration and maybe a worn collar on an old coat.

Pressing a towel soaked in cold water to her clotting scalp, Dianna considered the odds that someone might show up to set her free. She had a mental image of Dennis charging to her rescue, a triumphant hero in a lithograph from a turn-of-the-century melodrama. There would be a little caption below the picture: Rescued, and just in time, too!

Then Dianna thought, It's not going to happen. He's not expecting to hear from me until next weekend, and when I don't call, he'll probably feel bad for a day or so, then figure I stood him up and begin to forget about me.

Someone else could happen along, but the chain is probably across the front drive, and if someone does show up, it most likely will be Goody with some other member of the Wilkinson clan brought along to strangle me. There have to be a lot of other Wilkinson relations around here.

Dianna sat down to think through her options. She knew there was no allowance for mistakes—every decision she made would have to be the right one.

There seemed to be two broad directions she could take: eliminate the danger or escape.

For me to eliminate the danger, she reasoned, I would have to eliminate Esau, and maybe Goody as well. That's going to be both difficult and risky. The trouble with taking the man-thing on is that I could easily end up the one eliminated.

I am twenty-eight years old, not at all weak, but Esau's got to be maybe three times my weight. And he's very very strong. I am only in fair shape, and I wouldn't last two seconds out in the open, hand to hand against the man-thing. And he can certainly outrun me—maybe not in a sprint, say for fifty yards, but for any longer distance, he's going to run me down.

I've got the brains here; that's the advantage I've got to use. His weak point is his mind, or the lack thereof. He is the "beast that wants discourse of reason." Although, thought Dianna, remembering his cagey game with the key, he is not to be underestimated. He has shown a devilish shrewdness, a sense of survival strategy that in the city you'd call being "street smart." She remembered how the man-thing had faced Lancelot. He was a perfect fighting animal, completely instinctual, killing with deadly accuracy and no apparent effort.

Dianna exhaled, trying to dispel some of her mounting tension. Her hunger was beginning to distract her.

Let's just say for the sake of argument that I want to try to eliminate Esau. What could I do? I could stab him, or shoot him, but I don't have a knife or a gun. Club him, hit him in the head, knock him out long enough for me to get to the road. But what if I only hurt him? The creature could go berserk, turn wild with pain like a wounded animal.

Dianna remembered what Esau had done to Jacques. *I certainly have seen the kind of killing the man-thing is capable of doing.*

That left "escape." But in order to get out of here, Dianna realized, *I'll have to come up with a terrific plan and try to second-guess what Esau might do to get in the way.*

Dianna swallowed hard. How long had it been since she had eaten? Out of habit she glanced at her watch. She took it off and tossed it in her suitcase. It felt strange not to be wearing it. Her wrist felt incomplete.

Hunger. If I'm going to get out of here, I've got to get something to eat soon, as soon as possible.

She began by taking an inventory of everything around her, paying particular attention to items that might be useful as weapons or tools.

One brass floor lamp, one cast-iron fire set with poker, tongs, broom, and shovel. Matches, fire ring of firewood of various shapes and sizes. Paintings, one Bobcat head, a set of dueling pistols. . . .

This has possibilities, Dianna thought. She tried to pull the case off the wall, but it was securely fastened. She took the poker, pried the mounting screws out of the plaster, and opened the back.

Along with the ancient pistols, there was a mold for making ball, a ramrod, and some other assorted tools that Dianna assumed were used for repairs or cleaning. In the mold she found three lead balls. She pulled the cap off the ornate powder horn and tried to shake the contents out on a sheet of paper. Empty. She realized it wouldn't be wise to leave something as volatile as gunpowder hanging in a frame on a wall.

Dianna remembered how her grandfather used to fire the old guns in his collection. Once when she was just seven, Grandfather had let her shoot one of his replica antiques at a black powder gun club range in Delaware. Dianna remembered the tears that had come with the loud report of the firing of that first gun, but after a few more attempts she had gotten used to the sound and had even occasionally hit the paper targets.

She knew the old pistol first had to be cocked. Dianna tried to pull back the hammer, but it wouldn't budge. Then, using the strength of both thumbs, she managed to draw it back until it clicked in place.

Clamped onto the hammer was a piece of sharp rock. That must be the flint, she thought to herself.

She pulled the trigger, but the hammer moved only sluggishly. The other pistol was even more difficult to cock, and the hammer hesitated as the trigger was pulled. A gunsmith's marking on the barrel gave the date 1769.

Great, a two-hundred-year-old gun. I can just see the thing blowing up in my face.

She continued her inventory—one set of ashtrays, stool, two chairs, small desk, books, magazines. They hadn't gotten around to packing up her belongings. The laptop was there with disks, paper, one pen, two pencils, her Louis Vuitton handbag, scissors, a small tube of Super Glue, and nail polish remover.

Holding the bottle of polish remover to the light, she examined the label—"Contents: acetone, water, alcohol; keep away from children; keep away from eyes; harmful if taken internally." The bottle was almost full. In the corner of the bathroom was a spray can of Lysol, also labeled "keep away from eyes."

Altogether, it's not much to work with, she thought, but there must be other useful things in the room I'm overlooking. I have light, heat coming from the electric baseboards, and hot and cold running water. I can also build a fire.

The phone rang downstairs. The phone, of course, she realized. If I could only get to it, I'd call the police or the fire department. The phone continued to ring. Where was everybody? Dianna wondered who was on the other end. Could it be Agnes calling in for Goody? And what would the caller do when no one answered?

The phone kept ringing. A sound came from the hall. Dianna, maintaining a safe distance, neared the hole and looked out. Esau was awake and listening. She had an odd déjà vu of her early days in New York, when she would jump whenever the phone rang, hoping it was ringing to tell her of an audition or a callback.

Suddenly Esau hopped to his feet and ran downstairs. Probably it's Esau's agent, she thought, with a starring role for him in a new movie—something like *Quasimodo Does Dallas*.

The ringing stopped abruptly.

Why wasn't there a phone in the room? One call and she could have had the police on their way to get her out.

Moments later Esau came back up the stairs. In his hand was the telephone receiver, its torn cord dangling behind him. He promptly walked up to the hole in the door and offered it to Dianna. Oh, great, it must have been for me.

When Dianna declined to reach for the offered receiver, Esau shrugged and tossed it aside. So much for calling the cavalry.

Esau rubbed his stomach and moved across the hall to Goody's door. To Dianna's amazement he knocked. Where did he get those manners? she asked herself. Goody, of course. That woman could teach etiquette to swine.

When there was no answer, Esau pounded on the door with his fists for a while, then hesitantly turned the knob. It opened. Esau went in and made little whimpers, looking around the room.

Dianna watched him through the open door. The bed was unmade and the room was a little messy. That's strange, thought Dianna, Goody has always seemed so orderly. When Esau didn't find the room's occupant, he curled up at the foot of Goody's bed and went to sleep.

38

Dianna dried her hair in front of the bathroom mirror. She considered making a second mad dash for freedom, waiting until Esau was in a deep sleep, then simply sneaking out of the room and sprinting for the highway. But she rejected the impulse, deciding that she needed more time to come up with a plan.

There was something about the man-thing's instinctual behavior that warned Dianna he would be difficult to fool. He seemed sharply attuned to smell and all the nuances of the environment, and getting away even while he slept would be risky. Her next move had to be well thought out and carefully executed.

It was important that she get to know her enemy. She had to discover his every weakness. There was so much animal in him. Who was this misshapen creature? What went on in his mind? Should she conceptualize him as more man or more animal? More animal, she decided. I'd say I should think of him as about two parts gorilla . . . one part cat, one part dog . . . with maybe two parts human being thrown in.

Where under heaven did the man-thing come from? she wondered. What gene pool produced this kind of creature?

Was it Esau's karma to be born in this form? she wondered. Roshi Takahashi would say it was.

He was certainly among the most deformed of men—a living Caliban, Yorick's ill-begotten offspring, an Elephant Man. Even Esau's face was marred with an ugly, jagged birthmark.

The man was a cruel mutation, a jest-in-the-flesh of some black-humored, sadistic god.

If the concept of karma is valid, wondered Dianna, what could Esau possibly have done in his past lifetime to warrant his heinous form? Who was he before—Hitler, Vlad the Impaler, Attila the Hun, a waiter at Joe Allen's?

I'm crazy. Any second I could be broken into small pieces, and I crack stupid jokes and chortle at them. It's got to be hysteria.

Her thoughts continued along the same lines. What about *my* karma? Am I here in this room because of my actions in some former incarnation? Roshi Takahashi says that even two people brushing sleeves in the street is the result of their behavior in past lifetimes.

Am I the guilty one here? For having an affair with a married man? For turning my back on Catholicism?

I won't accept that, I just won't, she thought. Karma is just a way of handing down guilt from one generation to the next—an ancient Asian way of controlling the masses. "It's your karma to be a member of a low caste, therefore you should be content to spend your life cleaning up the excrement from the street." It's only bullshit. Or is it?

Wasn't Machiavelli or somebody like that supposed to be my ancestor way back there on Father's side?

And, Jesus, what about the Dupres? Shipbuilders since the Revolutionary War. Supposedly they let nothing stand in the way of their rise to wealth and power. And weren't there a few historians who claimed that the Dupres got the Unites States into a number of major military actions (including the Spanish-American War) for the sole purpose of selling warships? During the Depression, Grandfather Dupre quadrupled the family fortune buying parcels of tax-defaulted property at a fraction of its worth.

In a way, Esau and I share a common karma. His family exploited mill workers; my ancestors ruthlessly speculated in ships and real estate.

Stop, Dianna, you're being ridiculous—everyone has got to have black sheep on their family tree.

Suddenly she felt cold.

She reached for the light switch, then stopped herself,

realizing that she might get a shock because of the wet floor.
The moment she pulled back her hand, the idea came.

A shock from a wall socket probably wouldn't kill the
man-thing, she admitted, but if I could figure a way to touch
Esau with an electric charge, I could keep him at bay. I could
use it like a rancher uses a cattle prod. It was a defense to be
looked into immediately.

Dianna searched the room. There was only one extension
cord and a couple of short lengths of wire that powered the
lamps. She plugged the extension cord into the bathroom wall
socket and measured the distance to the outside door. She was
far short of her goal.

Dianna had begun sawing at one of the lamp wires with her
nail file when the realization hit her, You fool, you've got to
unplug it first.

The wave of anxiety that followed made her see that the
game she was now playing was potentially lethal—dangerous
for the hunter as well as the hunted.

After connecting the severed wire to the extension cord, she
was still short by about three feet. Dianna removed the wire
from another lamp, stripped the insulation off the end, and
spliced it to the other two cords.

In college Dianna had pulled a B in stage lighting, and she
realized this was one of the few times she'd had an occasion to
use what she'd learned.

She bared the end of her makeshift shocker and pulled the
strands apart so that one could be held in each hand. Dianna
recalled from her stage lighting theory that for the current to
flow it always had to make a circle. By holding the end of one
wire in each hand, and holing it carefully, by the insulation,
she would be able to touch the two bare copper tips to Esau.
His flesh would them complete the circle.

There was still a problem—two sections of bare wire were
exposed where her homemade splices joined the lamp cords.
Dianna knew it was important to prevent the copper strands
from touching one another and thereby shorting out the circuit.
She ripped a dry washcloth in half and tied the pieces over the
two splices.

The hurt in Dianna's head and arm made her want to wake
Esau up just to give him a good shock, but she decided her
chance would most likely come soon enough.

Dianna tested the two windows in the bedroom. She raised the one that looked out at the barn. Both windows were large enough to get through, but if she tried to jump, she was sure to end up with a broken leg. A ladder of bed sheets. That was an idea she filed away for future use.

But even if she got down, and the question continued to nag at her, what would she do then? She couldn't take the risk of Esau catching her defenseless.

A gutter ran along the eaves on each side of the gable where the window protruded from the roof. Dianna put a hand out to see if the gutter might support her weight, but it creaked and bent under the slightest pressure. She gave up on the windows and moved to the closet.

Dianna noticed that by opening both the bathroom and the closet doors she could mask the view into the room from Esau's side of the door hole. In the closet were shelves with a few sheets, towels, and an extra blanket. Curiously, there were scuff marks all over the wall.

Looking up, Dianna saw a trapdoor in the ceiling. The shelves were reinforced and served as a ladder.

The attic was pitch-black and musty. Dianna could feel a thin layer of dust on whatever she touched. She crawled across boards that were laid over the ceiling beams. In the darkness, using her hand as eyes, she discovered several rolled-up rugs, stacks of boxes of moldy books, and an assortment of old wooden chairs.

From the far end of the attic came a glimmer of light. Dianna groped her way toward it on the assumption that there might be a window and a possible way out.

Suddenly her hand pressed into thin air, and she toppled forward.

Her mind flashed, This is it. I'm falling to my death.

Just as she was about to go completely over the edge, Dianna hooked her foot around a floorboard and regained her balance.

She had almost fallen into the elevator shaft.

Far below her she could just make out the roof of the elevator car.

Moving with much more caution, she continued her journey to the source of light.

On the way, her hand touched a dust-covered wooden handle. Her fingers groped its heavy shape. The object seemed to be some kind of hammer, but opposite the nail-pounding head was not a claw for pulling nails but a heavy steel spike tapered to a chisel-like edge. Dianna slipped the tool in her belt.

The source of light proved to be a disappointment. It was only an air vent that faced her former prison, the icehouse. And instead of being the exit she had hoped for, the metal slats were well-seated, and they resisted Dianna's efforts to push them out.

Leathery wings flapped around her, and she dropped prone in the dust. Bats.

She dragged a box of books toward the attic entrance, thinking, That's all I need, a case of rabies.

Back in the room she brushed herself off. Well, it's a good thing I bathed. Her clothes were caked with dust from collar to cuffs.

She took a moment to examine her newly found tool. The hammer seemed heavier than the ones she had used building sets for her college theater. On the shaft was the label Mason's Pride. It's for chipping bricks or stones, Dianna realized. The two-inch-wide edge was rusty and dull.

Dianna turned to go wash up, then jumped back, dropping the hammer into the box of books.

Esau was glaring at her though the opening in the door. His attack resumed—pounding, slamming, thrusting his hand as far as it would go into the hole.

The door was strong, but Dianna knew it wouldn't hold forever against this kind of onslaught. She plugged in her jerry-rigged shocker and, brandishing exposed copper in each hand, stood to the side of the hole.

Esau reached in to pull at the edge of the panel. He broke off another bit of the wood. One wire to the pinky, one to the index finger. Flash, zap, the smell of ozone, and the hand was gone.

Esau whined and, sucking his finger, gaped in surprise at his booteful.

He grunted and, now able to get his hand through the door hole, made a grab for her face.

One wire to the wrist, one to a finger. Flash, zap, the arm was instantly withdrawn.

"Garrrrah-ga!" he growled and thrust his other arm into the hole, snatching at the air.

Dianna couldn't get the wire into position. She scrunched in the corner and tried to dodge the hand, but even so, Esau caught a piece of blouse and ripped off a sleeve.

He wasn't holding still long enough for her to make contact. Dianna stretched the cord to its full length in order to get farther over to the side.

The flailing hand paused for an instant, and quickly she touched the forearm in two places. Flash, zap, again the arm vanished.

Dianna smiled and stepped back toward the bathroom. Flash! Zap! She walked into a bare wire of her makeshift splice.

The current surged from her lower back up through her chest and out her arm where it touched the door frame.

Dianna couldn't move. For a moment she felt her heart clutch and her diaphragm muscle paralyze.

She could not take a breath.

The lights in the room blinked out.

She staggered, released from the grip of the current as the circuit went out. Only the wall kept her from falling.

Dianna had no idea how long she leaned there, unable to breathe. With a gasp, her breathing began again.

She felt a dull tingle in her body, along the path that the surge of current had taken, and it felt as if someone had pounded all those muscles with a heavy rubber mallet. Looking behind her, she saw what had caused the shock—a rag had come loose around one part of the improvised splice, baring a wire.

My body took a jolt that was strong enough to blow the fuse, she realized, and put the room in darkness.

The fire in the hearth brought warmth and light.

The electric baseboards would not come on; evidently they were wired into the same circuit as the rest of the lights. Dianna still had hot water, and across the hall in Goody's room and throughout the rest of the inn, the lights were burning. The blown circuit only affected Dianna's bedroom.

She stoked the fire with the last of the wood and put in a few books from the attic, realizing that her supply of burnable items would not last very long. Dianna placed the tip of the poker into the hottest part of the flame and thought, It won't hurt to have a red hot weapon around.

Eat. Eat. Eat. The pangs of hunger came again, this time with more force, with more insistence. I've got to eat soon. For now, she knew, the next best thing was to rest, or she would have no strength left for future battles.

Even sleep, she realized, was always going to be a calculated risk, but one she would have to take. A cautious check through the hole revealed Esau lying on the floor, nursing his wounds. Maybe the shocks will keep his hands out of the hole, she thought. Dianna opened the bathroom and closet doors to block Esau's view and climbed under the covers of the big bed.

Her arm ached, her head pounded, her torn scalp felt as if it were on fire, the muscles of her arm and shoulder still throbbed from the power of the shock.

Dianna lay in bed, turning. The "sleep that knits the raveled sleeve of care" was not going to come that easily, if at all.

North by Northwest or *Rear Window*, she thought, that's where I am. I'm in a Hitchcock film and I am one of his victims of circumstance. Or am I? Wait, that's not right— Hitchcock's protagonists were usually in some subtle way deserving of their fate, like the Cary Grant character in *North by Northwest*. His flaw was having a career in advertising. Yes, that was Hitchcock's subtle way of getting in a dig at Madison Avenue.

Guilt. Guilt. No, I am not guilty. But then am I totally innocent? No way, she admitted, thinking through the facets of her situation:

My motives for escaping New York City were self-centered.

I didn't give the office the number where I could be reached, because I didn't want the FM tracking me down to give me more work.

I've been having an affair with a married man. Granted, the wife happens to be a bitch, but I am still the one fooling around with the husband.

But nothing I have done makes me deserve to be murdered. But then neither does working in advertising—or does it? She chortled at her jest, then thought, Stop it, Dianna. For God's sake, get a hold of yourself. Stop the laughing.

Dianna wondered what kind of match Arthur would be for Esau. I'd give him exactly three seconds until Esau had reduced him to pink Jell-O.

She couldn't visualize the Roshi physically engaged in combat with Esau either. Takahashi would come at the problem from some obtuse angle. Yes, she thought, like the bedouin desert tribes who say the shortest distance from point A to point B is to use A and B as one side of a square and then make the journey by taking the long route around the other three sides. No, somehow it would not be necessary for the teacher to exert himself.

Takahashi would find some unlikely solution . . . like making Esau laugh. Yes, Dianna thought, that's the kind of thing the old Zen master would do. In seconds the Roshi would have Esau laughing and giggling, and they would be rolling together and playing on the floor like a pair of preschool best buddies.

Esau's voice called out from the first floor of the inn. "Goody? Ag-ga? . . . Goody? Ag-ga?"

Dianna wondered, Where in God's name are the two women? Another thought came to Dianna, What about Dennis? Was there a chance he could come? If Dianna didn't call and he sensed something suspicious, he might. It was a lot to hope for, she realized. But then, he was looking for his sister. What if that ringing phone was Dennis trying to call me? No. There's no reason he would try to call; he thinks I'm in Maine.

Dianna carefully turned over on her side, feeling a shot of pain run up her arm.

No, no one's going to help me, she told herself. I can't count on it. If I am to make it through this, I'll have to do the work myself.

As she fell into a restless half sleep, her empty stomach growled and began to churn in growing spasms.

"You are what you eat," she thought. She saw how much truth there was in that saying.

You are all the strength, the intelligence, the sharpness of mind, that you take from the food you can find, or grow, or steal . . . or hunt.

In her half dream, the concept of eating suddenly became

clear and took on a very basic and primitive significance that
had never before had bearing on her life.

Eating was survival.

Eating was existence.

Eating said "no" to death.

39

Esau awoke with the rays of the sun. His arm hurt, and there were blisters where the current had burned the skin.

Like a stalking tomcat, he crept up to the hole. He listened. The sound of Dianna's deep, steady breathing told him that she was asleep.

Booteful sleep. Good time Esau get in.

He carefully pulled on the edges of the door around the hole. The panel made a loud cracking noise.

He stopped and listened. Dianna slept on.

Esau stuck his hand in timorously, then quickly jerked it back, remembering the shocks. When nothing happened, he cautiously put his arm through, trying to reach the ends of the slide bars or the lock. All three were out of the range of his fingertips.

Esau went into Goody's room and grabbed a coat hanger. Working clumsily, but manipulating the tough wire as if it were string, he reshaped the hanger so that it formed an elongated handle with a hook at one end.

Do like Jacques.

He had seen Jacques do the same thing once when the Frenchman had locked himself out of the horse van.

Back at the door hole, Esau again listened for a moment, then reached in with the wire. It kept slipping off the curved end of the bar. Finally, he got a grip and gave a tug.

The bar creaked and moved half an inch. The wire dropped out of his fingers, and he had to go back to Goody's room and fashion another one. The second time he caught the slider, he was able to pull it back another inch.

Good. Esau in soon.

Dianna awoke with a jolt. What was that noise? she thought.

Silently she moved so that she could peek between the masking bathroom and closet doors. There was Esau's forearm through the door hole, his hand working with the coat hanger.

The poker, she thought in panic.

Dianna grabbed it from the fireplace; the steel was cold to the touch. The fire had been out for hours.

She heard the coat hanger scraping against the bolt.

Looking around wildly, she spotted the nail file. Holding it in both fists, she quietly squeezed between the two masking doors, and with all her force she plunged the file into the busily working hand.

"Ooooooo-aaaag-aaaahhhh!"

Esau dropped the hanger and jerked his arm out of the hole. The file had penetrated clear through the back of his hand.

Dianna slid the bolt back in place.

Esau took the file, which jutted out of his palm, with his good hand and, making a grimace of pain, yanked it out. Blood spurted on his poncho.

"Gaaaaaaarga! Garrrrka-garkooooaaaaaa!"

Esau went wild.

He began throwing himself at the door, screaming and yelling, crazed with anguish.

Dianna knew she had to stop the attack before the door gave way. She held up the useless wire shocker.

But Esau paused only a moment and then seemed to get even more enraged at the sight of it.

Pointing one of the dueling pistols at Esau through the door hole had no effect either. He seemed to have no awareness of the gun as dangerous.

In desperation she grabbed the can of Lysol and sprayed it toward his eyes. He stopped and fanned the air in front of his face, sniffing, blinking, and squinting.

He charged again, and once more Dianna sprayed. He swatted at the air and almost lost his balance. Esau's hands went to his eyes, leaving a trail of blood from his palm running down his face.

When he realized what the warm liquid was that dripped from his chin, he fell back into a sitting position in the far corner of the hall by Goody's room.

Who would have thought that something as banal as air freshener could stop such an onslaught? The chemicals must have hurt his eyes. Well, I'll take any break I can get, she thought, no matter how temporary.

Licking his bleeding palm, Esau looked up at her, tears of pain in his eyes.

Dianna was unable to tell whether the tears were from physical sensation or from a sadness at being so viciously rejected.

Again I was foolish, she admitted to herself. I was caught off guard. The fire was out, the poker was cold. Last night I blocked my view and my hearing by opening the closet and bathroom doors.

Things might not work out so well the next time, she realized.

Determined to keep a small blaze going and the weapon ready, Dianna rebuilt the fire and set the poker on the burning logs.

The storm door downstairs slammed, and she rushed to the front window in time to see Esau disappear around the corner of the inn.

Dianna's hunger was overwhelming. She felt weak from exhaustion and starvation and knew without a doubt that it was dangerous to go much longer without food.

I promised myself I would plan a careful escape, she thought, but if I don't eat soon, I will be too run down to even think straight, and I'll never have the stamina to carry out any plan.

Whatever the risk, I've got to get food. Now.

Dianna pulled the bars back and turned the key.

40

On her way out Dianna positioned the door so that it could be entered and locked quickly. As she paused to listen for any sound of Esau, the thought nagged at her, You don't have a plan; this is stupid and irrational.

Then she heard the Roshi saying a favorite phrase, "To know is to act." He had been describing the highest form of spontaneous action, where an individual is so at ease with himself that he has no need to consider a response.

But if that is true, she reasoned, then my non-plan of action couldn't possibly have an iota of Zen. I don't "know" anything and I'm not at all at ease with the situation.

Near the top of the stairs, Dianna saw that the door to Jacques and Agnes's room was open. The contents were in shambles. Her eye went immediately to a gun cabinet.

She was afraid that it would be locked, but it opened with only a tug. There were three weapons inside—a shotgun, a .22, and a deer rifle. Her hopes fell. On all the guns were chrome trigger locks. The Wilkinsons would have probably always kept them locked, she realized, because of Esau. Dianna set the shotgun in the hall to be picked up on her way back.

The stairs creaked as she moved down. Lying on the bottom step was the pay phone. Esau had ripped the whole unit off the wall. She muttered to herself, "He must not have gotten the part."

She entered the dining room. The tables were set for dinner, and the bar was stocked with packages of peanuts and pretzels, which she hurriedly stuffed into a paper bag. She slipped a small paring knife, for slicing lemons, into her back pocket,

189

and paused at the wine rack to grab a bottle of Pouilly-Fuisse.

I've got to find the kitchen, Dianna thought. Then I can get some real food and maybe a butcher knife.

Where was it I saw Goody wheeling the tray of dirty dishes? She must have used the elevator, and that means the kitchen must be in the basement.

Dianna stood in front of the elevator door, looking for the controls. There didn't seem to be any. At her back, under the staircase that led up to the second floor, was another metal door. That, realized Dianna, had to lead to a staircase, which leads to the basement.

She tried the handle, but it was locked, apparently from the other side. Dianna's frustration grew as she realized that this door was another route to the kitchen and food.

Desperately feeling along the wall, she discovered two buttons behind an oil painting. Dianna pressed and waited. The machinery came to life with a loud clunk and a grind.

Dianna panicked. The sound, she thought. Esau will hear the elevator. She was just ready to retreat to the safety of her room when the door to the lift opened.

Goody sat rigid in the old wheelchair. The woman's mouth was open and her yellow teeth set in a silent death scream.

Goody's soulless eyes, the whites now a dull gray, gaped in a slightly cross-eyed leer. The smell of death and putrefying flesh hit Dianna like a breeze from hell.

The chair creaked and wheeled a few inches out into the hall.

Goody's head was thrown back, looking toward heaven, her expression set in a questioning grimace of panic and terror, as if in the woman's last moments she had desperately sought answers from somewhere upward and beyond, as if Goody's last question had been directed to God, asking, "Hey, why did you do this to me?"

Dianna fought the urge to scream and then gagged. The elderly woman must have had a heart attack in the elevator.

A sound came from behind her.

It was Esau. He was at the front screen door.

Dianna stepped out of sight, her back against the wall opposite the elevator. Esau fumbled with the door handle.

With a sense of relief she remembered, The storm door was locked when I tried to get in after running from the barn. The lock is probably set so that the door only opens from the inside.

Should I wait or try to make a run for it?

Dianna was about to sprint for the steps when she heard the sound of breaking glass. The storm door opened and closed.

She could hear Esau in the entranceway, playing with the door handle.

What to do? Make a mad dash out the back door, or through the bar into the dining room, or down the hall and up the stairs to her room?

Dianna stole a quick glance around the corner. Esau was still in the entrance area, but his interest had shifted to an umbrella. Laughing a stupid little laugh, he opened and closed it roughly several times until some of the ribs broke and it fell apart. She heard him toss the umbrella and start up the stairs.

That's it, I'm finished, she thought. He'll discover I'm not in my room and come after me. Dianna's breathing was so hard that she was certain Esau would be able to hear her panting.

But Esau paused on the third stair and came back down to go into the dining room.

As soon as his footsteps left the foyer, Dianna crept along the hall toward the foot of the staircase. She heard the crinkle of cellophane as Esau tore open a bag of potato chips. Dianna took four silent steps, realizing that any second Esau could walk out and grab her.

The dry wood floor started to pop. Dianna lurched into a run toward the stairs.

As she grabbed at the banister, her paper bag broke, strewing the junk food contents over the steps. She hesitated but heard heavy footsteps coming from the dining room.

Dianna charged up the stairs and into her room, forgetting to retrieve the shotgun. She threw the bolts back as fast as she could.

Seconds later Esau was at the door, pounding away. Lysol only slowed him down; the effect of the spray was clearly lessening.

Dianna brandished the paring knife. He clutched his injured hand, launched into a fit of rage but kept his distance.

Dianna had returned with very little to show for her efforts—no food except the bottle of wine, which she had somehow managed to hold onto, and one small knife. But she had gotten information. At least I know where the kitchen is, she thought, and I certainly don't have to worry about Goody coming back.

That last bit of knowledge was reassuring, but at the same time it meant that one door of hope was closed. Though Goody might have been the one to give the orders to kill her, the old woman had at least been a voice of reason. And she seemed by the sheer force of her will to be able to control Esau.

So, Dianna thought, it is less likely than ever that the curtain will fall on this act with a deus ex machina ending. It's up to me, the mere mortal, to shape my own destiny.

The plan hadn't gone that badly, but she realized it could easily have ended in total disaster. She swore to herself that from now on she would be more careful.

Dianna stoked the fire and made several trips to the attic, bringing down all the boxes of old books for fuel. She took every piece of furniture in the room and the wooden kitchen chairs that she found in the attic and broke them up into burnable lengths. When finished, she had a respectable supply of splintered chair legs, smashed desk drawers, and other miscellaneous furniture parts. The thought of dismantling the bed occurred to her, but there was no way she could take the massive four-poster apart, let alone cut it up into pieces that would fit into the fireplace.

Dianna studied the bar on the front door, remembering Esau's earlier attempt with the wire. Using the mason's hammer she drove a wedge-shaped piece of wood onto the space between the bar and the door. Dianna tested the bar by pulling back on it with all of her strength, but it wouldn't budge. He won't surprise me again, she thought.

From outside in the hall came the creaking sound of Goody's wheelchair.

Dianna listened in amazement. That woman had been very dead.

At the hole she saw Esau rolling the wheelchair down the hall. Goody sat looking upward, gripped by rigor mortis, her eyes and mouth still locked in her bizarre grimace. This time the wide-eyed corpse seemed to simply ask, "What happened?"

Esau wheeled the chair into Goody's room, smoothly lifted her up, and set her on the bed. He dropped to his knees and looked up at her. "Goody Ma-ma," he uttered.

He took her hand, having to bend her stiffened arm to get it into the right position, nuzzled it, then placed it on his face.

"Ma-ma."

With his head on Goody's cold lap, he grinned and sucked the wound on his injured palm. He held it out to Goody as if he were showing her stigmata.

"Peeeeza, Goody, peeeza."

He held his hand out again, putting it right in front of the dead woman's face.

"Peeeeeeeeza! 'Oooody?"

After a time, Esau stared into Goody's death mask and whined longingly. He poked at her with a finger. As his cries grew in intensity he grabbed her shoulders with both hands and shook her violently.

"Gooody. Eeeee-ahaaaau. Peeeeeeza."

When there was no response, he became quiet and sat beside the cadaver, his arms embracing it. He smiled, swaying from side to side, rocking the body as a mother rocks her baby.

Goody's cold and immobile face seemed to mock his need for closeness.

After a time he set Goody in the bed and forced the brittle corpse into a reclining position. Esau covered her gently with a blanket, then, like a contented dog, reassumed his place at the foot of her bed.

He glanced across at Dianna's door, then slowly closed his eyes.

In his sleepy mind Esau's thoughts turned. *Why booteful not want play with Esau? Why she not let him in her room? Esau a very booteful man, but she only hurt Esau.*

Why Goody not help him? She lie so still. Goody dead? Esau hope not. But maybe she dead. Goody Mama smell dead. Please, no.

No one feed Esau. He eat what he find.

Esau glad Jacques dead. Esau want Jacques dead forever, but Esau hope Goody wake up soon.

Esau 'ove her so much.

Touched or revolted, thought Dianna, what should I feel? Then she decided that she didn't care and that it didn't matter—nothing mattered except her exhaustion and her now raging hunger. *Hunger! Food!* Her only thought, her only care was satisfying the primal command of her empty stomach.

Sitting on the bed, she managed to push in the cork on the wine bottle and pour herself a tall glass. About one hundred calories, she guessed.

The wine hit her in seconds. Dianna went to the side window and raised it. Outside it was still, and dense fog obscured the tops of the trees.

The geese were on the pond behind the barn. She looked at the fat, juicy birds and imagined a warm slice of goose breast. Her mouth was a waterfall of saliva.

The landscape blurred. Dianna almost passed out and had to grab the windowsill to keep on her feet. She thought, It's the combination of the wine and not eating.

In a frenzy Dianna grabbed the curtain rods and pulled them off the windows. Then she unhooked all the curtains and unthreaded the draw cords out of the pulleys. By tying the cords together she made one that was at least thirty feet long.

She tightened a loop at one end around a bedpost and tugged on it, trying to determine how much weight the cord would hold. One of the knots pulled apart. Dianna triple-tied each knot and tugged on them until they were all tight.

Feeling a light-headed rush, she staggered and almost fell. I'm really high, she thought. The alcohol must have gone straight into my bloodstream.

Dropping the snare to the ground, she thought, Now all I have to do is to get a goose to step into it. "A goose to goose-step," she commented aloud to herself and laughed drunkenly.

Dianna tried throwing ashes and wood chips out the window, with the hope that the geese would think it was feed, but got no response. Then, remembering the call that Agnes used to gather the flock, she shouted and honked with all her strength through her nose. "Here goose (honk), goose (honk), goose (honk)!"

The flock had not been fed for two days, and making a loud nasal ruckus, they charged around the back of the house to their usual feeding area. Great, that's just what I need, thought Dianna, sound the Klaxon.

As she had expected, Esau soon came around the side of the inn. He scanned the grounds, searching for the cause of the flock's disturbance. Abruptly glancing up, he saw Dianna poised in the window.

After a momentary pause, as if some new idea had occurred to him, he hurriedly disappeared around the side of the house.

Dianna resumed the calling. "Goose, (honk), goose, (honk), goose, (honk)!" The flock aimlessly strutted about, unable to locate her voice. She threw down a few more wood chips and kept the call going. One of the geese spotted a falling chip and ran for it, bringing the whole gaggle behind it.

They wandered around below, eating the chips.

Dianna's first two tugs got nothing, and she had trouble resetting the loop in the midst of the converging flock. The third pull snared a heavy bird by the foot, and Dianna hauled it up.

She was bitten on the hand and pecked in the face as the bird came into the room.

After closing the window to cut off the animal's escape, Dianna stood looking at the indignant bird, who was apparently unharmed by the journey up the side of the building. It paced the room with arrogance, as if its pride had been hurt, but it was too pompous to let it show.

God, thought Dianna, what do I do now?

The haughty goose with the draw cord still looped around its leg strutted across the room and defecated on the carpet.

Tears came to Dianna's eyes as she took up the paring knife and pulled in the rope, hand over hand.

41

Dianna squatted before the fireplace, holding a singed piece of pink meat with the tongs. She kept it in the heart of the flames from a little stack of burning, moldy books. Her blouse and jeans were caked with blood and feathers.

Bits of down floated in the room. Soot and ashes covered Dianna's face and hands. She popped a chunk of charred flesh in her mouth. It tasted fantastic, delicious, better than any Thanksgiving bird Dianna could remember.

Even as she ate, the remainder of the goose carcass pulsed and jerked in occasional remembrances of life.

The image of the goose's neck breaking would not leave Dianna's mind. Just as the bones had cracked, the animal had seemed to look into itself, in a moment of total resignation. At that second—just before death took hold, but when it was certain—all resistance stopped. It was as if the goose had understood and found an inner peace, a kind of acceptance, a profound realization of what it meant to die.

There was no rage, only a wistful sadness, a heartbeat of looking inward and a quiet self good-bye.

What exactly was that moment? Dianna wondered, half wishing she could have shared the animal's thoughts during those last, parting seconds.

I felt detached from the killing. I, Dianna, did not commit the act. It was as if the goose had been slaughtered by some third party, she realized. I was only present as an observer.

As the pangs of hunger eased, she looked at her gory clothes and the burnt hunk of goose flesh in her hand. I am an animal, she thought. It only took a few days for me to lose all

self-respect and become an animal. I feel like a lady gladiator.
I have been captured by the Romans and put in the arena.
That's who killed the goose; it wasn't Dianna née "The
Humane" of Westchester, it was Dianna "Captured-and-
forced-to-kill-and-willingly-does-so" LaBianca, iron woman
unchained, lady butcher.

I should have at least set the bird out on a table or something
and tried to have some semblance of a civilized meal. Dianna
took a swig from the wine bottle. "Fuck it," she said aloud.
"Who am I kidding? Sitting down at a table wouldn't have
made the goose feel any better."

How can I have so little guilt over the bird's death? she
wondered. She did feel some remorse, but it was distanced,
tucked away in the far corners of her mind. Yes, it was
somehow safely removed, like her recollection of the act of
killing.

My principle-betraying deed, Dianna concluded, was wholly
justified. It was necessary. What I did was vital to my survival.
. . . Sweet Jesus, is it possible that I am actually accepting
this as a part of myself? She bit off another mouthful.

How quickly is idealism sacrificed to the call of the stomach.

A dull clatter came from the other side of the house. She had
been hearing random noises from that direction since she had
started plucking the large bird. Dianna gulped the last mouthful
she could hold and noted that she had finished three-quarters of
the bottle of wine.

The fire was blazing, and she stretched out in front of the
hearth, absorbing the heat and luxuriating in her inebriated
feeling of fullness. It's amazing how a round stomach and a
bottle of wine can produce a rosy glow of optimism. I've
always been such a goddamn civilized person. I am a perfect
specimen—the end product—of the selective inbreeding of
intellectual society.

Why did I ever bother to study theater in college? All it did
was fuck me up. I should have elected more practical studies,
tangible courses, like Skinning and Gutting of Poultry 101 or
Knife Fighting, Advanced Studies or Methods of Negotiation
with Pituitary Hunchbacks.

Why couldn't I have had a hobby like firearms or electron-
ics? she thought. Even if I had been a runner or had gone out

for some sport like track, or a martial art like karate or aikido, it would be an asset right now.

Dianna remembered a day when she had been walking along upper Broadway with the Roshi. They passed a bookstore, and Dianna made some comment about wishing she had more time to keep up her reading.

The Asian gentleman smiled and said, "Do not think that book knowledge is everything. It is important, but it is not everything." He launched into a story:

"I had a best friend at the university that I attended in Osaka. He was a brilliant student. He could talk on any subject and had read all the books of philosophy. He studied all his life, every day. He knew the history of the world in great exactness. He could even read the plays of Mr. Shakespeare in English, while I, myself, have plenty of difficulty reading them in Japanese.

"This man had an incredible, staggering treasure of knowledge, but . . . he died."

The punch of the story took Dianna completely by surprise.

Then Roshi started laughing. Dianna stared at her teacher, not quite believing that was the end of the story; then, realizing his point, she joined him—having a near fit of hysterical laughter.

Both of them carried on laughing together for five minutes over the story, like two insane fools, leaning against the stone wall of an office building, cackling wildly, tears coming down their cheeks, as passersby shook their heads in wonder.

A noise outside the window took Dianna away from her thoughts. The tip of an aluminum ladder projected above the window ledge.

He wants to get me to elope with him, was Dianna's first thought, and despite the danger she chuckled at her own joke. With the wine came reckless courage, and a kind of dull, half-fuzzy assurance that she could handle almost anything.

Getting up with a drunken nonchalance, Dianna forced herself into action, but the effects of the feast slowed her down and left her with a feeling that she was moving underwater. After turning the lock on the window, she grabbed the hot poker and the knife and waited.

Glass chunks sprayed into the room as Esau's hand smashed through. He thrust his face in, and Dianna slapped the dull red fire tool into his neck.

Esau jerked back, cracking his skull on the windowsill. He screamed and reached for her. Dianna let him grab the end of the poker and saw the smoke of scorching flesh as his hand closed around it.

Raging with pain, he struck out, hitting the unbroken parts of the window.

Dianna burned his fingers as he yanked out leaded panes. She swung the poker down with both hands, cracking his knuckles and scorching his skin.

Esau grabbed the poker along the shaft and jerked it away from her, throwing it out into the yard. As he started bashing at the center crosspiece of the window frame, Dianna tried to stab him with the paring knife.

The sight of the little weapon sent Esau into a frenzy. The pain in his hand, very swollen from the nail file stab, was a constant reminder of what a blade could do. He fluttered his hands fearfully and emitted a babble of little screams.

Dianna, faced with such an impossible target, missed and plunged the knife into the lead frame, breaking off the blade at the handle.

In desperation she backed off. Esau was putting his full weight on the window frame, and it was creaking and giving way.

Dianna thought of the can of Lysol but immediately knew she needed something much more effective.

Could I push the ladder away from the wall? she thought. There wasn't anything in sight long enough to do the job without her having to get close to Esau.

Using the shovel from the fire set, she scooped up a pile of glowing ashes, carried them to the window, hauled back, and threw them in Esau's face. Scoot, ashes, and red-hot coals went in his hair, nostrils, and mouth.

Esau coughed and roared. He beat his head and spat ash.

Another shovel in the face. Coals fell on the floor of the room.

A third shovel.

Blinded by the ash, Esau retreated down the ladder by feeling each rung with his feet.

As he descended, Dianna dumped more coals on his head.

Esau lost his footing and fell three steps onto a rung below. With a pinching noise the metal ladder buckled in the middle, crashed forward into the wall and then to the ground. Esau fell with it, landing on his side.

He lurched up, smoke billowing from his poncho, ran to the goose pond, and jumped in.

Dianna smothered the hot coals on the floor with a blanket.

She paced, taking a final hit of the wine, draining the bottle, and looked around the room. It was becoming less and less habitable.

With most of the furniture smashed and only the altarlike bed standing in the room, by the stone mantel, the place was starting to look like a combination of settings—for a heavy metal music video, a Sam Shepherd hotel room, and a Camus novel.

Already the room was chilled from the broken window. Dianna put a blanket over her shoulders and thought, How simple my life has become.

Right now, I couldn't care less about how much money I'm making, whether or not I like my job, or if people are impressed by the clothes I'm wearing.

I don't give a damn about nuclear power, the environment, starvation in the world, or war in the Middle East.

I am not in the least interested in what's opening on Broadway.

My life is cut-and-dried: eat, stay alive. Maybe that's what I needed all along—one or two overwhelming problems.

Simplicity. Isn't that what the Roshi is always saying? Is that the secret of happiness—eating home-killed goose and being alive in the midst of adversity?

No, thought Dianna, that kind of contentment is as momentary as any other. It's all relative, isn't it? Happiness is only a change for the better. And if tomorrow is only more goose, will I be equally happy? Certainly not.

How perverse are our human requirements for bliss.

The sounds of restless horses came from the direction of the stable. They had not been fed or cared for in many days. Her heart went out to them, trapped, as she had been, without food.

Dianna had a flash of the boards that had been kicked out of the barn wall that day. . . . It seemed like a lifetime ago when she had been there with Goody. Could I get through the hole? she asked herself, and began to formulate a plan.

Footsteps sounded on the roof overhead. Dianna, surprised

that she felt so calm, looked up at the ceiling and thought, What in God's name is he going to try now? Can he get at me through a window?

Just in case, Dianna took the wedges off the bars to give herself an exit and stood waiting, with her last shovel of ashes in hand.

Esau's attempt was rather halfhearted and, remembering his last debacle, he moved cautiously. He had gotten onto the roof by shinnying up a cedar tree that grew near the house. But there was no easy way to get down to Dianna's room, because the windows were flush with the walls of the building.

Esau want in. Booteful 'ove him if he in. At least Esau think so. But Esau not sure now. What is wrong? Why booteful not see? Maybe booteful just stupid. Like goose.

He felt around the eaves, trying to get a grip for support, but nothing protruded from the wall to hold onto. Esau tested his weight on a rain gutter and almost fell as it broke away from the side of the building. The gutter on the other side of the window withstood his bulk. He put a foot in the rain trough and reached over, trying for a handhold on each side of the gable.

For a moment he succeeded, and Esau's body covered the entire expanse of window. Then with a crack the gutter tore away from the building. His huge hands found a grip on the window ledge. Esau tried to pull himself up, but it was obvious that he could not.

Dianna raised the window and, poised with a shovel of coals, looked down at him.

Esau cowered, anticipating the burns.

Dianna stood immobile.

Slowly he lifted his head, and their eyes met. His hair and blankets were soaking wet from his cooling-off dunk. His face was blistered and burned, one eye bright red.

What is going through his mind? she wondered. He knows I can dump the contents of this shovel on him whenever I choose, yet he isn't begging, and he doesn't even seem that concerned by the situation at the moment.

The dull lust was still evident in his eyes, but there was something else, too—an appraising coldness like that with which a tomcat eyes a difficult female. It's all the pains I have caused him, Dianna realized. They're starting to add up. It explains his even gaze. He is becoming afraid of me.

Theirs was no longer a game, but an obsession—a fight to the death between grim veterans.

Dianna felt the now-familiar icy-handed spasm knead up her back. She tried to shake it off as an athlete tries to shake off a minor injury. But there was no stopping the chilling contraction. It wound its way, on its certain course up her spine, with a feeling of cold fire.

When it had passed, she casually slid the hot coals out of the shovel and onto Esau's hands. He seemed to expect this and gave her an angry look as his flesh burned. He quickly changed his grip on the ledge and flicked his fingers to shake off the bits of hot coal.

The man-thing's determination was intense.

Sudden fear cut through Dianna's alcoholic fog.

She realized that Esau was not going to let the pain stop his progress. He lifted himself up, trying to raise his leg to get a foot over the window ledge.

The smell of burning flesh and clothing filled the room. Adrenaline pumping, she darted in a circle, looking for a weapon.

Where was it? Somewhere with the books. Dianna thrust her hand into the pile of rotting hardcovers and paperbacks from the attic and wrapped her fingers around the haft of the manson's hammer.

At the window, she paused and rotated the weapon in her hand so that the hammer head was facing her and the brick-and-mortar chipping flange faced away from her.

She raised the hammer to one shoulder and brought it down in an arc. She was trying to bury the tool in his wrist, maybe cut an artery, but she misjudged the weight of the hammer and the blow fell short. Instead of hitting Esau on the wrist, she chopped off the tip of his pinky and the last joint of the adjacent ring finger.

The two bits of finger flew into the room with a spurt of blood.

For a moment he was incredulous—immobile and openmouthed, staring at the blood squirting from his left hand, where the ends of his two fingers used to be.

It reminded Dianna of one of those frozen moments from a cartoon when the coyote hangs, anticipating a fall, a thousand feet above the canyon floor, just after the roadrunner has cut away his rope bridge.

Esau seemed to drop the twenty feet to the soft earth in slow motion. His fall crumpled the rain gutter into a twisted and flattened V.

He ran like a madman to the duck pond and thrust in his hands, cooling the severed fingers and burns in icy water.

He roared like a bull elephant in great agony.

"Gaaaaaaaaaarrrrr-gaaaaaa!"

Why Esau hurt so much? How can hand hurt so much?

The pain made Esau wild, and a rage to kill was building within him.

Booteful make so much hurt. Esau start to think booteful be like dog or Jacques. Why she not understand?

Why does she not feel his need? Why does booteful not see Esau is booteful?

Why Ag-ga not come back and Goody sleep so long and not wake up? Goody fix Esau's hurts.

He felt the sores on his body and sucked at the bleeding, throbbing agony that was his mangled hand.

Esau want 'ove booteful or break booteful?

Many things Esau not understand.

In her room, Dianna scooped up the two bloody finger parts in the ash shovel and threw them into the fire.

PART IV

A kanji that is formed of two basic calligraphic components—the upper right symbol being the character for a human head, the other sweeping slash, a stroke that means to advance or to move forward.

A crying lost child
Stumbles over
Dark fields
Catching fireflies.

—Ryusui

Jade and man
Both are shaped
By hard tools.

Chinese proverb

42

Now there was a steady draft blowing in the room through the broken window. Dianna wedged the door again, and as she put some pieces of a smashed chair into the fire, she realized that her supply of wood was already getting low.

Dianna took down all the pictures and paintings from the walls and wiggled the hooks and nails out of the plaster. Using the mason's hammer, she nailed up the bedspread over the opening. It helped to cut the wind, but in places, the fabric flapped between the nails. Unless it was warm outside, the bedroom was going to stay chilly.

The portrait of Thomas Wilkinson stared up at her from the place she had set it on the floor. The eyes in the work were noticeably similar to Esau's. Dianna smashed the painting's frame, threw the pieces on the fire, then set the canvas on the mantel. She decided to keep the portrait as a target, a grim summation of Esau's character, a reminder that he was as capable of selfish and deadly action as his ancestor depicted in the painting.

Dianna remembered the hatred and the growing taste for vengeance that she had seen in Thomas Wilkinson's great great grandson's eyes. How long would it take before Esau's feelings would turn completely cold? The thought of the man-thing jumping on her body, as he had done to Jacques, breaking her bones, crushing her internal organs in a fit of rage, was not a pretty image.

Dianna opened a book, tore it in half, ruffled up the pages, and fed it to the fire. As she started to tear a second book she realized it was the room's copy of the Bible. She opened it to the Old Testament and looked for "Jacob and Esau" in the page headings.

In Genesis 26:16 she found the story of Jacob and Esau, the sons of Isaac. Jacob was a smooth-skinned, plain man who dwelt in the fields. His older brother, Esau, was a hairy man and a hunter of beasts. Isaac loved Esau, and Isaac's wife Rebekah loved Jacob.

One day when Esau came home starving from the hunt, Jacob convinced his brother to sell his birthright for a bowl of potage. Dianna thought, Esau must have had an impulsive appetite or else he must have been very, very stupid.

Years later, when Isaac was old and his eyes were dim, the time came for him to pass on the birthright to one of his sons. Rebekah put the skins of goats on Jacob's face and neck and dressed him in Esau's clothes, so that Isaac was deceived and lawfully passed the birthright to Jacob.

There's no way the trade of potage for birthright could have been completely on the up and up, Dianna realized. No, the deal didn't seem like one that would have "stood up in court," so to speak, or Rebekah wouldn't have had to go to the trouble of costuming Jacob. It stood to reason that Isaac probably would not have recognized the birthright/potage deal as binding.

I'm sure Esau had no love lost for his mother when he found out how she had been in on the scam. Yes, admitted Dianna, Goody picked the perfect name for her grandson. It's probably got five thousand years of bad karma.

She took down the old volume of *Curiosities and Anomalies of Medicine, 1901,* one of the few books remaining on the shelf in the room, and checked the appendix. Information about humpbacks was in a chapter called "Minor Terata."

The chapter began with a section dedicated to the ancient belief of divining the future from the birth defects of newborn infants. The writer of the book cited Cicero, who believed that a child born with a deformity was the inevitable consequence of the positions of the stars and the planets at the time of the child's birth.

Therefore, deduced Cicero, the observation of newborn human monstrosities was as significant as the observation of the astrological phenomena. And thus, by studying the births of deformed infants, one could predict the future with the same certainty as one might predict the future from various movements of the stars and planets themselves.

The book went on to translate, from ancient Babylonian writings, various astrological predictions based on the births of deformed infants:

"When a woman gives birth to an infant that has the beard already grown out, the land will be blessed with abundant rains."

"When a woman gives birth to an infant that has six toes on each foot, the people of the world will be injured."

"When a woman gives birth to an infant that has no well-marked sex, calamity will seize upon the land; the master of the house shall have no happiness."

"When a woman gives birth to an infant whose back is bent, affliction will seize upon the countryside and the master of the house will die."

Interesting, Dianna thought, that the ancient writers started each sentence with "When a *woman* gives birth to a . . ." What an insidious way of putting all the blame and the guilt for the child's deformity on the woman's head. It says nothing about "When a man fathers an infant who . . ."

Later, in the "Minor Terata" chapter, under a paragraph heading "Curvatures of the Spine," "Kyphosis," the proper medical term for a humpback, was defined as being the condition of having a posterior curvature of the spinal column.

The book further commented that there were several medieval superstitions concerning humpbacks—commonly held beliefs that the touching of the hunch of a humpback could

   . . . bring a person good luck.

   . . . make a barren woman fertile.

   . . . cure impotence in a man.

The writer attributed all of these beliefs to the similarity in shape of the hunch of a humpback to a pregnant woman's stomach.

The book nauseated Dianna. She tore its brittle backing into several pieces, crumpled the pages, and added the tome to the flames.

43

After the baseboards had gone out, Dianna discovered she could heat her room until it was nice and cozy by filling the tub with scalding water. The blown fuse obviously didn't have anything to do with the water heater. The moist air spread the warmth very well, and now, with the broken window, Dianna realized that she was going to have to keep the tub filled all the time. The only drawback was the constant presence of condensation on the walls, which was starting to incubate little splotches of black mold.

Taking a bath continued to be slightly frustrating to Dianna. She could never relax and shake off the need to be alert. So, with an ear out for trouble, she lay in the hot water and considered every possible angle of a plan that was formulating in her mind. It depended primarily on surprise and required that she be up and out to the barn in the wee hours of the morning while Esau was still sleeping.

One problem would be how to get herself up before dawn. Dianna hadn't brought a travel alarm, and there was no clock in the room. She had never been good at waking herself up, but this time she would simply have to will herself to do it. Dianna focused her mind, trying to set it like a clock.

She did aerobics for forty minutes, concentrating on legs and upper body strength. Afterward, she felt good, a bit achy, but much better prepared to run.

Dianna laid out a pair of jogging shoes that she thought would be the best for wet grass and dressed in the clothes she would wear in the morning for the attempt. After setting out her wallet with all her cash, she climbed into bed.

Now, as she pulled herself up onto the high mattress, the impression was even stronger that the towering oak frame was like an altar. Lying back in the center of the bed, Dianna had a feeling she was one of those long-dead Renaissance noblewomen, stretched out on a subterranean sarcophagus, arms crossed in sleep, immortalized in stone below some towering French cathedral.

She saw herself as a petite, girlish carved figure, as she had appeared in her early teens, like many of the effigies on the tombs. To make the illusion complete, thought Dianna, the echoing chant of a requiem should be heard.

In seconds she had drifted off into a light, dream-charged sleep.

In her dream Dianna was hurled down into a pit, or was it up to heaven? In the vague nature of her dream, she couldn't be sure of the direction, only that she was catapulted back through the religious history of her youth.

The familiar but forgotten voices of nuns and priests from her parochial school and her parish came at her in the night.

"Thou shalt love the Lord thy God with thy whole heart and thy whole soul and thy whole mind."

"Children who die without baptism are deprived of the . . ."

". . . *Spiritus sancti.*"

"Devotion to Mary has always been an integral part of Catholicism. . . ."

"Pray for one another and the healing of your souls."

"False teachers will be thrust down to hell, chained there in the abyss, to await . . ."

"*In nomine Patris et Filii . . .*"

"It will be noted that in these scriptural references the concept of eternal punishment is always . . ."

She awoke to consciousness for a moment and remembered snatches of her vision. I wonder if I should have prayed before getting into bed, she thought, then drifted off again.

It proved to be a long night of cruel and restless sleep. Dianna tossed and turned, caught between an unconscious fear of oversleeping, and dreams of stations of the cross and the receiving of sacraments of goose flesh from the hand of a faceless pontiff.

44

Dianna awoke with a jolt. The dawn sun hung just below the horizon. A few geese were honking, and the horses were wild with hunger, kicking at their stalls and whinnying. She estimated she had overslept her ideal waking time by an hour.

After silently lacing her shoes, Dianna went to the door hole. Esau lay in Goody's room, on his spot at the foot of the bed, his back to Dianna.

A log was lying on the hall floor. What is that doing there? she thought, immediately on her guard.

Esau must have brought it up in the night without my hearing. Was it a battering ram to break down the door? But the log seemed much too long for that.

Besides, Esau's attempts on the door seemed to be easing off. Not managing to break down either this door or the door to the icehouse may have discouraged him. Also, Esau's hands had to be giving him a lot of pain.

After taking the time to quietly restoke the fire and to review the steps of her plan, Dianna pulled out the wedges and slowly drew back the bars.

The hinges popped.

Every little noise of her feet on the floor seemed like thunder.

She kept an eye on Esau through the hole, but he was still breathing regularly.

Dianna opened the door only enough to squeeze out.

Expecting at any second to have to retreat to the safety of the room, she studied Esau's back, but the man-thing didn't move.

She eased out the door and was heading down the first step

when Esau walked out of Goody's room. He was wide awake.

He looked at her and grinned a grin of victory.

As Dianna almost fell headlong down the stairs, she saw him pick up the long length of log.

What was he going to do with the tree trunk? she wondered in terror. But she had no intention of hanging around to find out.

The bastard had been faking sleep, she realized. Her plan was out of the question—there was no way it would ever possibly work now.

Remembering that the elevator car was still on the ground floor, she bolted down the stairs and around to the metal door. She pulled away the painting and hit both buttons on the wall.

The elevator door, moving slower than Dianna thought possible, opened.

As fast as she could, she entered and pushed Door Close. Seconds later Esau's fists were pounding outside the elevator car door.

Dianna hurriedly considered her alternatives: up to the second floor or down to the basement? Without a workable plan she was lost.

She pressed 2. Improvise, ad lib, it was like being on stage alone when another actor fails to make an entrance—keep talking, keep moving. And most importantly—get back to the safety of your room.

As the car moved upward she could hear Esau banging below. Evidently, she thought, the workings of the elevator were kept secret from him. That was why the buttons were hidden behind the painting. That knowledge gave her something to work with.

The car door opened, and Dianna panicked. The length of the log was jammed between the door to her room and the opposite wall.

That was his plan. The man-thing had figured out a way to keep her *out* of her sanctuary. There was no way she could get into her room without removing the log. It had to weigh over a hundred pounds, and she knew from the way it was pushing against the wall that Esau had wedged it in place with considerable force.

Esau, alerted by the sound of the elevator door opening, came rushing up the stairs.

Dianna pushed B, the car door shut, and the elevator moved downward. The lift seemed to take forever to reach its destination. At least he doesn't know how to operate this thing, she thought.

With a shock Dianna realized that she hadn't replaced the oil painting on the first floor, and Esau might see the buttons. I've got to keep the elevator door open, she thought, so that Esau can't summon the car and follow me into the basement.

Finally the lift opened onto the basement kitchen. Dianna positioned a bench so that the elevator couldn't close.

The automatic door kept opening and shutting, slamming into the bench. As long as it was in place the car would not move.

Dianna studied the well-equipped room. Along one wall stood a number of large refrigerators—some not in use and others with frozen meats and vegetables.

A hallway led from the kitchen to a ramp that rose to a metal door that Dianna knew opened into the backyard. But the metal door was padlocked from the inside, and the basement windows were only narrow slits too small to get through. "So there is no exit," Dianna said to herself.

I'm safe here for a little while, she thought, but the slamming elevator door made her nervous. From the refrigerator she took a carton of milk and drank. Then another noise began.

Running to a stairway that led up from the basement to the first floor, she saw at the top of the stairs another metal door. Dianna realized that she was looking at the door that faced the elevator on the first floor above.

Esau was trying to bash it in. On the inside was a bar that dropped into metal brackets set in the door and door frame. It didn't look as if it would hold for very long.

Thinking she could find safety there, Dianna rushed into the elevator car. But she realized immediately that she would go crazy if she had to hide in the confined space of the small box. Besides, she thought, Esau might eventually find which button to push to open the doors.

Then she noticed the ceiling of the elevator. Over her head was a square trapdoor.

Knowing she had only seconds, Dianna grabbed a bag and

stuffed it full of groceries and an assortment of kitchen implements, including several butcher knives.

After tossing the goods, along with a bar stool, into the elevator, she hurriedly checked the first-floor door at the top of the stairs, only to find it almost caved in. Dianna jiggled the bar and decided that she could lift it, even though the brackets were now slightly bent.

Timing would have to be perfect if her plan was going to work.

She returned to the elevator, pulled out the bench, took a deep breath, pushed 1, and let the door close.

A second after it left, Dianna pressed the Up button to summon the car back after it made its stop.

She raced up the flight of stairs to the battered first-floor door, listened, and heard the car open at 1.

Esau had ceased his pounding as soon as he heard the car move. Through the crack under the basement door, she watched the shadows of Esau's feet. He did exactly as she had expected. He stepped into the open lift.

As she heard it close and start downward, Dianna tried to raise the bar on the metal door.

It was jammed from Esau's attack. Dianna was frantic. She pulled with all her strength—heaving, straining, and hitting the metal brackets with her bare hands.

It didn't move. Just as she heard the elevator door in the basement slide open and Esau step out, the bar clattered open.

Next came the big gamble. Dianna launched herself out the cellar door and pushed the Up button on the first-floor wall control panel. Then she ran down the hall toward the stairs that led to the second floor and her room, but instead of going up, she broke off to her right and hid against the wall in the dining room.

Esau stomped up the stairs from the basement. Thinking Dianna was heading for her room, he passed her by and took the stairs to the second floor.

Dianna circled the other way through the dining room into the bar, returning to the first-floor elevator door. She could hear the car coming, but it was taking more time than expected.

She took a second to quietly rehang the oil painting so that Esau would not discover the controls.

The elevator stopped on her floor and opened. Dianna

pushed 2, held the door open with her foot, and called, "Esau, Esau, I'm down here, on the first floor."

As soon as she could hear his footsteps thumping down toward her from the second floor, Dianna let the elevator door close.

When the car next opened on 2, Esau was downstairs pounding on the first-floor elevator door.

She glimpsed the shotgun where it lay outside Jacques's room and was about to step out and get it, but Esau had caught on. He rounded the turn from the hall on the first floor and came up the stairs toward her three steps at a time. His weight hit the elevator door seconds after it closed.

Inside the elevator Dianna stood on the stool and opened the narrow escape hatch in the ceiling. It proved to be a tight squeeze for her, so she was confident that Esau would never be able to get through.

The roof of the car when it was on the second floor was just a little below the attic beams. She shoved the groceries up through the small opening, pulled herself up, then carefully closed the little escape door.

On her hands and knees Dianna pushed the groceries along the floorboards in front of her, causing small clouds of dust to puff up around her in the dry attic air.

Her sensation of optimism was complete, exhilarating. Dianna couldn't ever remember a time when the taste of victory had been quite as delicious. Nor had she ever enjoyed making a fool out of an opponent—but this time had been different. That's what must trigger the competitive instinct, she realized—the opiate high of success and triumph.

A flurry of bats were returning from their night excursions. She casually waved one away with her hand, opened the trapdoor to her room and wondered, Are bats edible?

45

As the sharp high of adrenaline euphoria wore off, Dianna's satisfaction over her foray and her nice haul of food and utensils slowly turned into a dull fatigue of anger and frustration.

After all, she was still a prisoner, still under a sentence of death.

Her escape attempt had not gotten off the ground, and she had never once had an opportunity to take the initiative.

Esau had tricked her, first by feigning sleep and then by blocking the door with the log.

Dianna's face flushed with rage, and frustration. That sneaky son of a bitch, how dare he try to barricade me out of my room. Biting off mouthfuls from a dry loaf of Italian bread, she called to him, "Esau. . . . Esau."

He quickly found the sound of the voice, and his mouth fell open in amazement when he saw that she was back in her room.

Dianna did an imitation of Esau's growling and began mocking him. "Gaaaaaagha-gooo!"

She made a face out the hole, parodying his ogling eyeball. "Poor Esau. *Poverto,* Esau. I feel so sad that little air-head Esau is so horny."

Switching to a Southern accent, she said, "My, but aren't you just the most degenerate thing I ever laid eyes on."

Esau stood listening, his head cocked at an angle, straining to understand.

She continued, "What a big, filthy, sleazy, slimy fella you

217

are. And such a stupid cretin that you actually think you make
my little heart go pitty-pat, pitty-pat."

"Pit-ti-pat," echoed Esau and smiled at his verbal accom-
plishment.

"That's right, you son of swine, pitty-pat, pitty-pat. Why
don't you just put your fat scarface next to this little hole in the
door, and I'll give you a nice lethal present right between those
big, ugly-as-shit brown eyes?"

Dianna took a long butcher knife and held it behind her
back.

Esau came closer and started to put his face to the opening,
but he stopped. He was wary from the spray and the ashes. He
grabbed the doorknob and shook it.

"No, no." Dianna's grip tightened on the handle of the
knife. She smiled and said, "Come here, you scum-sucking
hunk of carrion, and booteful will give you a great big surgical
kiss."

Dianna put her lips next to the hole and puckered. "Come
on. Come to Mama. Come to 'Mama the Ripper.'"

Esau hesitated.

She made kissing noises that sounded more like a plunger
clearing the drain of a sink.

He hesitated.

She made more kissing noises.

He just stood looking at her with his head cocked to the side.
The pain of his hand and the hurt of dozens of burns and sores
were very much with him.

Dianna's anger was seething, ready to explode—she was
being driven by a desperate need to even the score, to strike
back with all the venom and disgust that raged within her.
Conscience and reason were gone, washed away by the red
heat of a desire to hurt, to cut her opponent viciously—to the
quick and through the bone.

She baited him. "Oh, come closer, *merde* breath, let me do
a little plastic surgery on your face."

Esau took the door handle and shook it again.

Clever bastard, thought Dianna, he's got some kind of sixth
sense. She kept her sweet tone of voice. "Come here, Esau.
Kiss, puke, kiss. I want to give you a nice little eyeball shave."

Esau moved closer.

"Yes, scabhead, come try to kiss booteful." She put her lips to the hole again. Her hand with the knife was trembling.

Esau put his mouth to the hole. Dianna's hand was shaking violently; she could hardly hold onto the weapon. She stood a moment watching his grotesque mouth trying to kiss through the hole, then she slashed at his face.

The blade struck the wood, and Esau jumped back with only a tiny cut over his lip. He felt the bleeding spot and looked at her, not sure what had happened.

Esau's romantic mood was undaunted by the incident. Dianna thought, He must not have seen the knife, or fully realized my intention.

She kept the blade hidden and tried to lure him within striking range with a number of different approaches, but her efforts were only rewarded with longing looks from the man-thing, who steadfastly remained at a safe distance.

Her inability to even the score ate at her, enraged her even further—and made her lose control. The urge to lash back exploded in her brain, a nova of white-hot light. She threw the knife at the wall and yelled in frustration, "Aggggggggh!

"Do you know what your problem is, Esau?" she said.

Esau stared, understanding the inflection of her words but not their true meaning.

"You're ugly, that's your problem. You're ugly as dog shit. Do you understand 'dog shit'? Well, you're it. You are a notch *below* ugly dog shit. Understand?"

Esau looked at her with a big, pouting frown. "Ugly" was a word he had learned all too well from the neighborhood children. He hated the word. The word was a lie.

"There isn't a woman on this planet or in hell for that matter that would want such an ugly thing as you to put a finger on her."

He looked at her, deeply hurt.

"You're probably the ugliest motherfucker that ever called himself a man."

"Esau boo-te-ful," he said emphatically as if it were a fact obvious to all.

Dianna let out a high-pitched, cackling laugh that went on for a solid minute.

Esau cringed against the wall.

Dianna went to the bathroom and took down a framed

mirror. "Come here, you ugly piece of shit. Look at yourself. You have an asshole for a head."

She mocked him, "Esau ugly." She got into the meat of the word. "Uuuug-leeee."

Esau moved in closer.

Dianna put the mirror over the hole saying, "You don't believe me? Come on, take a look at yourself in the mirror."

He had seen mirrors before. But to him a mirror was a thing that lied. That's what Goody had always told him. That the reflection was wrong. Goody always said that Esau was booteful.

"Look at yourself," said Dianna. "That's you in there. And you are one uuuug-leeee cadaver fucker."

Goody lie? No, Goody no lie.

But why booteful say these things?

Tears ran down Esau's cheeks. His mouth puckered, and his chin quivered like a baby.

"Uuuug-leeee," jeered Dianna. "Uuuug-leeee."

Abruptly Esau turned and ran down the hall and into Jacques's room.

Dianna collapsed on the floor. She felt disgusted with herself. I didn't have to do that, she thought. The LaBianca mouth strikes again. It was like kicking a retarded person or a little boy.

Stop! Stop! her thoughts screamed. He's not a boy. He's a murderer and would-be rapist. He deserves a quick and painless death or at the least imprisonment for life.

Then why do I feel guilty? she asked herself.

How can I assess a person's responsibility for their actions when they have one-quarter of a brain? He's not even a human being.

Yes, he is.

No, he is not!

Her thoughts came in a torrent of rationalizations.

How am I supposed to react to a killer-child? . . .

Or is it a retarded killer? . . .

Or is it a killer-beast that merits only extinction?

It thinks, it feels, it loves—at least it loves Goody.

But it is evil, a flesh-craving he-devil.

If I escape alive from this inn, he has got to be caged—

locked away from all human beings for the rest of his "unnatural" existence.

Fool! I'm a fool. If I behave as if I have even a hint of a conscience, I am going to end up very dead.

I've got to steel my thinking, she avowed, and when it comes to dealing with the man-thing, I've got to be as cold-blooded as the blade of a guillotine.

Dianna was furious with herself. Why did my hand shake? I had nothing to fear. If I had stabbed Esau, I could have seriously wounded him with no danger to myself. The game might have been over. She made a fist with the hand that held the knife. Jesus, I am still trembling.

I cannot let myself be afraid to kill him. No, "kill" wasn't the correct word; "execute," she decided, was the word she should use in connection with her purpose.

My life is on the line. This man could fatally hurt me in ten different ways, or he might rape me, or he might kill me out of vengeance or sheer hatred.

Dianna couldn't believe what she saw as she replaced the mirror on the bathroom wall: a stranger, ten years older than herself, with dark rings under the eyes, large bruises on her forehead, a chunk of raw scalp showing, and a face puffy and covered with splinters and small cuts.

A triangle of hair that pointed backward on her forehead had turned silver. My God, I'm going gray from fright, she thought. The face in the mirror seemed alien to her, and yet it bore a resemblance to someone else, someone she couldn't quite place.

Then she made the connection: it was the Wilkinson face in the canvas on the mantel that she looked like—particularly about the eyes and hair. Mr. Thomas even had a touch of gray on the forehead. Yet the likeness was not so much of the features of some attitude or inner quality.

Dianna laughed and said, "It's Dianna LaBianca now appearing nightly at Fenwick's beautiful Wilkinson Inn. Come see her right before your very eyes transubstantiate into a Wilkinson." The problem is, thought Dianna, how do I keep the show from closing in Fenwick? The last thing I want to do is "die out of town."

• • •

In the room down the hall, Esau dug through the closet that
Jacques and Agnes had shared, selecting items that caught his
fancy.

Esau ugly?

He moved before the wall, trying to find the right place to
stand in order to cast the perfect shadow. The white plaster
didn't hide as much as the fieldstones in the cellar, but after
many awkward contortions he figured out how to make his
image pleasing and symmetrical.

*Why the booteful not see Esau booteful? Maybe booteful has
eyes like Goody that need glass over them to see.*

He opened a tube of lipstick. *Esau show booteful he not
ugly.*

After defrosting some packages of vegetables on the fire,
Dianna had a mini-feast. Along with food to last a couple of
days, she had four butcher knives, a spoon, three forks, a pair
of tongs, and a nasty-looking meat cleaver.

I should just dig in and wait it out, thought Dianna. With
Goody dead, someone has to appear in a few days. And where
was Agnes? What had happened to her and the van?

Dennis? Wait a minute, what day is this? It took her a few
minutes to think through the morass of days and nights. "It's
Friday! How can that be?" She thought it over again. . . .
Monday to Wednesday morning in the cellar, Wednesday night
and Thursday night here. . . . "Yes, today is Friday."

Dennis was expecting my call by this morning. Is there a
chance he'll try to call me at the inn when I don't call? If he
does, he'll find the phone out of order. Would he then drive
out? No, not likely, certainly not right away. He'll stay in
Boston and wait for me to call.

Eventually someone will show up, but when? Today, tomorrow, in three days, a week? But "when" could be too late—in
an hour could be too late.

A knock sounded on Dianna's door. Esau stood at a
respectful distance from the door hole, dressed in a ridiculous,
eclectic ensemble. His hair was brushed back, giving him the
appearance of a madcap classical composer.

He wore lipstick and reeked of cologne. The poncho blanket
was replaced by a lumberjack shirt haphazardly buttoned and a

tie that instead of being under the collar circled his bare neck.
Over the shirt he had somehow just managed to get on a tuxedo
jacket. The seams were split at the shoulders, and the sleeves
were four inches too short for Esau's long arms. A belt was
buckled across the shirt at the level of his chest. The trousers
were a pair of Jacques's work pants and had been put on
backward. The length of the pants was too long by five inches,
and Esau was walking on the cuffs with only his bare toes
showing. Neither the shirt nor the trousers reached to his waist,
and there was a hairy band of skin exposed below his navel. On
his head was one of Agnes's flowered hats, and around his
neck were various pieces of jewelry. Two ribbons adorned his
ears. In one hand he held an assortment of plastic flowers
gathered from the table settings downstairs.

He held them out to her. "Booteful."

"Well, well," said Dianna, "if it isn't the malformed
gentleman caller."

"Pit-ti-pat," he said.

I'm being courted, she realized, by a fool.

Esau struck a series of ludicrous poses. At first Dianna
couldn't figure out what he was doing. Then he flexed his
biceps, and it dawned on her that he was imitating his pictures
of fashion models.

Dianna sang, "There he is, Miss America." The deep curve
of Esau's spine, his short legs, and his hairiness, combined
with his animated actions, gave the impression of a demented
circus bear. Or a Charlie Chaplin doll created in the genetics
laboratory of some grandson of Dr. Frankenstein.

Esau leaned casually against the wall and said, "Esau
booteful."

The ridiculousness of the situation wasn't lost on Dianna,
but playing this game was beginning to grate on her frazzled
nerves.

Esau offered the bouquet again, "Booteful," and jiggled the
handle of the door, begging her with his eyes.

This thing, she thought, this creature dares to woo me with
goddamn *plastic* flowers. All the frustrations of the last days
came to a head. She stood and looked at him with glaring eyes
and thought, Perhaps it's time to even up the odds. He thinks
he can seduce me, she thought, well, let him think for a
moment that he has succeeded.

She calmly took a small bottle from her purse, carefully unscrewed the top and set it within easy reach. Then in a deep husky voice she summoned him, "Esau. Esau."

He watched her hopefully, keeping his distance. To give him a better view, she moved back to the center of the room, which she knew would let him feel secure enough to glue his eye to the door hole.

Turning her back and imitating a belly dancer, she cast seductive glances at him over her shoulder. Dianna pulled off her jacket, spun it around, and tossed it in the corner. Coming around to face him, slowly, one button at a time, she opened her blouse.

Esau's eyeball at the hole was bugging out of his head.

Dianna presented her back, slipped her arms out of the blouse, and as she turned to face him held it up to cover herself. She tugged at one corner of the shirt with a finger and pulled it languidly across her body. Her hands caressed her hips and went into her jeans. Popping the snap she pulled the zipper down inch by inch. Dianna circled away then slid her hands coyly down to her hips. With a slow dance movement, she crossed over to the small bottle and hid it in her palm. She reached out with both arms and did a high stepping walk toward the door.

As she neared the hole, Dianna was amazed to see Esau move back a few inches. For a moment she was angry: Come on, sucker, don't lose interest now. But when she saw his face, she knew why he had retreated, and it wasn't out of lack of interest.

His features were distorted with ecstasy. Esau was leaning against the banister, eyes half-shut, legs apart. The work pants were around his knees. His hand stroked himself rhythmically.

Dianna thought, His testicles are hungry. Yes, that's what happens when a man gets horny—he gets hard when his balls begin to crave like two ravenous little stomachs.

She remembered the greedy blood-eating plant from *Little Shop of Horrors*. Yes, that's what a man's sexual drive is all about—it's a ruthless "feed me" impulse of the two hungry stomachs hanging below his penis.

Esau began pelvic contractions, and beads of sweat gathered on his face. He groaned and snorted. The palming motions increased in tempo and intensity. With his other hand he reached down and began kneading his balls. Throwing his head back and bellowing, he began to finish his business.

As Esau dropped to one knee Dianna took a mouthful of nail polish remover and spat it in his face. It hit him in the right eye, and he slapped his hand over his eyelid as he screamed and came at the same time.

Dianna couldn't read his reaction. Was it pleasure or pain? For a short time the burning of his eye seemed to heighten his enjoyment. Then he began clawing at his eye and, raging in anguish, slammed into the wall.

Spitting and gagging, Dianna ran into the bathroom to rinse the polish remover from her mouth. Saliva ran down her chin from the effects of the chemical. She knew the acrid taste would linger in her mouth for a long time, but the image of Esau in the throes of passion would stay with her forever.

46

Her heart pounding, Dianna wrapped herself in a blanket and sat on the bed.

I lost it; my hatred and loathing got to me and overcame my reason, she admitted. I should never have gone to that length, even to win the slightest victory.

Something bestial and primitive in her had been stirred—though not by Esau, she realized, but by her own charade. As an actress, she possessed the right instinct, which was to play a role from the inside. To portray a stripper, she knew that she had to think like a stripper. She had put her head into the kind of dull-eyed come-fuck-me thoughts that she knew were a part of the stripper's act.

Dianna wanted to masturbate and vomit at the same time.

The awareness that some small part of her had been turned on filled her with both guilt and self-hate. I should be in control of this kind of reaction, she thought. Dianna remembered acting classes and the times she had played hookers or sensual characters. It always got me going, she recalled.

There should be a switch in my body—an off/on "turn on" switch. Then when a situation arose like this one, or even when she was in a relationship with a man like Arthur, the switch could be set to the desired "off" position.

Becoming aroused was my own stupid fault, she admitted. My striptease for Esau was unnecessary. I could have come up with some other plan that would have lured him within range of the nail polish.

She had wanted just one good clear shot at his eyes. With

Esau as blind as Oedipus, the odds would have swung to my favor. It would have been worth it if the plan had worked.

An unpleasant thought struck her: Was I turning him on as a cruel way to attract him, or was I just turning him on, for a selfish reason? Dianna knew there had to be an element of domination in what she had done. I did have momentary power over Esau. I had the control and the total attention of that bulging eye.

Esau thinks he is handsome. What a joke.

Then Dianna laughed and wondered, What if he is? What if Esau is the quintessential example of living beauty? Perhaps he is the normal one.

He could be. Why not? Esau is convinced that he is handsome.

Perhaps I am the one with the misconception. *I* could be the monster. I could be the misshapen freak.

No, Dianna, no. You are losing it, you are simply losing your grip. She tried to reassure herself, "No, Dianna, you are not the beast.

"You are a child of God. A daughter of Christ and of Buddha. And of whatever is out there. . . ." Her voice trailed off.

Dianna was not at all convinced. She was sure of nothing.

A sprinkle of April rain fell lightly outside. A light wind rustled the budded branches.

She knew the rain would be good for the seedlings. The newly set-out plants seemed to quiver with joy as the falling drops hit their wilted leaves. She looked out the window: The tree and the young plants had become Jacques's umbrella. And he is returning the favor by feeding the roots of the sweet william and the sugar maple with his essence. What an unlikely end for Jacques—a reincarnation into sugar.

Suddenly there was a disturbance among the geese. They honked and ran in a clump toward the pond. At the edge of the forest, stalking out of the thick brush, was a red fox. What does he think he is doing? she thought. Wait a minute, how do I know that's a "he"? It could just as easily be a "she." As the animal crept in on the gaggle, Dianna leaned out the window and shouted, "Get out of here! They're mine!"

The fox looked up at Dianna in surprise, turned tail, and ran.

The sun kept popping in and out between rain clouds, causing momentary brilliances of sun showers. What time of day is it? she wondered. Is there a time? Is time being held still, while I step outside of my real life? I have been in this satanic room forever and will continue to be here forever.

The Hitchcock premise continued to nag at her. Is the victim always—in some petty way—deserving? But even if I bought that premise, she asked herself, why would I be deserving? Because I'm in the "Theater"?

Am I guilty because I am a dilettante in the business of supplying pleasure to other dilettanti?

It's true I don't do any real work, not in the sense of manual labor, or of supplying useful, life-sustaining services. But, she chuckled, if I am deserving, so would be Hitchcock—after all, we're in the same business.

How long would the door continue to hold up?

She peeked through the hole, looking for Esau. He lay curled at the foot of Goody's bed. Though his right eye was slightly swollen and half-closed, he didn't appear to be in pain. If I'd only gotten both eyes, she thought. Damn. Esau's head nodded, and his one working eyelid sagged. Typical male, thought Dianna, he doesn't want to stay up and talk—he comes, he falls asleep.

Twisted dreams, visions reflected and re-reflected by distorted mirrors, passed though Esau's mind—Dianna taking him to a baseball game. A game like the one he had gone to with his Dada so long ago.

Esau and booteful together. Together fun.

He saw Dianna and himself eating the wonderful hot dogs in the giant ballpark and riding home in the backseat of the red car. That night they slept together on a rock floor covered with fresh straw.

Booteful 'ove Esau.

Esau smiled in his sleep as he pictured the two of them running hand in hand through fields of yellow flowers. He saw them both dressed like the couples in his magazines. Together they ran to the cemetery, where Dianna gave him chocolate bars and let him lie with his head on her lap, and they sat side by side on his Dada's grave.

Booteful sad too. She understand.

A moan came from Esau as he dreamed of Dianna lifting up her skirt and offering herself to him over a tombstone. He wildly entered her, thrusting and thrusting, but before the great pleasure came, she had transformed into Goody and was calling him a bad boy and hitting him.

Then Dianna became a skeleton with a pitchfork, who kept jabbing it into Esau's hand and then into his eye and then kept sticking him with it again and again until he tore the skull off the figure of death that was torturing him.

And Esau stomped on her skeleton, breaking it to pieces, and then he scattered the bones everywhere across the fields and forests of the inn.

PART V

A kanji which can mean "a journey that will lead to knowledge."

I am so sorry
To have to die
At this time
When plum trees bloom.

—Raizan

To light a lamp before Buddha
First extinguish yourself.

Chinese proverb

47

When Dennis arrived, Dianna was going over details of the layout of the barn, trying to remember where everything was located. She had the hot water on full in the bathtub, letting it pour down the overflow drain as she tried to warm up the bathroom.

If she had heard Dennis drive up to the front of the inn, she could have warned him. But she wasn't expecting him and had no idea he was there until he called out . . . and then it was too late.

That Tuesday night at the antiques store, when Esau terrified Dierdre and slammed the store's owner against the wall, the hunchback had created a local commotion. The elderly man had gone to the hospital and was recovering while wavering in and out of consciousness. During his waking moments he only managed to babble a few words.

Reports of a red-faced monster on the loose, terrorizing the Vermont highways, hit the local papers and earned a small mention in Thursday's *Boston Globe*. Dennis, who was always hoping to hear some news that would relate to Anne, kept a close scrutiny on the press in the area. Dierdre's picture in the article reminded him a little of his sister, and he called to check into the story.

By Thursday he had connected with local officials who informed Dennis that the high school girl was rational and that she appeared to be telling the truth. Dennis made the decision to drive out Friday morning. The next call he placed was to the Wilkinson Inn, to see if he could get a room.

The phone line was busy and stayed that way. When he asked the operator to try the connection, Dennis was informed that the line was out of order.

Dennis was annoyed that the phone wasn't working, because he had found the inn convenient. He figured that if he just drove out there, he could probably talk Agnes into giving him a room.

Friday morning en route to meet with Dierdre, Dennis stopped to turn into the inn from the highway but was surprised to see the chain padlocked across the drive. He made a decision to pass by later in the day, after he had looked into the story.

Later that afternoon, Dennis beeped into his Boston answering machine and was surprised and disappointed to find there was no message from Dianna. He had no desire to make the long drive back to Boston and again tried to call the Wilkinson and found the phone still out of order. The operator told him that they were planning to send a repairman out to take a look as soon as possible.

Dennis was sure someone was at the inn and decided to drive himself there—chain or no chain, reservation or not.

Near one of the stone columns beside the highway entrance, Dennis managed to flatten some of the brush, which was damp from the intermittent showers, and was able to drive around the padlocked chain.

As he came up the circular drive in front of the main building, everything seemed quiet and normal. The grounds and the downstairs of the building were dark, and there were a few lights on upstairs and no vehicles out front, which confirmed Dennis's theory that Agnes and Jacques had gone off somewhere, leaving Goody alone. As far as Dennis knew, Dianna was in Maine, and he had left a special message for her on his answering machine, asking her to leave a number.

As Dennis parked he couldn't see the bent and broken ladder below Dianna's window around the side of the building, but he did notice that the glass of the front storm door was broken.

At first, he thought a robbery had taken place, and he had an impulse to turn around and get the police, but he realized that technically he was trespassing and he might have some trouble explaining himself. Dennis decided he should find out what exactly was going on before he spoke to anybody.

• • •

Esau was in the basement, cleaning out the last carton of ice cream that was left in the freezer, when he heard Dennis's car come up the drive. He hoped it was Agnes and crept up the basement stairs excitedly and peeked out the front window. He was disappointed and angry to see that it was Dennis.

How well he remembered the scent of the man from the grounds and the glimpses of him through his icehouse window. And the times he had walked too close beside Esau's booteful. And the night when he had almost taken the booteful away.

Booteful Esau's now. She his.

He uttered a low-pitched, quiet growl, similar to the warning he had directed at Lancelot before their final encounter.

Esau break man. Break man dead.

Esau put down the ice cream and crept off into the darkness of the first floor.

Dianna was still upstairs, and the noise of the water pouring in the tub obliterated all sounds from outside. The black mold was multiplying in blotches the size of fifty-cent pieces on the tiles.

Dennis was uneasy as he opened the broken front door. The day had been strange enough already. Before leaving Boston he had gotten the press department to print up credentials that would get him in to see Dierdre.

What Dennis had told Dianna about his career that night over dinner was only partially true. He had realized that he would never be able to fool Dianna into believing he was a writer. But his family did in fact own a part of a publishing company, and he was employed at a major newspaper, paying his dues until he would go into management. Dennis was working in business affairs, however, and his identity as a travel reporter had been completely fabricated.

That afternoon his crime reporter's press card had gotten him an interview with Dierdre, and her description of the face behind the glass of the front porch of the antiques shop had been macabre and seemed genuine. What made her especially convincing was the fact that she had been consistent in the retelling of her story, in every detail.

Dennis opened the front door and walked in. He flipped a wall switch, but it was on the same circuit that Dianna had blown, and no lights went on. He stopped and listened, hearing only the distant muffled sound of running water.

The umbrella stand was overturned and one of the umbrellas lay open and broken. There was a melting, half-eaten carton of ice cream sitting on the front desk.

The smells of the inn were all wrong to Dennis. There was a little of that strange animal aroma in the air—the one he had noticed in Dianna's room the night he had left. Then there was a trace of another smell—repulsive and awful—a scent of fetid meat.

Dennis listened for a few seconds, then called out, "Hello. . . . Hello."

There was no answer.

Dianna in her bathroom, behind two doors, with the hot water faucet wide open, sat trying to draw a map of the interior of the barn. She heard nothing.

Dennis called out, "Mrs Wilkinson? Agnes? Hello?" and he moved up the first two steps toward the sound of running water. There was a loud pop, and Dennis's foot crunched down on a small bag of potato chips.

Esau crept up silently behind Dennis, coming out of the darkness of the dining room.

Dennis could smell Esau before he heard him. The repulsive odor crept up from behind over his shoulder and shot up his nose.

Dennis whirled, and from the blackness loomed Esau's face. Dennis knew at once that it was the same face that Dierdre had described—the red birthmark made him certain.

A second after Dennis looked around, Esau's fist shot out and caught Dennis on the side of the face. Dennis's sudden turn caused Esau's hand to miss its mark and saved Dennis from being knocked out with a single blow.

Stunned, Dennis fell back on the steps for a second. Then he was up and half crawling, half running up the stairs.

Esau grabbed at Dennis's foot but only came away with a shoe in his hand.

"Agnes!" shouted Dennis as he raced to the top of the stairs. "Goody!"

Dianna, hearing his cry and recognizing the voice, shot out of the bathroom. "Dennis! Dennis! Look out! There's a man out there who will kill you!"

"Dianna!" shouted Dennis.

"Look out, he's strong and dangerous. He killed Anne!"

Dennis just missed tripping on the log in front of Dianna's room but went hurling headlong into the front bedroom. His mind was still a blur from Esau's blow.

Dennis's foot caught on a throw rug near the entrance to the room, and he went down to the floor. The smell of decaying meat was heavy in the air.

Esau was through the door a split second later and leapt toward Dennis, trying to jump with both feet on his enemy's back.

Dennis rolled out of the way just as Esau's hair-covered feet crunched down on the floor. As Dennis pulled himself up, his face rose beside the bed, inches from Goody's bulging eyeballs and her gaping mouth.

The foul odor seemed to be coming right out of the dead woman's mouth like a hideous exhalation of bad breath.

Dianna watched for a second from the door hole. She wanted to rush out to help, but the log kept her wedged in. She had to do something. She pulled on her shoes, grabbed a butcher knife, and climbed up the closet shelves toward the attic.

Gagging from the cadaver's face and smell, Dennis lurched to his feet, grabbed a lamp, and threw it at the large red-scarred face that crouched in the near-darkness a few feet away from him. His head was starting to clear, and he could see the size of his opponent and the animal-like focus and hatred in the eyes. Dennis had seen boxers with eyes like that, street kids, who fought like demons and never cared about getting hit.

The fear caught Dennis by surprise, a sudden unanticipated kick in the groin. This was a devil he was fighting, a formidable terror, not someone to trade blows with.

Dennis feinted to the left and went dashing out the door. Esau was fooled for a moment, long enough to let Dennis get by, but then Esau was running after Dennis down the hall.

Dennis took the turn at the top of the stairs. Get to the car! Got to get to the BMW!

Three steps behind him Esau saw the shotgun. The dark blue gun metal reminded him a little of his baseball bat. He snatched it by the barrel and went after the man four stairs at a time.

Out the front door and Dennis was sprinting for the car. His fingers fished in his pockets, trying to find his keys. Which pocket had he put them in?

He looked behind him—the huge man was only a few steps away. He had a gun! A shotgun he was holding by the barrel.

Dennis's hands went into his pockets. Did I drop the keys? Where are they! I'm dead without the keys!

Got the keys! They had been mixed up with his change. Get the door open. In the driver's seat fast. Lock the door, fast! Dennis was in the BMW, his fingers fumbling with the set of keys.

Dianna jumped down from the tiny door into the elevator car, which was still parked on the second floor. She pushed the Door Open button.

A smashing crunch—the driver's side window exploded in at Dennis in a burst of flying glass. Glass in his face. Glass in his eyes. Glass everywhere.

Esau was playing baseball, hitting hard. The shotgun was his bat.

God, no, there is glass all over me. My eyes! Can I see? His panic began to take over. He tried to narrowly open his eyes; there were a dozen tiny flakes of glass on and under his lids. Get the keys in the ignition. His fingers groped the steering column, trying to feel for the key slot.

Another smashing crunch, louder. Dennis couldn't see it, but he could tell from the sound and the direction of the pieces of glass that hit his face that the windshield had been shattered.

He had just got the tip of the key in the ignition when Esau raised the shotgun again. Esau lined up his target. He was the batter and Dennis's head was the baseball.

Hit ball out of park.

Dennis got the key in and was just about to give it a turn when Esau swung down through the gaping windshield. This blow Dennis heard but never actually felt. When the wooden gun stock hit his head, it merely sounded to Dennis like a dull thump. The blow slammed through Dennis's skull, numbing the area of his brain where the sensation of pain was received and deciphered. As a result Dennis felt only the first instant of a surge of pain that immediately shut off.

For three seconds, he just sat there wondering, "What was that strange thudding noise?" Then he slumped over the steering wheel, totally brain dead.

Dianna reached the front door just as the fatal blow was struck. She stayed out of sight behind the darkness inside the storm door. She saw Dennis fall and watched Esau open the door and drag the body out of the car.

Continuing to use the shotgun as he would a baseball bat, Esau walked in a circle around the car, smashing every single window with an expression of delight and abandon.

Dianna wasn't sure what to do. Suddenly there wasn't anyone to help anymore. But she was out of her room, inches away from escape.

Should I try to run out the back door? Or get in the BMW and get it started? I could be miles away in minutes.

Esau sat in the driver's seat of the car, turning the steering wheel and making motor sounds.

The inside overhead light of the BMW was on, and the buzzer sounded a warning that the key was in the ignition and that a door was open. Dianna tried to guess how long the car battery would last with the drain of the buzzer and lights.

Suddenly Esau glanced in the direction of the inn and began sniffing the air. Dianna turned and as quickly and as quietly as possible ran back up the stairs into the elevator car and up through the attic to her room.

48

Dianna sat in the gloom, listening to the sound of the warning buzzer of the BMW. It seemed that every moment the buzz became fainter. She heard a voice call from outside her window.

"Booo-tee-ful," came like a quiet three syllable grunt from below. Then again, "Boo-tee-ful."

Dianna looked out her window. Esau was standing on the ground, waving up at her, holding onto Dennis's leg by its shoeless foot.

Esau pulled his victim over to the old water pump. Moving the body like a boy would manipulate a toy action figure, he tried to stand Dennis against the pump. But Dennis's corpse was not cooperating, and Esau had to compromise, sitting the body on the ground with its back resting against the handle of the pump and the legs spread-eagled.

Dianna knew that she shouldn't be giving him the satisfaction of her attention and felt a little guilty to be an observer. But what did it really matter? What was the difference if she looked on or didn't? She felt as if she were watching a bad late night TV movie simply because there was nothing else more interesting to do.

Esau got behind the body and, throwing looks up to see if Dianna was watching, began to animate Dennis's arms, making the corpse do a little puppet dance in celebration of Esau's victory.

Dianna turned away and closed the blanket over the window.

As she studied her map of the barn, a weak whinny came from the stable. She realized that by now the horses must be half-dead from starvation. Normally I would be hysterical over an animal that went unfed, she thought. Why don't I seem to feel anything more than a passing concern?

I should care about their suffering. Why don't I? Has saving my own skin made everything else insignificant? Why, suddenly, is "I" and what affects "me" all that matters?

Fear, hunger, rain, the cold—these were elemental things she had never before dealt with on a life-sustaining, everyday basis. Now these once-taken-for-granted forces dictated her very existence. In the city, she realized, the worst thing she usually had to deal with was not being able to catch a cab.

For a moment she saw a flash cut of herself starring in a little scene from Bob Fosse's film *All That Jazz*. It was a shot of her face and bare neck and shoulders as she was silently zipped into the blackness of a body bag.

Perhaps I should end the struggle here and now, she thought. Why should I subject myself to more pain? I merely climb into a hot bath, take a razor blade . . . That way I get the last laugh. All Esau would have is another corpse for a puppet.

Dianna took up a chrome butcher knife and studied her reflection in the polished blade. There is, she admitted to herself, definitely something appealing and even sensual about suicide. One cut and I simply drift off into a dark sleep with my honor intact.

That would be the proper Japanese way—seppuku.

On the other hand, suicide conflicted with her catechism. The Catholic God had "set his cannon 'ginst self-slaughter." Light glinted off her chrome-mirrored knife, onto her face.

But the idea of seppuku, ritual suicide, seemed so ultra-civilized, such a "nice" sportsmanlike manner of taking one's good-bye. Dianna felt it was too prideful and too polite, the sterile choice of an unemotional intellect.

She placed the cutting edge on her wrist and slid the blade sideways, leaving a tiny track of blood. One thing that put a damper on her impulse was the tinge of pain that she felt—along with its promise of a much greater pain to come.

And then there was the mental picture that came of Esau molesting her cadaver. The image seemed to strip all the honor from the deed.

Apart from her intellectual reasoning, Dianna could feel her newly awakened survival instinct beginning to grow. The more she seemed to slide downward into an animal-like life-style, the more the need for vengeance grew like a dragon in her gut. It was a burgeoning need to fight back, a need that whispered in her ear, like the whisper of the Fool from *Lear*, that suicide was merely an idiot's desperate punt—too easy and too final.

Her baser drives shouted at her. . . .

Live!

Live to avenge!

Live to kill!

Live!

The *now* body is more important than the soul or the conscience or the promised lives that could yet be lived.

Dianna moved to her blanketed window on the world and looked out.

Dennis sat in flaccid stillness against the side of the pump. His head was bowed slightly, as if he were in the midst of a prayer. There were little glass cubes from the broken windows in his hair and on his clothes. The sun came out, and for a moment the shards glistened like a sprinkling of diamond dust from a wave of a good fairy's wand.

His shoeless, sock-covered foot, pointing up from the damp grass, looked cold. The breeze ruffled strands of his hair. Dianna had an impulse to go down and wrap a blanket around him.

Amazing how primeval the landscape has become, she thought, a collection of things elemental:

A nervous herd of geese huddling together for warmth in the rippling pond.

A little fountain bubbling up out of the earth where Esau had torn the water pipe from its place beneath the grass.

A sugary hanging tree.

A grave.

Adolescent flowers struggling to take root.

A corpse sitting in reverence, silently praying to some supreme being.

Life, death, a sense of flow, a sense of infinite time, a feeling of purposelessness, the unseen but still deeply felt presence of some God. All this was a part of the landscape's composition, and it seemed to fit naturally and fundamentally together.

Dianna wondered what the grounds of the inn had been like

a few thousand years ago, when they had been the home of the Indian. What stories could this land tell, she wondered, what blood has it drank? How many generations of savages have faced death on this very spot, in combat with each other or in a struggle with some fearsome beast? Some of the savages, a few, had endured. So would she.

She sat there for half an hour remembering her moments with Dennis.

The sound of Esau's footsteps came up the stairs and went into Goody's room. The fading noise of the car's warning buzzer broke into a series of chirps, then petered out. That's it, thought Dianna, the BMW's battery is dead. No driving home today.

The temperature quickly fell ten degrees, and clouds amassed above the inn, high, towering, anvil-shaped thunder pods, black and heavy with rain. The cold shot into the room, putting manuscript papers into a restless flutter.

Lightning flashed, and large raindrops blew in the shattered window. Dianna readied herself, dressing in many layers of clothing and a slicker. She put on heavy socks, laced her shoes tightly, tied the hood of the jacket over her head, and slipped a butcher knife into her belt. In one hand she carried the meat cleaver.

Through the door hole, Dianna studied Esau carefully, trying to decide if there was anything untoward in his manner. His breathing seemed regular but light, and there was no snoring.

Could he be feigning sleep? she wondered. As the thunder rolled, Esau's body twisted in little spasms. Those small jerky movements, she knew, would be hard for him to fake. He is really sleeping, she decided. The time was now.

Dianna knelt by the side of the bed and prayed, "Mary, mother of God, blessed is thy womb. . . ." She prayed partially from faith, but more from her need for success. The words of her girlhood ritual did not seem that reassuring to her.

Dianna had always disliked prayer. It was the "asking" part of prayer that bothered her the most. She had grown up with too many people who would *ask* for everything in prayer and then *do* nothing themselves to attain any of it.

So why am I praying? Dianna admitted that her stakes had never been this high.

Are there really no atheists in the trenches? she wondered.
I've never been in the trenches before, but I certainly am now,
and what am I doing?—I am praying like a saint.

Fear. That's what I am trying to master—creeping, insidious, unpredictable fear. But what is it exactly that I am truly
afraid of? Is it a fear of hellfire and eternal damnation? Or a
fear of being reborn as a cockroach?

No, she decided, it's more simple than that. I'm just scared
of the fact that maybe I don't go on, because I really don't
know for sure, do I? No matter what I *believe*, I don't *know* a
goddamned thing for sure.

"Oh, Lord," she asked quietly, continuing her halting
prayer, "why am I so ignorant and why do I understand
nothing? Why is my mind only chaos and confusion? Why am
I such a blind and helpless fool? Amen?"

She spoke the last word as a question in sotto voce, like an
aside in a play that would normally be spoken to the audience,
but in her head the aside was addressed to her vague and
generic God.

49

Dianna made certain once again that Esau had not awakened. Then, as quietly as possible, she climbed up the closet shelves to the trapdoor. Inching her way along the few attic boards that had not yet gone into the fire, she reached the elevator.

The high stool in the lift had been knocked over during her earlier climb out, and with no other choice, Dianna dropped to the floor of the car with a thump. She waited and listened. The rainstorm kept up with full force. But, she wondered, would the torrent be loud enough to cover her movements?

Dianna hesitated before pushing a button. The next move in her plan was dangerous and required that she get out on the second floor. Dianna was tempted to change her strategy and take the car down to 1. But that, too, had its risks. The grinding of the old elevator car as it traveled might awaken Esau.

Dianna was sure that Esau would be standing there waiting to grab her.

Inhaling deeply, she pushed Door Open.

With a crunch that seemed deafening, the door opened. No Esau and still no sound of movement within the building. Cautiously, keeping an eye on the entrance to Goody's room, Dianna stepped out.

Her heart skipped a beat as the lift door clunked shut behind her.

For the plan to work, she needed to buy herself time. Dianna calculated it would take three minutes to get down the creaking staircase and out the front door and at least another twenty minutes for the things she had to do in the barn. She had to keep Esau out of the picture as long as possible.

She moved slowly, a tiny step at a time, along the hall toward Goody's room, toward the sleeping Esau. The thunder worked to her advantage. She used the rolling sounds to mask the noises of her feet on the creaking floor.

After a full three minutes of softly creeping forward, she stepped over the log that jammed her door and peeked into Goody's room. Dianna half expected Esau to be awake and smiling at her, but he hadn't stirred from his position at the foot of the bed.

As she watched the sleeping figure, Dianna was tempted to abandon this codicil to her plan and turn and run. But then, with all possible care, she began to close the door to Goody's room.

Like Dianna's door, Goody's opened outward into the hall, and the hinges were almost as rusty. Breathlessly Dianna moved the popping and squeaking door an inch at a time, trying to hide the noise with thunder. At the halfway point, she removed the key from the lock and inserted it in the other side so that the door could be locked from the hall. That way if Esau suddenly woke up, she would have a chance of slamming the door and turning the key.

Dianna knew that the door wouldn't be too much of a deterrent. Unlike the situation in her room, this time Esau was inside and would only have to break a lock and not the entire door itself. It might not buy her many minutes, but even a few seconds could make the difference.

The door shut with a click. Dianna turned the key in the lock and pocketed it.

Alternating between a cautious tiptoe and a sprint of two or three steps, as the noise of the storm permitted, Dianna reached the downstairs front door. It opened quietly, but as it closed behind her a chunk of glass popped under the weight of her sneaker.

Cursing, Dianna broke into a run. She knew that the clock was moving against her.

The grass was wet and slippery. Rain beat on her face, and her jogging shoes were soaked after only a few steps.

There was no way to estimate how much time she had. Esau might not catch on for two hours, or he could be up in two minutes. Dianna kept feeling Esau's eyes staring at her back.

Around the side of the stable she came to the loose boards

where the old swayback had kicked them out. One board hung by a single nail and was a simple matter to yank off. The other would also have to be removed to give her enough room to squeeze in, but it wasn't going to be as easy. The plank was long, and most of it was still nailed firmly in place.

Dianna tugged, using even the strength of her legs to do the pulling, but the boards acted like a strong spring and would only come an inch or so away from the wall.

Obviously she would never be able to break the board, but it might be possible to pull out the nails that held it. The piece of barn planking she had first removed caught her attention. Dianna wedged it between the barn wall and the loose end of the second board. She pried downward, using the plank as one of the crowbars she had learned about in her stagecraft courses.

The rain made the wood slippery, and the work progressed slowly. Twice Dianna's fingers lost their grip, forcing her to start over again.

She looked through the darkness and thought, How vulnerable I am out here. If Esau comes, I will have no choice but to stand and fight. Part of her wanted to set out running for the highway, but it had to be a solid two-mile run, and it would be too easy for the man-thing to overtake her. Checking to be sure the knife was correctly positioned in her belt and the meat cleaver within easy reach, she continued her efforts.

The board arched farther and farther away from the wall as Dianna forced the makeshift crowbar into the widening gap. The loose end of the long plank protruded about eight inches. With a creak of rusty nails, the board tore away from the upright posts and fell to the ground.

Dianna went quickly through the opening. The stable smelled foul from five days' accumulation of horse urine and manure. The old swayback lay in his stall on his side, eyes closed, hardly breathing.

Now that Dianna was inside, it was a simple matter to get out. At each end of the stable were identical double doors held shut by wooden bars. Inside each set of doors was a long swing gate that opened inward.

The interior of the barn was too dark for her to do her work, and it took several minutes for her to find the light switches. She knew a light could attract Esau's attention, so she only turned on a single bulb, low on the wall near the centrally located harness room. The light cast eerie hard-lined shadows, black spokes that fanned out from the source onto the walls and ceiling.

She hoped she could find a horse that was still strong enough to get her away from the inn. She ran down the length of stalls, examining each animal.

The saddle mounts were in terrible shape—two were dead, and the ones that had any strength left were at the stable doors weakly begging to be fed. They hadn't been able to get water from the automatic spigots as the English horses had. All the thoroughbreds were standing.

"I'm sorry," she said. "If I get out of here, I'll see that you all get dinner."

The work she had to do required both hands. Dianna put the cleaver aside, took down a saddle, and said to herself, "Please, God, let me make the right choice."

One gelding seemed to be having trouble with a hind leg, probably, thought Dianna, from kicking at the stall. That left two possibilities: Lady Ann or Crumpet.

Lady Ann was glassy-eyed and calm, obviously very weak. As Dianna watched, the horse staggered and almost collapsed to her knees.

Crumpet, on the other hand, seemed spirited. Perhaps too much so, thought Dianna. He had a wild look about the eyes. But, she decided, the one thing I can be sure of is that Crumpet will run, and that's what I need.

Putting the bridle on took more time than expected because the hunger-crazed animal kept trying to pull free, and saddling proved to be impossible until Dianna tied on a feed bag. To keep Crumpet from gorging himself and getting sick, she allowed him only a small portion of oats.

Dianna sensed Esau's presence even before the horses did.

In a moment of clear intuition, she was sure the man-thing was outside the stable and that he knew that she was within. A half second of alertness and a momentary restlessness among the horses reinforced her instinct. The loud thump of a fist hitting the double door nearest the inn was the final confirmation.

Crumpet sauntered sideways, but the rest of the horses didn't seem to care anymore.

Every experience Dianna had faced with Esau had led her to

expect this. During the planning process, she had warned herself not to count on getting away without being detected.

She had a good idea how the scene had been played out. Esau awakened, found the door locked, and broke it down in a few minutes. Once he discovered Dianna was gone he undoubtedly tracked her to the barn with his nose.

She had developed a scenario to allow for this. It called for her to lure Esau to a set of doors at one end of the stable, and then, once she knew he was in position, she would ride as fast as possible to the other set of doors, open them, and be away before Esau could get around to the other end of the long building.

The howling wind and the sound of Esau's fists on the stable walls blended into an insistent and malicious-sounding din—as if all the elements were on Esau's side and conspiring against her.

Dianna felt displaced in the black-and-white-horror-film atmosphere of the barn, isolated from the world.

Crumpet, wanting more oats, became unruly, but Dianna goaded the horse to the exit farthest from the inn. She dismounted before the set of double doors and approached a swing gate.

The fencelike swing gate was designed to be used in warm weather, to prevent runaways while the large barn doors were left open for ventilation. The gate was hung with a spring so that it automatically stayed closed, blocking the exit.

Dianna had to attach a hook from the gate to the stable wall in order to keep the swing gate in the open position. Once that was accomplished, she tested the bar on the large barn doors, making sure they could be opened without trouble. Then after double-checking everything and taking the time to adjust her stirrups, she rode to the other set of large doors at the opposite end of the barn.

Dianna reined in the horse alongside the large double doors and rapped on them.

"Esau, Esau," she called. Dianna heard him at the small entrance on the side of the stable and shouted, "Esau, here I am. Over here at these doors."

His pounding stopped, and for a few seconds there was only the noise of the storm. Dianna was about to call his name again when Esau's weight slammed into the door beside her.

Crumpet jumped, and Dianna reined the horse sharply. Now's the time to make my move.

She spurred the thoroughbred into a gallop through the length of the barn. Crumpet was fighting her, but she drove him with all the tricks she knew, trying to gain every second.

Even before Crumpet halted at the other end of the barn, Dianna had dismounted. As she lifted the bar and pushed out the large double doors, Crumpet tried to pull away.

The wind caught one door and blew it open, tearing the hinges out of the wall. It dropped onto the grass.

At the far end of the barn it was quiet, then:

"Gaaaaaaaaarrrrrh!"

Esau had figured out what Dianna was up to.

. Crumpet reared up. His eyes rolled wildly. Dianna held onto the reins of the terrified horse and was almost lifted off her feet.

She knew that Esau was on his way to her end of the barn and that she had only seconds to spare.

Crumpet kicked out with his hind legs, then reared up. Dianna put her entire weight on the reins, but the animal, crazed with hunger and fear, crashed sideways into the barn wall.

As the horse dragged Dianna away from the door, into the barn, his hindquarters bumped open the latch to the swing gate.

Forcing Crumpet's head down and taking advantage of a momentary pause in his frenzy, Dianna mounted up. Before starting forward, she watched in horror, in a helpless kind of slow motion, as the fencelike gate swung closed, blocking her escape.

The gate stood over five feet high, and there was no way out except to jump it.

Crumpet stood calm. For a second Dianna hesitated, staring at the exit in terror.

There before her was the open path to freedom. All that held her back was a shoulder-height of fence.

One jump.

She held her breath and spurred the horse forward. Her approach was good, her form flawless.

In spite of the animal's condition, the jump was perfect. Dianna kept low in the saddle to avoid hitting a beam over the stable door. As the horse cleared the top of the gate, she was suspended in a moment of elation and joy.

There was nothing but a clear bridle path ahead of her.

Just then Esau came around the corner.

As Crumpet touched ground, the hunchback made a running dive and caught a rear hoof in a tackle with his massive arms. The horse's legs went out from under him and Crumpet went down in the mud.

Dianna flew over the horse's head, slid twenty feet in the slop, and felt a stab of pain in her right elbow as it cracked against a fence post.

Esau's arms were almost wrenched from their sockets, but he held on and was dragged along by the momentum of the animal.

Dianna got to her feet and reached for the knife in her belt. The pain in her right elbow made her drop the weapon and retrieve it with her left. Esau and Dianna stood face-to-face, covered with mud, dimly backlit in halos from an amber yard light.

The dark rain beat on them, sending little dribbles of muck down their arms and legs.

Thunder broke overhead.

Esau took a step toward her.

Dianna brandished the knife and shouted. Her voice came out like a voice from a crazed animal or a demon—guttural and full of venomous hatred. There was no mistaking the conviction behind her words.

"If you come near me, I'll cut your fucking balls off."

Esau took another step toward her but stopped.

They stood facing each other in the deluge—baptized head to toe in mud and falling rain.

Dianna cocked her knife arm like a gunfighter ready to draw. She felt roots growing from her feet into the bowels of the earth. She was a rock, immovable, and at that moment she was invincible.

Esau was happy he had won. Booteful played hard, but Esau had won. Now all he had to do was step over and make her his.

Yet something told him this was not the time. Something was wrong. He sniffed the air. The booteful's smell was different. Why? There was no odor of fear.

Booteful look strange. She mad Esau won.

He knew that feeling from the times he had himself lost, but there was something else that made him hesitate.

Booteful look cold. Booteful look hard. Like Goody Mama look when Esau bad.

Booteful's look was like that but much stronger, even more frightening. Esau was somewhat intimidated by the knife, but that was not what stopped him.

Something in booteful's words shut down fire between Esau's legs.

A shiver coiled its way up his crooked spine, through his hump and into his back. He felt no want, no need to play with the booteful.

No play now. Maybe play later.

Like a subservient dog bowing to the leader of the pack, he flopped down, legs spread in a puddle, and splashed muddy water on his thighs.

Dianna turned and, cradling her injured arm, walked slowly toward the inn.

She knew the moment was hers.

She knew she would not be touched.

Not at this instant. She was too proud, too strong, too much for anyone on the face of the earth to take on. Without so much as a glance back, she covered the distance to the front door.

Esau splashed the water on his face to cool himself off and grinned after her. His eyes gleamed with the assurance that his ultimate and total victory was not far away.

50

Dianna dragged herself up the stairs toward the second floor. The shotgun, its stock chipped and battered, was lying against the banister. Dianna figured that Esau must have used it to break out of Goody's room. Dianna entered the elevator car and pushed the button to close the sliding door behind her. Out of breath and exhausted, she collapsed in the corner of the lift. Her elbow was bleeding slightly from surface abrasions and causing her excruciating pain.

I almost made it work, she thought, but almost doesn't count. Coming in second has no meaning in this game. A split second would have been the difference. Dianna hung her head and thought, I wasted the precious moment myself, ogling at the jump. I had the opportunity and I was afraid. That instant of hesitation destroyed the plan and maybe my last chance of escape.

Her sense of failure was tempered with a realization that she had experienced something out of the ordinary—perhaps even a glimpse of what it meant to exist outside the "box" of human desire that the Roshi always talked about. For a moment I had it, I felt it, didn't I? she admitted to herself.

Standing in the rain and even while I was walking back to the inn, I didn't give a damn whether I lived or not. When I spoke, I wasn't afraid of him, and without fear, all my energy was focused into the words. In those few heartbeats I was stronger than he, and the man-thing sensed this and had no alternative but to believe my threat and to yield.

Where did that strength come from? she wondered. I just didn't care what happened to me. Could I do it again—summon up this momentary strength and use it on Esau? Dianna answered her own question. No, probably not. It's not something I know how to control.

Her momentary strength had been like that elusive floating feeling that she had had those two times during meditation, and she knew that she would not consciously be able to summon up the fearlessness that had come with her pain and anger. She knew, from her experience and her Roshi's teaching, that once she thought about it, once she *tried* to attain that mind-set, it would not happen.

Dianna thought back to the look on Esau's face after he had sat down in the mud. He had backed off from that particular confrontation, but he certainly was in no way giving up. There had been a sense of optimism and assurance in that expression. He believed he was going to get his chance later. He wasn't stopping to analyze or weigh the odds or feel any guilt at winning—he just *knew*.

In many ways I'm the schlemiel and Esau is the perfect Zen being, she thought. He doesn't think—he acts. He doesn't verbalize—he understands. He doesn't try. With all possible simplicity, he merely *does*.

There was no way to be sure that Esau wasn't now standing outside the elevator door, but Dianna had heard no movement on the stairs, and she felt reckless. She reached up and pressed a button. The door slid open. Dianna picked up the shotgun from the banister and took it into the elevator.

The passage from the small escape door through the attic and back into the room proved to be difficult and painful. Though she could open and close her right hand and move her arm at the swollen elbow, the slightest jostle caused considerable pain. Dianna decided it was a bone bruise or possibly even a hairline fracture.

Dianna paced the cold and ravaged room. Her feelings of failure and the pain in her arm drove her into a nervous and desperate spate of activity. She worked frantically in an attempt to remove the trigger lock from the shotgun. Using the butcher knives and other kitchen tools, she tried to pry off the lock. She picked at it with a hairpin and pounded it with the mason's hammer and fireplace tools.

But the mechanism was well designed and, like all trigger

locks, made of the finest case-hardened steel. It resisted her every attempt to get it off. All Dianna succeeded in doing was putting small scratches on the chrome.

Finally she lost her temper, and angrily grabbing the stock with her good hand, she smashed the trigger lock against the stone of the fireplace. Sparks flew from the impact, and the case-hardened steel left gouges in the rock.

She struck again. With a roar, the shotgun fired and leapt out of her hand.

Taken by surprise, Dianna dropped back to a crouch on the floor. The blast had blown out a big chunk of the plaster in the wall. A red mark appeared on her body where the stock had recoiled into her rib cage.

When she had recovered from the shock of the explosion, Dianna forced herself to reexamine the shotgun. There was no sign that striking the stone had had any effect whatsoever on the trigger lock.

I must have vibrated the mechanism in some way to set it off, she thought. If I had been holding the gun by the barrel, so that it was pointing at me, I could have blown myself in half.

Dianna tossed the shotgun on the bed. She knew she would never get past the trigger lock.

Esau called from the yard, "Boo-te-ful, boo-te-ful."

Sounds like it's show time again, Dianna thought. She pulled the blanket away from the window frame and looked out.

The rain had turned to a light icy drizzle. Esau stood on the lawn below in a pool of ghastly yellow halogen light. In one hand he held Lady Ann by her stable harness; in the other he carried a hollow tree stump.

Esau show the booteful how good it can be. Esau want her see how strong Esau is. If she see Esau play she want play too. Maybe the booteful not know how much fun it is.

When Esau was sure he had Dianna's attention, he dropped the stable harness and grabbed Lady Ann by the tail. Esau looked up at Dianna with a half-crazed expression, then set the stump down behind Lady Ann's hind legs and climbed up.

Dianna could see that the act was staged for her benefit. His intention was clear from the way he leered and grinned in her direction while flaunting his virility.

He is, she thought, superior to me in certain ways. Not because he is male—Esau's female counterpart would be equally formidable—but because of his bestiality.

He is perfectly programmed for survival in a primitive environment. He has the muscle, the size, the ultra-perceptive senses, and all the instincts necessary to keep him alive.

And his need to procreate is an all-consuming drive. I worry about the possibility of having kids in four or five years, while he has a driving need to impregnate everything that moves.

Why did God or Nature or evolution or whatever put those hungry testicles on man? she wondered. Why is the male drive so unfocused and uncaring? Is it really essential to procreation? Is the trait vital to the evolutionary process because it mixes up the gene pool with as many different combinations as possible?

Dianna watched passively, without the slightest impulse to turn away. She was not aroused; nor was she repulsed. Instead, Dianna found herself coldly objective. His technique is crude, she thought. I wonder how Lady Ann rates him as a lover? Dianna looked on and decided, She will give him a total pan.

She speculated on the possible offspring of their union—a hunchbacked stallion, a hunchbacked centaur, Bottom from *Midsummer Night's Dream* with a hump beneath his ass's head, a professional wrestler?

She wondered if, besides Esau's deformities, there were any other dark and insidious secrets hidden in his chromosomes. Perhaps Esau was a throwback to some extinct Homo erectus, the missing link between man and ghoul. When the performance reached its climax, Dianna leaned out and booed, giving him a thumbs down. Then she turned away, covering the window with the blanket.

Dianna sat on the bed and stared at the wall. She wished she could suddenly turn catatonic. Every muscle in her body ached, and her clothes, face, and hair were covered with drying cakes of mud. It felt like four in the morning, but her sense of time told her it was only early evening.

There was one option, she realized, that might satisfy her intellect and her non-Catholic sense of honor.

All it would require was one match.

Build a little fire in the corner of the room, say near the door. The whole inn would go up in a bonfire, and with it, Dianna

LaBianca. There would be no body for Esau to toy with, no possible loss of honor, no more pain, only sleep.

You suffocate, don't you, she thought to herself, before you burn? The flames use up all the oxygen around you, and you lose consciousness. A fire might even claim Esau, say if it was done when he was napping.

It's a possibility, she thought, "To be or not to be ashes." My best and final role, I get to play Jeanne d'Arc.

File that one away, she decided. It would only be a last resort.

51

Seeing the modern weapon and the antique dueling pistols lying together on the bed gave her an idea: there might be more shells somewhere inside the shotgun. Dianna tried opening a chrome piece on the side of the weapon above the trigger, but it wouldn't budge. Then she noticed a round knob with finger serrations. By turning and pushing at the same time, Dianna was able to remove the knob.

Dianna tilted the barrel toward the floor, and out fell two shotgun shells. My God, now I have powder, she realized. With the lead ball and the old pistols, I can put together a working gun.

Dianna laid out a sheet of clean paper and opened a shotgun shell where the cardboard was crimped together at the end. Little lead balls poured out, revealing another layer of wadding. She worked slowly and with care, afraid she might somehow explode the shell. Below, in the brass casing, was a thimbleful of silver-gray powder. She poured it on the sheet of paper and took up one of the pistols.

Dianna had never shot a flintlock, but she had watched them being fired on the range, and she had shot other kinds of her grandfather's black-powder pistols—the ones that used the little brass percussion caps.

She studied the gun, trying to figure out how the mechanism worked. Let's see: First I cock the hammer, then pull the trigger. That releases the hammer, which holds that piece of flint. I see, the flint strikes that little metal plate there and causes a spark. The spark ignites the powder in the barrel through the touch hole. Since the gun doesn't open up anyway,

I guess that both the powder and the ball have to be loaded through the barrel. Dianna remembered seeing shooters load their long flintlock Kentucky rifles by pouring the black powder right into the barrel.

She worked the action on the one pistol she thought might fire. After a number of tries, she saw sparks, and when she finished cleaning out the touch hole with a pin, she decided to load the gun. The question was how much powder to put in the barrel. She reasoned that when the weapon was made gunpowder was not as strong as the stuff in a modern shotgun shell. "If I use too much powder," she said to herself, "this antique could easily blow up in my hand."

Dianna decided to play it safe, thinking that if the pistol didn't fire with enough force, she could always reload and try again. She compared the size of the opening in the shotgun barrel with the caliber of the handgun. The pistol looked about four times smaller, and estimating that modern powder was about twice as powerful, she measured out an eighth of the charge from the shotgun shell.

Dianna poured it in the barrel and shoved it all the way down with a rod that was part of the pistol set. She remembered the layer of packing that had been in the shotgun shell and figured that it might be important in some way to make the gun fire. Dianna took the wadding from the cardboard cartridge and rammed it on top of the powder. The lead ball went in last and had to be pounded down the barrel with the rod and taps of the mason's hammer.

Dianna felt a surge of hope as she held the loaded pistol. She smiled and thought, For the first time I can take the initiative without having to risk my neck.

Brain triumphs over muscle. The equalizer is in my hand. It's simple now. I know Esau doesn't fear the pistols. All I have to do is lure him near the hole. Then I pull the trigger at my leisure. If I miss or only wound him, I reload and fire again. I have three more lead balls and plenty of powder.

Charged with elation, Dianna whirled around the room aiming the pistol, making shooting noises. She held in her hand a definite means to freedom.

Steadying the flintlock on the splintered wood around the hole, she sighted along the barrel at a picture on the far wall across the hallway. I've got to aim for an eye and hope the ball will pass into the brain.

Her elation cooled. It's not going to be a paper target I'll be aiming at, she realized. I'll be trying to commit cold-blooded murder.

Murder, execution, or self-defense? she asked herself. Dianna knew she could rationalize it several ways. Esau is keeping me hostage—that's kidnapping. He is attempting rape. In the process of either crime, I could easily be killed—that will be murder.

But is Esau really trying to commit murder? In fact, in his demented mind he probably thinks he's doing something that's good for me.

And can I really say that Esau is a person responsible for his actions?

Her hand holding the pistol began to shake.

"Oh, come on, Dianna," she told herself. "This is not the time for guilt. It is kill or be killed."

If only there were some other way out. But she was certain there was not.

Once again she tried to hold the pistol steady as she practiced aiming, but the muscles in her hand seemed to have a mind of their own. My shaking is psychosomatic, she concluded. My overdeveloped conscience is speaking to me through the muscles in my left hand, saying, "Thou shalt not kill," "Do unto others . . . ," "Life is sacred."

By the precise definition of the deed, in the eyes of God, she knew she would be committing murder, and premeditated murder at that. At the exact instant she would pull the trigger, her life would not be in danger; therefore, legally it would not be self-defense.

In the microcosm defined by Dianna's possessing the gun, she would become the killer, Esau the victim. I can't believe it, she realized. I actually feel guilty at having the upper hand.

Are there precedents for cold-blooded acts of self-defense? She didn't know. . . . Why couldn't there be some other choice?

"Aggggggggh!" She felt caught in a circle of logic—in a web of her Roshi's labels.

Why am I equivocating? Why am I even bothering to judge him as a man? That "thing" is a would-be rapist, and that deletes him from the category of human beings. Who in my situation would give a thought to a question of morality?

Dianna wished there were some wine left: What I need right now is about three-quarters of a bottle.

She warned herself grimly that the execution or act of self-defense or whatever it was called had to be a thorough job of killing. A wounded Esau was not a creature that she ever wanted to face. She knew she must shoot to kill, as cleanly and quickly as possible.

Dianna went to the door hole and, with a measure of solemnness, called to Esau. Her tone was determined but sympathetic, like that of a guard speaking to a prisoner as he tells him it's time to begin the last walk down death row.

It took Esau a while to wake from his deep sleep, but the softness in her voice was something new and piqued his curiosity. He lumbered near the door but cautiously stayed beyond the range of her usual defenses. Like a six-year-old, he rubbed the sleep from his eyes and reclined against the wall.

Esau was cautious. He couldn't detect any scent of fear, but he sensed something else. She seemed odd to him. She reminded him of the way Goody had once looked and smelled that time when she had forgotten to bring him food.

Dianna put the barrel through the opening in the door. Esau noticed the pistol with a wary curiosity but didn't move away.

Dianna had the sensation of being in a carnival shooting gallery. "Step right up, shoot the hunchback, three shots for a dollar," she whispered to herself as she pulled back the hammer.

Esau couldn't have been more cooperative. He stood, immobile, staring at her from across the hall—keeping his distance but still providing a perfect target.

Esau's injured eye had begun to heal, but it was still tinged with red. Dianna lined up the barrel with the white of his clear eye.

Then the shaking began again. Her left arm jerked with an irregular rhythm. The barrel bounced up and down, making a shot hopeless.

Dianna lowered the gun, switched it to her injured right hand, and shook out her left.

Nothing could relax the arm. She flexed her wrist, wrung out her fingers, and gripped the doorknob as hard as she could, trying to work out the tension.

I'm approaching this whole thing the wrong way, she realized. I've got to gain control by dealing with what is going on in my head.

She forced herself to picture Esau in the act of killing Jacques and Dennis and then recalled the image of Esau and Lady Ann. Lastly she made a quick mental list of all the pain Esau had inflicted on her.

Dianna's face hardened, her arm relaxed, and she looked out the hole.

Esau had inched in closer, and now the shot was ridiculously easy. It would be almost impossible to miss, even if she tried to. As Dianna put the weapon in position her arm felt weak but steady. She knew the violent shaking would not come again.

With the pistol aimed at Esau's right eyeball, Dianna pulled the trigger.

The weapon didn't fire. She recocked the hammer and took aim again.

With a flash and a dull thud, the powder ignited. Dianna instinctively squeezed her eyes shut and jerked her head to the side. The caustic smell of nitrate filled the air.

She peered out the door hole.

Esau stood a little way down the hall, looking at her with bewilderment. There was no sign of injury to his face or body. Dianna wondered, What happened? The flint had sparked, and the powder had definitely ignited.

She turned the pistol and peered down the barrel. There was the ball, an inch or so below the end of the muzzle opening. The force of the exploding powder had driven the lead only a few inches.

The flintlock worked perfectly, she realized, but I just didn't put in enough powder.

Holding the smoldering pistol, Dianna sat on the bed. How could I have known the bullet would get stuck in the barrel? Now I have no way of getting the ball out, and the pistol is useless. And I can't load more powder, because everything must go in through the barrel, and the ball is stuck in the way.

What's left for me to do? With a useless right arm, I have no chance to fight Esau with anything other than a gun. I am weakened almost to the point of physical and mental collapse. How can I make another escape attempt?

Dianna leaned against the wall beside the door. There at eye level she saw something that took her mood even lower.

The top hinge of her door, the door that was her first line of defense, had a long, wide, open split in the metal.

She ran her finger over the steel. All that was left holding the top hinge together was a tiny quarter-inch of metal. If Esau made the slightest attempt to break in, there was no way the door would hold.

Dianna took the other pistol, loaded it with all the rest of the powder, and repeated her shooting scenario. Esau was once again cooperative, but after thirty tries the gun still would not fire. Esau soon became bored with the game and sat against the wall, watching her cock and fire. Finally, in disgust, Dianna threw the weapon against the wall.

All hope exhausted, she broke down and cried. Esau's next attack was sure to break the damaged hinge. Her thoughts kept returning to her final alternative—suicide.

Esau trudged into Goody's room, and soon Dianna heard his snoring.

She dragged the blankets off the bed and lay down to sleep on the floor, with her back pressed up against the weakened door. She didn't want to take the chance that Esau would get in the room without her knowing about it. She set the pistol and the hammer within reach, put down her head for a moment's rest, and fell into a druggedlike sleep.

52

Dianna's sleep fell into a nightmare, an ever-changing vision. She was in a half-conscious, half-dream state and would later remember everything in exact detail. The events presented themselves in brilliant Technicolor, and each moment of the vision seemed true and immediate . . . as if experienced firsthand, as if lived.

Throughout the nightmare Dianna had an objective detachment, a removed but constant awareness that she was in fact only watching herself in a dream. But because the images were seen with such vivid clarity, and because the story unfolded with such plausibility, the act of watching in no way diminished the impact and immediacy of her nightmare.

The location of the dream often shifted abruptly. From past to present to future. From the real to the surreal.

It is the next morning, the day to come. Dianna is in the inn, in her room. She is resigned and slow as if she is moving through mud. She tries to manipulate her right arm. Her elbow is completely immobile, and the slightest movement brings a stabbing pain.

In another reality, a totally separate environment within her dream, Dianna sees herself kneeling behind a weather-grayed pew in an abandoned cathedral. Through a broken stained glass window, she sees a huge shadowed face float down from the sky—a face the size of a building that eclipses the sun. No features are discernible, only its shimmering outline.

• • •

Dianna takes the unfired flintlock and works the action. There is a sense of impending doom in her movements. When she pulls the trigger, the pistol still will not fire.

Dianna falls and falls and falls down through a heavy black rain.

Two butcher knives, one on each side, are put between the mattresses of the large bed. Dianna gets under the covers.

"Esau. Wake up, Esau." Dianna calls to him.
The man-thing rises and moves in toward the door.
"Move the log. You can come in." Her voice is detached, as if she were already dead.

A second-grade Dianna walks home from school with two friends. They stop and look in silence at a family of electro-cuted birds—a ruffled and twisted fivesome, lying together at the base of a telephone pole.

Esau heaves the log aside and jiggles the doorknob. The door opens a few inches.
The hunchback studies her with a cautious eye.

A gray face that was once Dianna is unmoving, the makeup thick, caked on. Her expression is cold and hard, locked in a tight-lipped, neutral smile. She is a corpse laid out in a silk-lined casket.

The eyeball at the door hole disappears.
Dianna's hand checks the position of the knife as she hears the log lifted and rolled aside.
The door to her room jerks open, breaks off its one good hinge, and comes crashing down, flat against the floor. Cautious as a nervous jackal, Esau shuffles into the room.

Her dream moves forward, Dianna's involvement in it growing deeper, while at the same time the awareness that she is in a dream intensifies.
In her half-conscious state she feels a need to "keep

watching," she has to find out what will happen, where her subconscious will take her and how it will project the events.

Esau takes a long moment to grasp the situation. Cautious, watching Dianna with uncertainty, he keeps his distance just inside the room.

She watches him—her eyes hard.

Moving to the end of the bed, he looks down at her, his body framed by the huge bedposts. His wary suspicion slowly turns to desire as he realizes she is his for the taking. His face brightens with a blackened-tooth grin of anticipation and conquest.

Dianna returns Esau's smile with contempt and loathing.

With a flip of the wrist, Esau reaches down, grabs the covers off the bed, and throws them at the wall. His eyes slowly roll across Dianna's body.

Esau's breathing grows rapid, and the veins on his head and neck bulge out.

Dianna stifles a cry of surprise as he grabs one ankle in each hand and draws her down to him at the foot of the bed.

Dianna falls and falls and falls down through a rain of blood.

Esau grabs Dianna's arm and ogles the pistol strapped to her wrist. Then his attention is distracted by Dianna's presence. He kneads up her calves, over her knees, and onto her thighs with his filthy hands. Large, broken fingernails close around the pants of her jogging suit.

There is the sound of tearing cloth and Esau rips away the garment.

Dianna's face is cold and impartial. She has sworn to herself to give him no reaction.

After rubbing his nose with the fabric, he lets it drop to the floor.

Esau whines, and he whimpers, "Booteful, booteful," his voice making an attempt to be soft and gentle.

There is a wildness in Dianna's eyes as her fear mounts. The terror starts to overcome her and she bites her lip to stay in control.

• • •

A black dog jumps out of a hedge and snarls at five-year-old Dianna. The girl freezes in her tracks. Somehow she senses that she should stay still. But the dog snarls and bares its teeth. She turns and runs in panic. The dog sinks it fangs into the flesh of her calf.

Esau pulls his poncho of ragged blankets off with a flourish. Except for his face, his body is completely covered with a thick mat of dark brown hair. The birthmark on his cheek and forehead burns crimson like a scab on an unhealed wound.

Dianna feels her stomach heave.

The curvature of Esau's spine pushes out his chest, thrusting and arching forward his sternum. The effect is like the great breast of a strutting pigeon.

And there on Esau's shoulder sits a hair-covered hump. The twisted mound of flesh throbs as blood courses through its gnarled arteries and veins. The hunch writhes with an existence apart from the rest of Esau's body.

The skin of the hump melts away and Dianna sees its contents: an evil pregnancy, a growing twisted brain in embryonic form, its placenta suckling on Esau's blood. It seems about to hatch from its dark and slimy incubator.

Climbing between the posts on the end of the bed, Esau positions himself in the V of her legs.

Putting one fingernail under the fabric, he rips away her underwear.

Grime-encrusted hands grab at Dianna's hips and thighs. Her fingers claw the mattress.

He leans over and tries to plant a sloppy kiss on Dianna's lips. The now-familiar rancid smell hits her like a belch of pollution from a garbage incinerator. Bile in her mouth, she turns her head away.

Just then Esau runs his hands roughly over her breasts, kneading the flesh like dough. He reaches down and grabs a handful of pubic hair. Dianna shouts in agony as his hand pulls her up off the mattress.

Relaxing his hold, he sits for a minute sniffing his fingers. Then he runs his thumbs over her nipples in a kind of wonderment.

As he moves to enter her, she quickly crosses her legs and commands, "Play. More."

Dianna puts the flintlock to the side of his head and pulls the trigger.

The hammer of the antique moves ever so slowly. There is no spark and nothing happens.

Esau puts his fingers in his mouth, paying no attention to the click of the weapon.

It is difficult to recock the pistol; Dianna's thumb strains as she manages to draw the hammer a second time.

Nothing happens when she pulls the trigger of the pistol, or the third time, or the fourth.

On the fifth try, the powder around the touch hole ignites. Dianna is sure that the gun will fire. But the powder merely fizzles and dies down.

Dianna's aching thumb can barely move the hammer. She panics as she realizes that she can't cock the pistol.

She turns her hips to the side, evading him. Esau's face contorts in frustration. His patience is beginning to wear thin.

Dianna inches her fingers toward the handle of a butcher knife between the mattresses. As her hand is about to touch the wood, Esau glances down. Dianna eases her hand back onto the bed.

Using her thumb and index finger, Dianna draws the butcher knife out from under the churning mattress. Just as the blade is about to slip free, the tip catches on the sheet, and as Esau lifts her to him, the blade drops from her grasp to the floor.

As Esau brings his face close to hers, Dianna turns her head to the side and closes her eyes, unable to acknowledge the presence of the man-thing that lies astride her.

Esau's expression turns to anger. His face becomes a grimace of determination.

Their eyes lock for a moment, in a communion of passion and hatred.

Dianna's aching thumb tries to cock the pistol. She cannot, but she must. She has to get both hands on the hammer of the pistol to use the strength of both thumbs.

With her injured arm she reaches around Esau's back in a weird embrace and puts both thumbs on the pistol's hammer.

Esau grabs her knees. Dianna cannot fight his overpowering strength.

The hammer of the weapon clicks into position.

Esau is poised, ready to make his conquest. He looks down at Dianna with his large brown eyes, like a dog in love with its master. His body tenses and he groans in anticipation.

A stone statue of Buddha, carved into the side of a mountain, has a face that is a white furnace of a star. Yet the outline of the Buddha's round head is familiar to Dianna. She has seen it before, but where?

The flint sparks. A flash comes from the powder around the touch hole. With an earsplitting roar, the pistol explodes.

The weapon misfires. Dianna looks in horror at her hand. Her palm is a bloody stump missing two fingers and a thumb.

Esau grins, grabs her by the throat, and begins to explode in spasms of pleasure.

Blackness.

Her dream is not over, but there is a slowing of the pace. The vision becomes a quiet thing where time is a plodding tormentor.

A Christmas wreath hangs on a window. Dianna is in a private clinic that occupies a brownstone in Manhattan's Turtle Bay area. Outside, a gray snow drifts quietly down between buildings.

Dianna falls and falls and falls, now gently, drifting down, down, down with the snowflakes.

A nurse on the floor enters and readies a stethoscope with a special enlarged cone. Dianna's stomach erupts in a series of violent spasms as the growing life within her punches and turns.

"How are the twins today?" asks the nurse.

"The same," remarks Dianna listlessly.

"One of them wants out," remarks the nurse.

"Always," replies Dianna.

"You look tired. Have you been getting your rest?" asks the nurse, noticing Dianna's sunken eyes and cheeks.

"No."

"Would you like something to help you sleep?"

"No."

The nurse checks the lump of bandages that covers Dianna's mutilated hand.

There is a knock at the door, and Dianna mumbles, "Come in."

The nurse leaves without a further word.

Arthur enters, or someone who looks like Arthur, but sometimes in the dream the face looks like Dennis's. The man sits in a chair facing her and takes her hand in his.

Arthur and Dianna sit quietly for a long time. They seem close, as if the event has bonded them together.

Arthur speaks. "The executor of the Wilkinson estate left papers for you to sign. You get control of everything if you bear a Wilkinson heir. From what I see, the estate is worth about three-and-a-half million, not counting the inn itself. Under the terms, you can't ever touch the principal, only the dividends and interest. But I estimate a yearly income of around four hundred thousand, and you are permitted to dispose of the money just about any way you want."

"I have a hump," says Dianna as she thinks over the terms of her inheritance and looks down at her stomach. "I have grown my very own hump."

"Maybe you should think about moving up to the inn," says Arthur. "It might be a better place to raise two . . . ah . . ."

Dianna interrupts, "You mean it might be a better place to raise one normal child and one monstrosity?"

She had been trapped by the situation. Her conscience wouldn't let her abort—murder a healthy child. And it wasn't possible to abort only the abnormal fetus—the one of her two fetuses that she knew would grow into a monster, a little kicking ghoul that would one day become like Esau and destroy all she knew and loved.

Arthur hangs his head, lost in thought.

Dianna begins laughing hysterically, convulsively, completely out of control.

Dianna sees herself in the hospital room as if seen from some place high above, from the seat of God.

She is a small, insignificant figure in a ceilingless cubicle surrounded by four walls. The four walls stand in the center of a void. It is a personalized hell, and Dianna is a damned woman living the first few seconds of her eternity-to-come.

The face of the Buddha head carved into the side of a mountain transforms. The white-hot furnace becomes the sun reflecting off the water, then a wash of black light, then a shadow that eclipses the sun, and then a metallic globe.

The outline of the Buddha's round head seems even more familiar to Dianna. She knows that face. She can almost place it but cannot. It changes slowly, developing recognizable features. The features become clear, large, dark eyes, a broad flat nose.

The god's face becomes the face of a child.

A hideous son of Esau.

Dianna's dream shattered. She lurched up, wide awake, in the huge bed, screaming and screaming and screaming.

It took a full thirty minutes for her to come down.

To put her feet on the floor to be sure she was not falling.

To check the one remaining usable pistol and make sure it had not been fired.

To feel her hand and see that all her fingers were still there.

To touch her stomach to be absolutely sure that she carried no throbbing hump of life about to give double birth.

To realize that in her dream she had done everything terribly wrong, that she had played the role of a total fool.

Remembering the dream sent a familiar paralyzing shiver up her spine. This time the spasm continued its journey up into her brain, where it felt as if it were entering the very core of her cerebellum.

PART VI

A kanji that may be translated as "the path that must be taken in the quest for art, enlightenment, and self-mastery."

A fallen flower
Returning to the branch?
Ah, a butterfly.

                    —Moritake

Into the chill of night
I spoke aloud.
But the voice
I did not know.

                    —Otsuji

53

The reality of the dream and the morning chill of the room brought Dianna to an acute state of awareness and gave her the feeling that she was in touch with all her senses. Heart still racing from the aftershocks of the nightmare, she stood at the window with the blanket pulled back, looking out and taking deep breaths to bring herself down and regain control.

Overnight, the weather had taken a silent and most beautiful turn. The grounds were dusted with a crisp snow that had stuck on the foliage and changed the barren trees and the greenish-brown grass into a fantasyland of white. The April cold snap had swept down from Canada, surprising the warming Vermont countryside with an unexpected blanket of snow.

Dennis's corpse had a salting of white that blended with the sprinkled cover of glass shards. The tree stump was now a small table holding a serving of white fluff.

The sweet william plants that Agnes had set out on Jacques's grave were buried under the snow—all except for one plant that stood strong and had a single deep-red flower on one of its thin branches. Despite the cold, the petals had opened in the night, an early and impossible bloomer defying the killing snow.

Dianna crossed to the hole in the door. Esau was breathing heavily, apparently sleeping, lying in his usual place at the foot of the bed, but Goody was nowhere to be seen.

Then Dianna spotted a shoe and ankle protruding from a hall closet. Strange, she thought. Why would Esau move Goody? Then she realized, Of course, the smell had finally gotten to him. It must have become a mighty and terrible reek, she conceded, to have made the hunchback move his precious Goody from her room.

The old woman's visible foot was poised with its toe pointed upward, as if Goody had been arrested in motion, in the midst of a kick.

Maybe that's what death is—a closet, Dianna thought. We are stuffed inside, and when we try to fight our way out, our bodies are stiff and all we do is kick at God and the moon.

The dark mood that hit Dianna was the worst of her life. The dream, the pain in her arm, the cold in the room, a fatigue that she could feel in the marrow of her bones, all these things added up and conspired against her.

Her depression, quadrupled in its effect by her battered body, came down on her head, covering her thinking with a black shroud. It dimmed her vision and blanketed the flickering light of her soul.

It set Dianna to work with a dark determination.

Moving sluggishly, she piled every last bit of remaining flammable material around the base of her hall door with the broken hinge. Dianna hoped that when she set a match to it, the fire would spread quickly, fueled by the dry timber of the inn and the strong wind that whistled through the window. If she was lucky, there was a chance she could catch the sleeping man-thing in a final embrace of flames.

As for herself, she could only hope it would all be over quickly or, at least, within the limitations of endurable suffering. Ideally, her life would be snuffed out in one of those spaces between breaths, between inhaling and exhaling—in that indefinable apart-from-time instant that she had tried to get a handle on, again and again, in all of her hundred thousand breaths of meditation.

When the makeshift pyre had become a small mound, Dianna took her dwindling box of matches and struck one. She leaned forward to touch the flame to the base of the pyre.

This would be it, she knew. Good-bye. There would be no turning back once the fire caught on. *Finito* LaBianca.

She saw the last page of her life, painted, like a bright Warhol or a Lichtenstein, in an artist's parody of comic-book style—a final spectacular full-page color drawing of the burning inn having become a death trap. The title of the work would be "Dianna's Adventure." The smoke would billow out of the frame all around the borders of the drawing, perhaps spilling even out onto the wall in a most existential manner. At the bottom of the frame would be a little scroll-shaped box with thin letters that simply stated THE END.

Dianna crouched down and stared into the eye of the burning match, transfixed. She studied the shimmering essence of the small fire, as it slowly worked its way down the wooden stick, and thought, There's a life in there, an echo of a soul finding expression through a chemical reaction. As the flame inched closer to her hand the heat hurt her fingertips and fingernails.

In an intense low whisper that was more like a growl, she spoke one word, "No." Then again, quieter but with even more certainty, "No!"

A vision came to her not of a specific plan but of a mind-set. It was, in effect, a manner of attack that was the primary tool and heritage of the earth's long bloodline of victors. It was an invincible attitude she knew she would have to embrace if she was to have a chance.

"Goddamn the bastard," she said to herself. "No one's going to make this decision for me. If I'm on my way to hell, I'm going to go with my head up, kicking and screaming, and I'm going in style."

"No!" she said one last time, and with a sizzle of burning flesh, Dianna put out the match between her thumb and forefinger.

The pain made her feel strong and supremely wonderful to be alive.

54

According to her Roshi, dreams always held a special meaning and truth. Her teacher, using his personal style of making everyday analogies, had once described dreams as telephone calls from the gods.

Dianna remembered being in class one night when Taka-hashi told a student at the Zendo, a brilliant young poet, that his writing abilities were a gift from the gods. The Roshi had gone on to explain that the gods honored the young student by speaking to him every night in his dreams; then when the poet was awake, he simply wrote down what the gods had told him. (As Dianna remembered it, the concept didn't sit very well with the student's ego.) The Roshi had told the young man that he was lucky—to have gods speak to him, his karma must be very good.

She massaged her injured elbow and forced it to move. The joint had swollen overnight to almost half again its normal size. For two hours she fought back tears of pain as she worked the elbow mercilessly—bending, kneading, doing light push-ups against the wall, slowly but certainly bringing the arm back into feeling and usefulness.

The dream was still very much with her, and Dianna recalled the overbearing atmosphere of negativity and defeatism. She knew this attitude had doomed her from the outset. But, Dianna wondered, were the choices in the dream mine, or as my Roshi might say, was I visited by some karmic spirit trying to show me what I am supposed to do?

"Fuck karma!" she shouted to herself. The stabs of fire shooting up her arm and into her shoulders from her elbow fueled her anger. Why should I accept that I have bad karma? Who says I've got to sit around and let anybody or anything—be it karma or the Fates or whatever—run my life?

"There are those who eat and those who are eaten," Dianna commented aloud as she busily worked away. "My karma is to be the latter of the two. I will it!"

Her anger raged. What philosophy is going to tell me I can't walk away from this? What deity has a right to predestine, to say that it *isn't* my karma to be victorious? Buddha? Or God? Or the Virgin? Well, if it is "their will," it's unfair, and unjust, and I'm going to use every ounce of energy in my protoplasm to change it.

Who says I'm guilty for something in a past life? That isn't me. I am here. Any guilt I have is only for the deeds of my own hand.

Take the idea of "woman as sinner" and ram it up a bull's penis.

If nothing else, I will at least have the satisfaction of leaving Esau nothing more than a dead piece of meat to necrophiligize.

When the arm had regained a good deal of its mobility, Dianna ate of the leftover scavenged kitchen food—lightly so that she wouldn't be slowed down, but enough to give her the stamina she knew she would need for the confrontation.

Dianna built a roaring fire in the hearth, set the tongs in the flames, and parked herself as close to the blaze as she could stand, savoring the warmth and drawing strength from it.

The portrait of Sir Thomas over the mantel stared down at her with its cold, superior attitude. Dianna broke up the picture's frame and stripped off the canvas. She folded the paint-cracked portrait neatly so the head was on top and set it in the fireplace. Dark burn spots grew on the Wilkinson face like leprosy and then began to devour the canvas. For a moment the cruel brown eyes seemed to look out, as if in horror, then the likeness of Sir Thomas Wilkinson was gone.

She cut two good-sized rectangles from the fabric of her windbreaker. With the needle and thread from her travel sewing kit she stitched two extra large pockets onto her denim jacket, one on the side and the other on the back. One pocket ran vertically under the left armpit down to the waist, and the other was behind the small of the back and accessible from the right side.

Analyzing the dream gave her a confidence, a little of the feeling of being a veteran, a recruit who had survived a first battle. Her fingers felt steady as she worked on a second seam of reinforcing stitches on the pockets, and when she held out her left hand, there was no shaking. Her right also did not shake, but the injured elbow felt very weak, and she knew it would be of limited use to her.

Dianna took the mason's hammer and began to hone its metal, scraping it against the rough stone of the fireplace. The rusty, dull edge of the curving chisel opposite the hammer head began to take on a sheen of bright steel. Dianna wanted the brick-cracking claw as sharp as possible.

As her honing fell into a rhythm, Dianna could feel the rasp of the tool on stone, right into her bones. The sensation was harsh and grating, but she found it grimly reassuring.

The pang of doubt came again. Is there a point in doing this? she wondered. Is it worth the effort to try my latest plan? What if my fate is written, set in stone, a thing that cannot be altered or redirected by any of my choices? Dianna realized she was pondering a worst case scenario—that human behavior does not influence human existence.

Wouldn't that be a kick? she thought. If all of humankind was nothing more than a congregation of slugs crawling blindly on the surface of the earth, leaving nothing more behind them than little trails of bluish slime. Wretched little clumps of flesh with no say whatsoever in the shaping of their destiny. Wouldn't that be the perfect cosmic joke?

She could visualize the mighty ones on Mount Olympus looking down through the clouds and chuckling away at all the effort and the simple misguided belief of the human race. "Hey, Zeus, come here and look at the fools. They actually believe the things they do or the words they say might really matter." Yes, thought Dianna, that would be the "cruelest cut of all."

Well, I'm not going to believe it. It just won't work for me. I would have no motivation but to lie around awaiting whatever wonderful or dismal things fate might have in store. It is not important that I have proof that karma can be influenced; I simply must assume that it can, and I must go forward accordingly. Otherwise, life—my life—would be pointless.

"Ignore fear, ignore negativity, press on," she told herself.

Dianna ran her thumb across the claw edge of the heavy mason's hammer. She didn't quite draw blood, but the keen, ragged steel left a bright abrasion on her finger.

Stretching, working her legs, more upper body exercises—Dianna drove herself into a mild sweat. She wanted to be loose and relaxed, with every muscle working smoothly. The workout, she knew, would make her feel positive and confident, and she wanted the endorphins to be at their peak when the time was right.

It's the smell that does it for him, she thought. I've to do something about that.

After emptying the contents of her Louis Vuitton bag onto the floor, she took the butcher knife and sawed a triangular patch out of the tough plastic wall of the purse. One side of the material was a dark brown, and the other was emblazoned with the small interlocking L-Vs. She made a little joke for herself: "the best for the best." Taking a razor and her tube of Super Glue, she disappeared into the bathroom.

When she emerged, Dianna could feel the effects of the exercise in her heart rhythm. She walked lightly on her feet, and her vision was extra sharp.

Taking the one remaining unclogged pistol, she smashed off the action with the mason's hammer so that the touch hole was easily accessible. A full load of powder from one of the shotgun shells went down the barrel followed by wadding and a lead ball. To make it easier to ignite, Dianna smeared a tiny bit of Vaseline all around the touch hole and sprinkled the sticky surface with a liberal covering of gunpowder.

The butcher knife went blade-first down the long vertical slit sewn under her arm. The mason's hammer she put into the other newly made pocket behind her back. When she practiced trying to remove the hammer, the claw caught on the fabric, and she had to rip the pocket open slightly along the top so that the hammer could be removed in a single motion.

When she had her weapons ready, Dianna began to set her belongings in order. She was about to throw the Kronenberger script into the fire when she caught herself. The Roshi had once told a story about a Zen sword master, Miyamoto Musashi, who had to fight a duel with a brilliant opponent.

When Musashi met his challenger at the place of the duel, the man took his scabbard from his belt and cast it into the sea.

Dianna remembered the knowing smile that the Roshi had at this point in his telling of the story. "It was at this exact instant that Musashi knew the victory would be his. You see, Dianna, a man who intended to win, would want to keep his scabbard to put his sword in after the battle was finished."

Thinking along these lines, Dianna carefully packed the script into her suitcase, with the few remaining belongings that had not been ripped or stained beyond possible use. She put everything in a bag and a suitcase so that it could easily be carried to the car or a taxi . . . or an ambulance. "No," she said to herself, "a hearse maybe, but not an ambulance."

She pulled the stuffed bobcat off the wall and tossed it into the flames. There was a hiss and the smell of burning hair.

"Dianna, keep it in mind," she told herself, "losers burn."

Ignore fear, ignore negativity, press on.

The laptop, she set beside her suitcase near the door, just as if she were planning to take it to the car. Then she came to a decision, picked up the machine, and dropped it into the center of the fire.

"Never again," she said to herself. Dianna watched with a great feeling of satisfaction as the plastic and metal melted, burned, and was reduced to a smoldering mass by the heat of the flames.

As she positioned her suitcase and handbag by the door, she had yet another flash of doubt. Once again she asked herself if she was doomed and playing out a pointless scene for a desperate audience of one. What's wrong with me? she thought. Why can't my courage hold?

To be able to set my suitcase in the corner by the door and not feel one iota of uncertainty, that would be true Zen. Or would it? she thought. Did that swordsman have doubts as he went to fight that duel? If he did not, how could he be human? But isn't that what Zen accomplishes—making frail and fickle Homo sapiens for a fleeting few moments into immortals, superhuman and God-like?

"Ignore fear, ignore negativity, press on. Shake it off. Do. Go."

She kept a constant watch out the door hole, but Esau remained in his deep sleep. She could see beads of sweat on the hunchback's face, and Dianna guessed that he had a fever from the infection in his hand.

Probably, if I could hold out for a week, she thought, he would be dead from gangrene or blood poisoning. But then who knows, with his bizarre chromosomes, he probably has an immune system impervious to any infection on earth.

Dianna took her bottle of nail polish remover, checked the top to see if it could be opened easily, and put it within left-handed reach in her hip pocket. She put the tongs into the heart of the flames to get them as hot as possible.

Dianna knelt by the side of the bed and whispered quietly.

"Dear God or Buddha or whatever, give me strength to be as strong as I may be. If there is an element of luck, or if there are other factors that may determine my fate, let them fall my way. If there is no factor such as fate or luck to be granted, give me the strength to create my own destiny.

"If there is no one or nothing listening to my words, then curse whatever science or force gave me life. Curse it for being so cruel. Curse it for not creating a warm and loving God.

"If there is someone or something out there who cares enough to hear my insignificant requests then, whoever or whatever you are, watch over me. If you have given me signs to be aware of your existence, forgive me for not knowing you and for not believing in you. If you see me and care, please try to understand my ignorance and my need and please give some more of your thought and consideration to human happiness.

"If all this is for nothing and I am not heard, let my words affect my own mind and thinking and give me the courage and the focus to live. In the name of the Virgin Mary, Jesus Christ, God the Father, Gautama Buddha, all other existing gods, and the truth of my own soul and existence, Amen."

Dianna felt a calm and had a sense of peace. Perhaps my religion is well expressed by my little Virgin Mary with the shaved head, Dianna thought. She has much of my own weird style of belief/nonbelief and is a pretty good summation of the confusion and contradictions of my irreverent reverence.

After filling the wastebasket half-full with hot coals, Dianna again stuck the end of the tongs into the heart of the flame. She wrapped the bottom and sides of the wastebasket in a heavy blanket and, after making a final check of her armament, she pushed her portable firebox up through the attic door.

Carefully sliding the simmering wastebasket in front of her, she made a slow and quiet journey across the attic floorboards. Dianna knew if she spilled any ashes in the bone-dry space, the inn would certainly go up in flames. Getting down into the elevator car was difficult and painful but Dianna took her time and managed it in silence.

Opening the elevator door was a minor trauma. She knew it was entirely possible that Esau would be waiting for her, ready to pounce.

With a clunk that seemed louder than ever before, the door slid open. No Esau. She crept down the hall toward Goody's room, her firebox in her arms, heating her chest and arms, causing a sweat to break out on her face.

Taking a deep breath, she looked around the corner. Esau lay in front of her, still asleep on the floor. If he so much as raised an eye, he would see Dianna. She studied his movements, half expecting him to stir. But Esau's breathing remained heavy and regular.

Ignore fear, ignore negativity, press on.

She set the wastebasket on its blanket, out of the way on the floor outside the door, took the flame-hot tongs in her right hand and the loaded flintlock in her left.

Esau still had not moved.

The first step in Dianna's plan was simple and direct. Attack—boldly and with no warning. Inflict as much damage in the first strike as could be inflicted. If at all possible, kill.

Step by step she inched closer to the sleeping man-thing. The floor groaned and creaked under her weight, and she half expected Esau to awaken at any second. When she was three feet away from the hunchback, Dianna aimed the pistol at his head. She would have liked to get close enough to press the barrel against Esau's scalp, but she kept just out of his reach in case he woke up.

Holding the pistol steady, she slowly brought the tip of the hot tongs up toward the touch hole of the flintlock. Her hands were not shaking and her aim was sure.

When the red-hot iron touched the powder, it ignited instantly, and the weapon exploded with a deafening roar. But just as she had put the tongs on the touch hole, the tip bumped against the flintlock and it slightly altered her aim.

The lead ball exploded out the barrel and tore into the side of Esau's head, taking away a large fleshy chunk of scalp and blowing Esau's ear to a pulp. A bit of the white bone of his skull was visible for a second before it was covered with a wash of red.

The force of the exploding shotgun shell powder was too powerful for the antique and split the barrel of the old flintlock. The recoil of the pistol hurled the weapon from her grasp and numbed her fingers. A steel fragment from the exploding barrel shot out, gashing Dianna's hand between her thumb and forefinger.

Esau lurched up, terrified, dazed, raging with a pain that hammered at the side of his head.

Dianna ignored the cut in her hand, and the hurt in her elbow, and pressed her attack. She swung downward with the tongs, and the hot iron smashed onto Esau's scalp.

As the metal struck home there was a scorching crackle, and the air was filled with the smell of burning hair and flesh. Dianna got in one more lick before Esau even knew what was happening.

"Good morning, booteful is here," said Dianna, giving him a shot of LaBianca mouth.

With a backhand swipe, the hunchback sent the tongs flying out of her hands and into the wall.

In a flash Dianna had the butcher knife out of her side pocket and held before her. She crouched, street-fighter style, the blade making little thrusts in Esau's direction.

They circled the room, their feet slipping on the throw rugs that covered the floor. There was blood running down the man-thing's face from the ragged shreds of his ear. A long reddish-black line of soot and burned flesh slashed across Esau's forehead.

Blood dripped from Dianna's cut hand.

Esau wanted to charge, but he was afraid of the knife, and his arms kept making circles of indecision as he wavered between trying to reach for her and trying to think of ways to stop the thundering pain in his head.

Dianna knew she had the initiative and was determined to keep it. Stepping in, she feinted for Esau's eyes and slashed at his outstretched infected hand. The blade struck home, cutting deeply into the flesh near the original wound. The knife lodged in bone, and as Esau pulled his hand away the blade went with it, jerked out of Dianna's grasp.

A screech of agony came from the hunchback, which, for a moment, terrified Dianna with its raw intensity. But it didn't shake her determination and she kept to her plan. She quickly unscrewed the top to the nail polish remover and capped the bottle with her thumb. She held it poised over her head.

Esau pulled the blade from his quivering hand, and a gush of puss and blood shot out of the wound. To Dianna's surprise he picked up the knife as a weapon of his own, waving it before him awkwardly.

Primitive man evolves, she thought with a bitter smile, from shotgun-used-as-baseball-bat to knife.

As they circled, Dianna's thoughts flashed back to the first day she saw the man-thing, when he had done battle with the German shepherd. The two creatures had faced off in a contest that could have only one possible conclusion—the extinction of one or the other.

Now, looking at Esau's face, cold with the hatred of his pain, Dianna knew that she was locked in that same kind of life or death situation.

Time to kill or die.

Dianna took a mouthful of the acrid-tasting polish remover and placed her thumb tightly over the neck of the bottle and its remaining fluid.

Now that she had experienced two different kinds of confrontation with the hunchback, one of staring into eyes that leered with lust, and the other of facing his anger and his rage to kill, she realized that she much preferred it this way.

She felt strangely content basking in Esau's hatred. The sexual element, she realized, had been debilitating. It had drained her strength, and the accompanying fear of humiliation and violation had diffused her aggression and sapped her will to resist.

Esau closed in and took a wild slash at her head. Dianna just managed to dodge the attack and felt a zip of air as the keen edge cut by her face. A second later she spat her mouthful at Esau's eyes. Esau turned his face away, and the stream missed his brown orbs but landed on the open wound of his mangled ear. The man-thing grabbed his head, the caustic chemical searing his exposed nerve ends.

Taking advantage of Esau's lowered guard, Dianna dashed the rest of the contents of the bottle all over his face, trying to get at least a drop or two in the eyes. The hunchback tore at his burning wound and retreated back to the safety of the corner.

Her first attack completed, Dianna bolted out the door and into the hall. The odor of fetid death hung like a cloud around the closet where Esau had stuffed Goody. The old woman's foot was still there, kicking in futility. Another reminder to Dianna of the merciless result of coming in second place.

Hurling the screen door open before her, Dianna burst out of the inn and into the icy air of the late afternoon.

55

The light ground cover of snow was everywhere, and the day's temperature had remained well below freezing. Dianna's footsteps kicked up little flurries of dry, loose flakes.

As she ran, the snowfall softly began again, and soon the air was a fluttering of white. Delicate snowflakes wafted gently down through the windless air, masking the grounds and buildings under a kind of living silk-screen veil, a quiet rain of tiny white flower petals.

She made for the barn and heard the slam of the front screen door behind her. It was a curious sound rising out of the blanket of snow, muted and thudding—a death knell nipped in the bud.

Dianna raced through the barn, hoping against reason that there would be a horse left that she could ride. In stable after stable she saw only the sight of inert, marble-eyed animals and smelled the stench of dead and dying horses. Lady Ann lay in stillness at the far end of the barn, her head twisted around at an impossible angle.

The broken neck must have been Esau's parting token of affection, Dianna thought grimly. She streaked through the length of the barn, and when she saw Esau enter the door at the opposite end, she continued her course out of the building, doubling back toward the inn.

She knew that Esau could not be far behind, yet there was not even a hint of footsteps—the snow sucked up all the sound, isolating her within a limbo of eerie silence.

Dennis's corpse seemed to look away, indifferent to Dianna and her problems, as she ran. She passed the stump, now seeming to belong in the yard, whitewashed and claimed by nature as a part of its domain.

Dianna never heard the sound of running feet coming from behind. It was the gasping wheeze of the man-thing that overtook her.

She looked back just in time to see Esau dive for her legs and pull her down in a tackle that sent them both sprawling and skidding through the powdery fluff to a spot just beneath the leafless, snow-covered branches of the sugar maple—the hanging tree.

Dianna felt his massive hands lock onto her ankles and knew that there would be no escaping that grasp. The fingers twisted her legs, spinning her around onto her back as if she were nothing but a Raggedy Ann doll.

The man-thing, his chest heaving, gasping for breath, looked down at her. The raw anger was gone, and there seemed only to be an ambivalence—more like the apathetic expression of a weary axe-man at a slaughterhouse.

Fine, Dianna thought as she fought for air. If this is the way it has to end, then just get on with it. She matched his apathy with her own iron-hard gaze of loathing.

They were immobile—he kneeling over her, she sitting propped up on her good elbow—for a solid three minutes. Blood ran down his cheek and dripped into a little red lake in the snow.

Her hand left a crimson streak on the blades of snow-dusted grass.

Their guttural gasps for air were the only sounds in the still landscape. Each breathed in a separate rhythm—two irreconcilable patterns that slowed together but did not fall into sync.

The woman and the man-thing shared a unique and bitter loathing—a feeling that might be known by old lovers who have had their affection decay into a deep and especially personal hatred.

She was the idiot, who at one time had thought he was merely a simple child who only needed a little understanding and compassion.

He was a fool, once believing she was the perfect one, the one who might see, at last, his true bootefulness.

Esau bent down over her, his hatred slowly mellowing.

Dianna knew the look. His thoughts were taking the direction that she feared but had anticipated.

Nothing seemed to daunt the man-thing—the cold, his hand, his fever, having his fingers cut, his face battered and burned, his ear and half his head blown away. She thought, His body has no nerve endings—he lives impervious to pain.

He is an animate construct of protoplasm, driven by a genetically preprogrammed brain with a single overriding command—procreate. He is a living sperm dispenser encased in a hairy leather hide, having no nerves and a flesh as insensitive as fossilized bone.

The hunchback's intention was clear as he knelt between Dianna's legs and tugged at her belt. With a yank that lifted her off of the snowy grass, he broke the leather.

Dianna's good arm inched its way to the small of her back.

Blood ran off Esau's chin, dripping spots onto Dianna's blouse.

There was a pop and a quick zip as he pulled open her jeans. His fingers seemed to move a little slowly, with a jerky hesitation. He wavered above her for an instant, and his eyes blinked and lost their focus, but then he caught his balance and continued.

Dianna's fingers curled over the haft of the hammer.

Esau ripped apart the zipper and, with the ease of tearing a sheet of newspaper, rent the denim along the seam from the crotch around to the back belt loops.

She slid the mason's tool from its makeshift pocket.

There was a meanness in Esau's eyes—a look that was similar to the time he had staged his little show with Lady Ann—a spitefulness that made her sure he was now trying to punish her for her actions.

With a slow and determined twist of his wrist, Esau shredded her pink underwear and tossed it aside into the snow. It lay there, a crushed corsage thrown on a great greenish-white sheet. Dianna supported the weight of her upper body with the strength of her stomach muscles so that she had both arms free to move.

Esau began to get hard.

Dianna looked him right in the eye and roared, "NO!" Then again, "NO!"

Esau hesitated, not knowing what to make of this.

Dianna hit him with the command again, screaming like a drill sergeant, "NO!" And again, "N-O-O-O-O-O!"

Esau looked at her in a daze.

This not right. Booteful sound like Goody.

Esau's hardness began to go away.

What happen?

Esau looked down at himself and stroked himself where it felt good.

Esau need smell. Need booteful's smell to make him hard again.

He reached down with his fingers to take her smell.

Why feel wrong?

Esau, looking down at Dianna, did a double take, not understanding what he saw. Moving in a kind of daze, clearly suffering from the loss of blood, he bent down to peer between her legs. There he saw the triangular patch of handbag material that Dianna had bonded to her flesh with the polyresin Super Glue.

Dianna had robbed him of her smell.

Confused, he leaned down to look closer.

The interlocking little LVs were the last thing he ever saw.

As the man-thing's fingers reached toward the patch, Dianna heaved the heavy mason's hammer high over her head. Its sharpened claw gleamed. She grasped it solidly with two hands and using all the strength she could get from both arms, she struck downward.

This time she didn't misjudge the blow, and it fell straight and true on Esau's head. A shout of rage and determination came from Dianna, erupting from the pit of her insides—a cry that told the world she was an existence that would not be ignored.

The sharpened edge chopped down, breaking through the thick bone and penetrating the skull, two inches into the brain matter.

With a slight twist of the handle, she jerked the hammer out, leaving a bubbling of blood.

Esau moving.

Esau floating up. Up into the sky.

Esau see his self lying so still in the snow.

What that mean?

How can Esau go somewhere without Esau?

Esau change.

A second hammer blow landed an inch from the first and drove itself into Esau's head with almost as much impact. It broke through the skull and sent bone slivers knifing into the part of Esau's brain that held his memories of smell.

Cut grass! Pine! Trees! Flowers!

Fresh, wild, wonderful smells!

Every good scent that Esau had ever smelled came rushing at him, exploding in his mind like bursts of fireworks.

Smells strong. Stronger than ever smell anything in whole life!

The aromas melded into one smell that overwhelmed Esau. With the blended scent came truth and cleanness and all the joy of living he had never known.

An aroma so pure and perfect it made Esau want to cry and made his heart break with a great sadness.

A scent that told Esau how filthy and how wrong and how bad his life had been.

Esau's body fell forward. His chin fell between Dianna's legs; his limp face flopped into the snow.

Raising the hammer a third time, Dianna buried the claw into Esau's hunch. It struck the deformed bone of the spine and wedged deeply between two vertebrae. The body continued to twitch.

Esau leave. Go away from self.

Why Esau have to say good-bye?

Esau getting smaller.

Good-bye, big place.

Good-bye, body.

Maybe it not so bad to say good-bye to body. Body not booteful. Body made Esau strange. Made Esau bad.

Esau body was bad thing. Yes. Body made Esau live like in scary dream.

Esau sad he bad. Sorry he bad.

Esau very small now. Esau tiny. A tiny seed.

Esau-seed would live? Seed grow again?

Or Esau-seed would die? No more Esau?

Seed live?

Seed die?

Esau going.

Esau no more.
Esau gone.
Esau . . .

Wet spots of Esau's blood passed the cold through her clothing as Dianna walked toward the inn. The snow fell now like down, a gentle dusting that drifted to the earth in the absence of any wind.

Wanting to make sure that the man-thing was really dead, she paused and turned to look back.

The mound of flesh that was Esau lay still.

A sprinkle of just-fallen snow gave the corpse a granitelike texture, like a monument in a winter graveyard. A statue of an insignificant man caught in a humble bow, his forehead pressed to the ground, struck down in the midst of some supplication. The hammer protruded from the hump like a prospector's tool used to stake out a claim.

The judgment was made. The sentence had been carried out and she felt no guilt.

The lone sweet william blossom seemed to rise with defiance, higher than before, fighting the pull of the earth. Its color matched the blood on the snow.

Dianna threw her head back and laughed. The laugh was loud and animal-like, more a cackle of victory and a warning to all who might hear.

The laugh cut through the air over the crumbling stone walls, past the overgrown pastures, to echo off the hills and the white-topped limbs of the distant forest trees.

Dianna saw the head of the Buddha from her dream, the head that was cut from the stone of the mountain, and now she could see the face clearly.

The face was not Esau's, and it was not like the other figures from her dream, elusive pools of light.

The face on the Buddha was a woman—a triumphant and living woman.

About the Author

John Driver studied Iaido, the art of the Japanese sword, and Zen philosophy for many years under the guidance of Sensei Yoshiteru Otani, attaining the rank of second-degree black belt in that discipline. An accomplished playwright and lyricist, Mr. Driver's interest in Asia has led him to write two musicals on the subject including the book and lyrics for the recent Broadway production of James Clavell's novel *Shogun*. Mr. Driver is a member of seven theatrical unions and has won prestigious awards for acting, directing, and playwriting.